PENGUIN TRAVEL LIBRARY

One's Company

Peter Fleming was born on 31 May 1907 and was educated at Eton and Christ Church, Oxford, where he gained a First in English Literature, besides being President of the O.U.D.S. and Editor of *Isis*. In 1935 he married Celia Johnson, the distinguished actress, and they had a son and two daughters.

After a brief sojourn in a New York business house, he joined an expedition which was supposed to be going to look for a lost captain in Brazil. This resulted in his first book, *Brazilian Adventure*, which has been translated into many European languages. As a Special Correspondent of *The Times* he travelled widely in Eastern and Central Asia. He served in the Grenadier Guards during the war – in Norway, Greece, S.E.A.C. – and later commanded the 4th Battalion of the Oxfordshire and Buckinghamshire Light Infantry (T.A.). He received the O.B.E. in 1945 and was High Sheriff of Oxfordshire in 1952. He died in August 1971.

Peter Fleming's other books are chiefly on travel and war history and include *News from Tartary* (1936), *The Forgotten Journey* (1952), *Invasion 1940* (1957), *The Siege at Peking* (1959), *Bayonets to Lhasa* (1961) and *The Fate of Admiral Kolchak* (1963).

One's Company is an account of his journey through Russia and Manchuria to China where he spent seven months with the 'object of investigating the Communist situation in South China' at a time when, as far as he knew, 'no previous journey had been made to the anti-communist front by a foreigner'. His book won widespread acclaim on its publication in 1934. *The Times* wrote, '*One's Company* should confirm the reputation won for Mr Peter Fleming by his *Brazilian Adventure*. In the journey through China . . . he exposed himself to experiences as novel and as dangerous as those in the earlier book; as before, he contrives to leave them none the less impressive for insisting every few pages that there was nothing out of the ordinary in his own energy and endurance', and the *Observer* called it 'a delightfully human book of travel and adventure in China, which gives the reader a living, colourful, and at the same time most accurate, picture of present-day conditions in that distressful country'.

PETER FLEMING

ONE'S COMPANY

A Journey to China in 1933

PENGUIN BOOKS

Penguin Books Ltd, Harmondsworth, Middlesex, England
Penguin Books, 625 Madison Avenue, New York, New York 10022, U.S.A.
Penguin Books Australia Ltd, Ringwood, Victoria, Australia
Penguin Books Canada Ltd, 2801 John Street, Markham, Ontario, Canada L3R 1B4
Penguin Books (N.Z.) Ltd, 182–190 Wairau Road, Auckland 10, New Zealand

First published 1934
Published in Penguin Books 1956
Reprinted 1983

Made and printed in Great Britain by
Richard Clay (The Chaucer Press) Ltd,
Bungay, Suffolk
Set in Monotype Baskerville

To the memory of
R. F.

CONTENTS

CONTENTS

Part Two
RED CHINA

FOREWORD

THIS book is a superficial account of an unsensational journey. My Warning to the Reader justifies, I think, its superficiality. It is easy to be dogmatic at a distance, and I dare say I could have made my half-baked conclusions on the major issues of the Far Eastern situation sound convincing. But it is one thing to bore your readers, another to mislead them; I did not like to run the risk of doing both. I have therefore kept the major issues in the background.

The book describes in some detail what I saw and what I did, and in considerably less detail what most other travellers have also seen and done. If it has any value at all, it is the light which it throws on the processes of travel – amateur travel – in parts of the interior, which, though not remote, are seldom visited.

On two occasions, I admit, I have attempted seriously to assess a politico-military situation, but only (a) because I thought I knew more about those particular situations than anyone else, and (b) because if they had not been explained certain sections of the book would have made nonsense. For the rest, I make no claim to be directly instructive. One cannot, it is true, travel through a country without finding out something about it; and the reader, following vicariously in my footsteps, may perhaps learn a little. But not much.

I owe debts of gratitude to more people than can conveniently be named, people of all degrees and many nationalities. He who befriends a traveller is not easily forgotten, and I am very grateful indeed to every one who helped me on a long journey.

May 1934 PETER FLEMING

NOTE – Some of the material contained in this book has appeared in the columns of *The Times*, the *Spectator*, and *Life and Letters*. My thanks are due to the editors of these journals for permission to reproduce it here in a different form.

WARNING TO THE READER

The recorded history of Chinese civilization covers a period of four thousand years. The population of China is estimated at 450 millions. China is larger than Europe.

When the author wrote this book he was twenty-six years old. He spent, altogether, about seven months in China. He does not speak Chinese.

Part One

MANCHUKUO

I

BOYS WILL BE BOYS

I ALWAYS read (I know I have said this before) the Agony Column of *The Times*.

I was reading it now. It was June 2nd 1933: a lovely day. English fields, bright, friendly, and chequered, streamed past the window of the Harwich boat-train. Above each cottage smoke rose in a slim pillar which wriggled slightly before vanishing into a hot blue sky. Cattle were converging on the shade of trees, swinging their tails against the early summer flies with a dreamy and elegant motion. Beside a stream an elderly man was putting up his rod in an atmosphere of consecration. Open cars ran cheerfully along the roads, full of golf-clubs and tennis-rackets and picnic hampers. Gipsies were camped in a chalk-pit. A green woodpecker, its laughter inaudible to me, flew diagonally across a field. Two children played with puppies on a tiny lawn. Downs rose hazily in the distance. England was looking her best.

I, on the threshold of exile, found it expedient to ignore her. I turned to the Agony Column.

The Agony Column was apropos but not very encouraging, like the sermon on the last Sunday of term.

'*Because it is so uncertain as well as expensive, I must wait and trust.*' The advertiser was anonymous.

I put the paper down. Normally I would have speculated at some length on the circumstances which evoked this *cri du cœur*, to-day I was content to accept it merely as oracular guidance. We were in the same boat, the advertiser and I; as he (or possibly she) pointed out, we must wait and trust.

From my typewriter, on the rack opposite, a label dangled, swinging gently to and fro in a deprecating way. 'PASSENGER TO MANCHULI' said the label. I wished it would keep still.

There was something pointed in such suave and regular oscillation; the legend acquired an ironical lilt. 'Well, well!' said the label, sceptical and patronizing. 'Boys will be boys. . . .'

'PASSENGER TO MANCHULI.' Had there been anyone else in the carriage, and had he been able to decipher my block-capitals, and had he been fairly good at geography and at international politics in the Far East that label alone would have been enough (for he is clearly an exceptional chap) to assure him that my immediate future looked like being uncertain as well as expensive. For Manchuli is the junction, on the frontier between Russia and Manchuria, on the Trans-Siberian and the Chinese Eastern Railways; and the latter line had recently been announced as closed to traffic, its ownership being in dispute between Moscow and the Japanese-controlled government of Manchukuo. In short, on the evidence to hand my hypothetical fellow-passenger would have been warranted in assuming that I was either up to, or would come to, no good; or both.

With the possible exception of the Equator, everything begins somewhere. Too many of those too many who write about their travels plunge straight *in medias res*, their opening sentence informs us bluntly and dramatically that the prow (or bow) of the dhow grated on the sand, and they stepped lightly ashore.

No doubt they did. But why? With what excuse? What other and anterior steps had they taken? Was it boredom, business, or a broken heart that drove them so far afield? We have a right to know.

But they seldom tell us. They may vouchsafe a few complacent references to what they call their Wanderlust. But chiefly they trade on an air of predestination; they are lordly, inscrutable, mysterious. Without so much as a Hey Presto! or a Houp La! they whisk us from their native land to their exotic destination; so that for the first few chapters the reader's mind is full of extraneous and distracting surmises, as a proctor's must be when he sees a chamber-pot crowning some ancient monument of the university. He overlooks the

situation's intrinsic interest, because he is passionately wondering how the situation was arrived at at all.

In this respect, if in no other, I intend to give the reader
a square deal. As my label suggested, I had in my pocket
a ticket to Manchuli. The reader will wonder why I had
bought it.

Not, I can assure him, from any love of the place. Manchuli
is a small, wind-swept village, lying in a vast, but naturally
not less wind-swept plain. The population is Chinese, Mongolian, and Russian (Red and White). In the autumn of
1931 I was held up there for a day, and during that day I
saw all that I wanted to see of Manchuli and of the network
of shallow ditches which surrounds it, whether for the purpose of irrigation, sanitation, or defence I neither know nor
care. In Manchuli, too, I read the greater part of *The Pickwick
Papers*, but that, after all, one can do almost anywhere.
Besides – as I say – I had done it. No; it would be idle and
dishonest to pretend that Manchuli aroused in me any of the
emotions that (for instance) Kentucky arouses in the saxo-
phonist or Bognor Regis in the poster-artist. The 'Come to
Manchuli' movement could count me out.

What was it then, not nostalgia? Simply this: that since
the railway east of Manchuli was thought to be closed, to buy
a ticket to, say, Harbin might well prove to be waste of
money. With the minimum of luck – and I had the maximum
– one could get to Manchuli; and there, after all, one would
find oneself on a frontier separating two nations whose
citizens are neither universally efficient nor universally in-
corruptible. So it would be surprising indeed, however serious
the railway situation, if one did not manage to penetrate
farther east.

But why penetrate farther east? We come at last to the
point.

I had in my pocket – or, to be strictly accurate, I thought I
had in my pocket – a document addressed 'To All Whom It
May Concern.' (Luckily, for I had left it behind, it concerned
nobody.) This document went on to say that I had been
authorized to act as Special Correspondent to *The Times* in

the Far East. I had acquired it in the following manner:

Two months before, I had gone to the Editor of *The Times* and informed him that the situation in China during the coming summer would be fraught with every conceivable kind of interest. (This was a howling lie; the situation in China during the summer of 1933 was as dull as ditchwater.) I was the man, I shamelessly implied, to tell the world about it; had I not been there before, and for nearly three months?

The Editor of *The Times* is a humane man. His first thought was for his colleagues. 'If I turn him down,' he said to himself, 'he'll go round pestering them. Then, when he finds that no reputable newspaper will give an excuse for going to China, he'll come back to me with some cock and bull theory about Ecuador being the Country of the Future. Much better get him out of the country at once.'

He did. I was duly commissioned to write a series of articles on China, each one more portentous and comprehensive than the last; they would be paid for at a generous rate. The *Spectator* advanced me £50. My publisher, a curiously gullible man, made good the necessary rest. To all these people who made it possible for me to pay my way I am very grateful.

That, then, is how I came to be on the Harwich boat-train, *en route* for Manchuli. I have presented my credentials. If the reader wants any further motivation, he can invent it for himself.

2

INTO RUSSIA

HOLLAND. On the Flushing platform tall draught-horses,
rather like the draught-horses you see in Japan, help the
porters with the luggage. The train pulls out and runs
through the evening sunlight across a flat country partitioned with a symmetry so emphatic as to be rather charming. But the flatness is overdone; privacy and surprise –
surely the two prime qualities in a civilized landscape – are
almost wholly excluded. Holland looks rather dull to me.

But not to the two little Cockney girls in the next compartment, unaccountably bound for Berlin. In an exercise
book they write down the name of each successive station.
'Oo, look!' cries one. 'There's a real Dutchwoman!' And by
God she is right.

I dine with a pleasant young Englishman. He claims to
know Warsaw, and we embark on a markedly one-sided
discussion of the Upper Silesian Plebiscite of '21. My
mission, when revealed, awes him. 'Manchuria!' he ex-
claims. 'But can you speak Russian, or Chinese, or Japanese?'
Alas, I cannot. 'Then how will you manage?' I say I do not
know. He eyes me with respect; a desperate fellow, this, he
is thinking. It is clear that he finds me Ouidan. I wish now
that I had not told him where I am going.

I wish that I had not told him, because the false values
which other people put upon one's activities are disconcerting. My own sense of proportion I regard as impregnably
established. In the light of it, a journey to Manchuria is a
perfectly normal undertaking: nothing to get excited about.
But the world at large persists in maintaining a set of values
which the simplification of travel, and the general standardization of most forms of external experience, have long
rendered obsolete. The far cry has still an embarrassingly

romantic lilt, and distance lends an enchantment which is in fact no longer hers to lend.

When we said good night, the young man wished me luck on My Adventures. I was afraid he would.

An atmosphere, congenial to me, of racketeering pervaded Berlin. Dark stories of the concentration camps, rumours of plots and feuds among the great ones, and an inexhaustible supply of jokes at the expense of Hitler were exchanged: but only when the waiter had withdrawn out of ear-shot. One looked instinctively for swastikas on the pats of butter.

I lunched with Wheeler-Bennett, Knickerbocker, and Duranty (on his way back to Moscow after a holiday), and concealed with only a partial success my ignorance of all European and most other politics. There was also present an American film-star, full of the ardours and endurances of Greenland, where he had been making a picture in a climate so unkind that two imported polar bears had died of exposure, martyrs to their art. He will linger in the memory by virtue of having told me the longest story about an operation that I have ever heard.

After an abortive attempt to get myself inoculated I left for Moscow on the night train.

A legend, blazoned in Russian across an arch through which the train passes to cross the Polish frontier, informs you that 'The Revolution Breaks Down All Barriers'. The truth of this is not immediately apparent.

The Customs House at Niegoreloje is decorated with large mural paintings, in which the devotees of agriculture and industry, curiously combining a tubular physique with an air of ecstasy, are portrayed in the discharge of their varied and onerous duties. 'Workers of the World, Unite!' is inscribed in gold letters and four languages round the walls. The second sentence of this now immortal exhortation – 'You Have Nothing To Lose But Your Chains' – is omitted; it would represent, my 1931 diary notes, 'a highly conservative estimate of one's potential losses in that place.'

However, I got my scanty luggage through the customs

without loss, if not without delay. The officials moved about their business, as they had moved two years ago, with a mystic and inconsequent air. Russia has never, I imagine, been very good at bureaucracy. To-day her functionaries, gravely inconvenienced by a newly acquired civic conscience, fall unhappily between two stools; on the one hand their fatalistic instincts bid them muddle through and cook the accounts at the end of the month, on the other the ideals of an exact and Prussian efficiency, forcefully inculcated from above, spur them on to higher things. By nature intro-spective and self-critical, the average Russian official is pain-fully aware that he was not born to fill up forms – or not, at any rate, to fill them up correctly. He is a kind of Hamlet, and in his relations with the traveller will veer unpredictably from the dogmatic to the perplexed, from the apologetic to the menacing. He is often likeable, but never, in any circum-stances, expeditious.

My brother Ian, recently returned from Moscow where he had been acting as Reuter's Special Correspondent during the trial of the Metro-Vickers engineers, had given me, by way of a talisman, a photostat copy of a letter he had received from Stalin. Stalin corresponds seldom with foreigners, and the sight of his signature, negligently disposed on top of a suitcase otherwise undistinguished in its contents, aroused in the officials a childlike wonder. Their awe was turned to glee when they found an album containing photographs of an aboriginal tribe in Central Brazil. Had I really taken them? Indeed? They were really very good, most interesting. . . . Even the Bolsheviks, it seemed, were travel-snobs.

I parted with the officials on the most friendly terms, but with a slightly uneasy conscience, for I had 200 roubles in my pocket. They came, like Stalin's letter, from my brother Ian, and they were contraband.

Now here we come to the question of what is called The Exchange. It is a question which I shall never understand. I yearn to do so. I would give anything to be able to write, or even to read, an article on 'The Future of the Franc' or 'The Peseta: Whither?' But I know I never shall.

In Russia the Exchange is a particularly unreal and complex bogey, and I will not here attempt to explain the difference between gold roubles and black roubles, for I do not know what it is, nor why it should exist. The only thing I am quite sure about is that if you are caught importing roubles into the country you are arrested; and that, on the other hand, if you change your foreign money at the official rate you don't get anything like as many roubles as you ought to. (The ten shillings which I changed at Niegoreloje, to allay suspicion, would not have covered the tip to my porter, had I employed a porter.) So the most economical, if not the most prudent, policy is to smuggle roubles in. Ian's 200 saw me across Russia.

There exists, of course, a most exact and comprehensive set of regulations designed to prevent this sort of thing. You have to declare all the money you have with you when you enter Russia, and when you leave it you are supposed to show up receipts proving that you have spent a certain sum (it used to be twenty roubles) every day. It sounds fairly water-tight on paper. But the Russians, as I say, have never been very good at bureaucracy, and on neither of my journeys across their country have I seen these regulations effectively enforced. Rouble-running would appear to be a likely career for a young man, with few risks and plenty of room at the top.

3

THE MIRAGE OF MOSCOW

'L'Europe est finie,' the little attendant had said when we crossed the Polish frontier into Russia; and so, it seemed, was June. Grey skies and a cold wind did nothing to enhance the attractions of Moscow.

Moscow is a depressing place. To me its atmosphere is somehow suggestive of servants' bedrooms. The analogy, however, is not one which I am qualified to pursue.

Public opinion in England is sharply divided on the subject of Russia. On the one hand you have the crusty majority, who believe it to be a hell on earth; on the other you have the half-baked minority who believe it to be a terrestrial paradise in the making. Both cling to their opinions with the tenacity, respectively, of the die-hard and the fanatic. Both are hopelessly wrong.

And who shall blame them? You cannot give a just verdict without considering all the evidence; and in Great Britain, unfortunately, there is only a tithe of evidence to hand. Our leading newspaper* continues to report the affairs of the largest country in the world through a correspondent posted outside its frontiers, so that its Russian news has much the same degree of interest and reliability as would distinguish a running commentary on a prize-fight at the Albert Hall if it were broadcast from the steps of the Albert Memorial. America, however (sometimes) misty with sentiment in her eyes, gets a fuller and less distorted picture of Russia than we do, because American newspapers print more and better Russian news than ours; it may be that their attitude would be less commendably detached if the Pacific Ocean were not so conveniently wide, but at least they have

*The policy, I should add, is in part dictated by the attitude of the Soviet authorities, who, though not hostile, are high-handed.

not made themselves ridiculous by first pre-judging, and then to all intents and purposes ignoring, a political, cultural, and economic experiment launched on an unprecedented scale.

In England authorities on Russia are about as numerous as authorities on Mars, and the knowledge of the former is about as exact and as comprehensive as the knowledge of the latter. Funnily enough it is much the same in Russia. Outside the Kremlin, where a handful of men, presumably able and partly Jewish, control (on paper) the destinies of the far-flung Soviet Republics, hardly anyone in Russia knows what is going on there, or why. They know, of course, what is supposed to be going on there. Education and propaganda – in Russia, as elsewhere, the two are becoming increasingly difficult to differentiate – are at their disposal in large quantities; they are stuffed with information, but starved of the truth. They can study history, but only history as Lenin would have liked it to have happened. They can learn about the present, but only as much about it as Stalin thinks advisable. Their home news, as a matter of fact, is concerned almost as much with the future as with the present; their newspapers announce ten projects to every one achievement. It is remarkable what a great deal is perpetually on the point of being done in Russia.

I have no wish to mock the Five Year Plan or any of its progeny. All human endeavour is in some degree laughable, and the most gallant enterprises are often also, in their inception, the most comic. To the hasty and hot-blooded critics of Soviet Russia – to that monstrous regiment of clubmen for whom all Muscovy is peopled by a race of bullies (whom they call 'Bolos') equipped by Mr Punch's cartoonist with knouts and bombs – I would recommend a 'Let the dog see the rabbit' attitude as being both wise and fair. To the Russians I would suggest that it is about time they produced the rabbit.

No one can travel, however perfunctorily, in Russia without appreciating the magnitude of the task she has taken on. That portentous experiment is not, as is widely supposed, primarily political and economic; it is primarily psychological. Here you have a people almost none of whose national characteristics can be held likely to contribute in any way towards the success of a project like the Five Year Plan. Most of them are by nature inefficient, irresponsible, and feckless. The enormous practical difficulties involved in rationalizing and industrializing Russia – the backwardness of the people, the country's lack of communications and capital – are minor obstacles compared with the fundamental components of the national character and outlook. Can the Russian peasant be galvanized into something approaching robot-hood? Can he, on the crest of a wave of enthusiasm or at the point of a G.P.U. pistol, slough off his native apathy, his charming but hopeless inconsequence, and turn go-getter?

It appears that, for a time and partially, he can. Prusso-American ideals of drive and efficiency have proved infectious. Progress has been made. A nation proverbially composed of dreamers has shown itself capable of toeing the line, biting the bullet, and punching the clock. Too often, alas, it has been the wrong line, the wrong bullet, the wrong clock. But the intention behind the gesture was sound even if the gesture went astray.

Will the gesture survive as a habit? Will the Russians transform themselves into robots? The visitor to Moscow wonders. But he wonders less and less. The bath in his hotel is out of commission. The lavatory is under repair. The lift does not work. The service is awful. The telephone exchange is impossible. Only one match in three strikes. . . .

Eventually he stops wondering altogether.

I regret to say that I am extremely bad at sight-seeing. My regret, I would add, is sincere. This is not often the case.

To glory in – even to admit – a proficiency at sight-seeing is, to-day, to court the charge not so much of eccentricity as of affectation. In a world which is being sucked inexorably into the maelstrom of standardization – in a concentric labyrinth of which all the paths are beaten – the sophisticated traveller is at pains to parade his independence of the herd. 'Of course,' he says, in a deprecating tone which underlines his latent arrogance, 'it's very obscure – it's not at all the sort of place that foreigners go to', or 'I'm afraid we didn't do any of the *right* things; we just poked about on our own, in the native quarter. It's so much less tiring . . . ' In his feverish anxiety to be different, he eschews the temples and the tombs, the cathedrals and the palaces – all the honourable and enduring landmarks for which the place is justly famous. He would not be seen dead on the Bridge of Sighs; to gaze on the Pyramids seems to him as unpardonable as to blow on his tea.

But I am not like him. I have an honest, conscientious desire to do those right things; right up to the moment of my departure I go on fully intending to do them. But I am lazy – lazy, and also wholly lacking in either an historical sense or the ability to appreciate architecture. The eyes of Boswell, that man of feeling, once filled with tears of spontaneous emotion at the mere mention of the Great Wall of China. I am not like that. The sight of any edifice, however imposing, however drenched (as they say in Stratford-on-Avon) with historical associations, merely embarrasses me. It stimulates my powers of self-criticism. Why does that even flow of dates and names which the guide is reeling off mean nothing at all to me? How comes it that I am still, after all these years unable to distinguish with certainty between an ogive and a reredos? And who the hell was Henry the Fowler?

I gape dutifully, but without pleasure, without profit.

So in Moscow, though I stayed there four days, or nearly twice the length of time considered necessary by those intending to write a book on Modern Russia, I saw none of the things that I should have seen. I can only tell you what Moscow looks like to the uninitiated.

The reality falls midway between the pictures drawn by the *Morning Post* on the one hand and the Intourist travel agency on the other. Moscow is a drab, but not a desolate city. At first you are surprised by its ramshackle and untidy air; then you realize that this is a symptom not so much of decay as of reconstruction. A great many buildings are half pulled down, a great many others half put up. Of the completed new ones there are probably fewer than you had supposed. Those futuristic, those tortuously embattled blocks of flats which photograph so well, are rare exceptions to an architecturally unimpressive rule. The streets are dull and forbidding, and their surfaces are bad. There is an atmosphere of rather ill-coordinated and precarious improvisation, such as pervades the wings of a theatre.

The people you will find oddly colourless and oddly likeable. Their curiosities are limited by their fatalism, and the stranger discovers with gratitude that he is not stared at. That agonizing sense of singularity which afflicts (for instance) the Englishman who carries gloves and a rolled-up umbrella through the streets of New York does not attend his wanderings in Moscow. He is far better dressed than anyone he meets; he is clearly that rarity, a bourgeois. But nobody takes much notice of him; he is not made to feel a freak and an intruder.

The people of Moscow are neither well nor picturesquely dressed. Apart from the blouse, which is quite often worn by the men, their clothes are conventionally, though ineptly, cut in the standard European style. In the centre of the town at any rate, there are no rags, no bare feet, no human skeletons. The streets are perpetually crowded, but the crowd is nondescript and unexciting. It drifts, chattering in a subdued way, and forms readily into patient queues at the tram-halts and outside the co-operative stores. In its eyes you can read no very explicit hope, and only occasionally despair. It is a phlegmatic, philosophical crowd. No doubt it needs to be.

One of the most curious things about modern Russia is the startling and universal ugliness of the women. Bolshevism appears to be incompatible with beauty. Across the frontier you will find the night-clubs of Harbin and Shanghai packed with the most ravishing creatures, all Russian, and mostly (by their own account) Romanoff. But in Moscow you search for a pretty, for even a passable face in vain. It is impossible not to admire the sagacity of their rulers, who have decreed that among Soviet citizens the married state is not to be looked on as a permanence. I do not see how it could be.

Even in the theatres you will draw blank. The Russian actress takes her art seriously. Years of intensive training are considered necessary to qualify her for a leading role, and our *ingénues*, who are in electric lights before they are out of their teens, have no counterpart in Russia. Moscow salutes no stars under the age of thirty; most of them are much more.

There is another curious thing about Soviet Russia, and that is how bad she is at window-dressing. I use the words figuratively, for the fault goes deeper than the Moscow shop-windows.

One has always imagined that the Russians, though never much good at putting things through, always had a talent for carrying things off. A talent for carrying things off implies a capacity for making a good impression on the superficial observer, and that capacity underlies the great and increasingly important art of salesmanship. Now the rulers of Russia to-day – the men of real power – have almost all got Jewish blood in them, and who make good salesmen if it is not the Jews? It is, I repeat, a curious thing that the Russians should be so bad at window-dressing.

For they are bad. It requires an effort to look into the Moscow shop-windows. Those piles of wooden cheeses, that dummy ham, the cake on which the icing is enamel – surely they might be displayed to better advantage round the inevitable bust of Lenin? Surely that imposing frontage of plate glass, disfigured though it is by a long crack clumsily patched with plaster, need not reveal an array of goods quite so fly-blown, quite so unprepossessing? . . .

Across the street a big new building is nearing completion. Above its roof a huge red banner floats proudly on the breeze; or did so float a month ago, when they first hoisted it. Alas, it was made of inferior material; the winds have eroded the stuff, and the flag is now a shoddy and a listless fringe upon the naked pole. One more gesture has missed fire. . . .

The Kremlin, castellated and cupolaed with dentifricial abandon, has the splendid, compelling assurance of a strong place which is also a beautiful one. From the river bank opposite one admires its crouching outlines unreservedly. But why, oh why, does the clock which crowns a central tower announce the time as 12.15 when it is really half past five? Why do they *never* carry things off?

I do not know the answer to that question.

4

DRAMA

NOTHING very memorable happened to me in Moscow.

My stay coincided with the closing days of an international drama festival. Some of the delegates were staying at my hotel, and I used to look forward immensely to breakfast, when they could be heard discussing whatever play it was that they had seen the night before. The play almost always had a monosyllabic but arresting title, like *Blood*, or *Mud*, or *Youth*, or *Rust*. The conversation about it used to go something like this:

An American Lady With Teeth: Well, Professor, wasn't last night a wonderful experience?

The Professor (a tall, thin, mild Englishman with very short trousers): It was certainly a most – er – unusual piece.

Young Mr Schultz (in a rasping voice): The lighting was bum. (*Mr Schultz is a very dapper Jew from Columbia University. He once had a one-act play performed in Watertown, N.J., and is inclined to be Olympian with the others. He sits at a little table by himself, pretending to read a novel in Russian.*)

Miss Possey (a very intellectual girl from Leeds): It wasn't the lighting so much as the cyclorama. One would have thought Boguslavsky would have got further than the cyclorama.

The Swiss Delegate (a human enigma): Yes? No?

Helen (the Professor's daughter. Fearfully keen, but a little out of her depth): Which was the cyclorama? The old woman with a wheelbarrow? I didn't like *her*. I thought she was just *silly*. I mean, there didn't seem to be any . . .

Young Mr Schultz (aggressively oracular): The cyclorama is a permanent concave backcloth, on which the light-values . . .

The American Lady (who disapproves of Young Mr Schultz): But the emotional *calibre* of that play! It left me quite limp. Didn't it you, Miss Possey?

Miss Possey (who is made of sterner stuff): Frankly, no. I found the symbolism overstated.

The Professor: My egg is bad. Oh, dear.

Helen: Never mind, Father. We'll get another one.

The Swiss Delegate (in a burst of self-revelation): The works of Shakey-speare! I love them greatly!

(*This bourgeois admission creates an awkward silence. The Swiss Delegate glances round him like a haunted thing, blushing.*)

The Professor (coming to his rescue): I confess I was a little puzzled, last night, as to what exactly was the significance of the young sculptor.

The American Lady: But surely that was obvious enough. He stood for – well, for sculpture . . .

Helen (brightly): And for youth, too, don't you think?

Miss Possey: I fancy there was rather more to it than that. The young sculptor seemed to me to be the playwright's answer to the whole question of what should be the place, what should be the function, of the plastic arts of a community absorbed in the process of industrializing itself. The young sculptor's failure came when he threw those fish out of the window; and his failure surely symbolized the failure of the plastic arts to justify . . .

Young Mr Schultz (with gloomy satisfaction): He wasn't a sculptor. He was a geologist.

(*While all are rejoicing at the discomfiture of Miss Possey the Swiss Delegate leans over to the Professor and says, in a stage whisper of the utmost urgency: 'You have some toilet paper, please? Yes? No?' The meeting breaks up.*)

I myself was not, except vicariously, involved in the drama festival. But I did go to one play. It was at the Kamerny Theatre, which has a reputation for sophistication, and at which, two years ago, I saw a farcical comedy called *Sirocco*, which owed nothing save its title (and that unintentionally) to Noel Coward. The interior decoration of the theatre recalls the gun-turret of a battleship. This time the play was *Negro*, a translation-cum-adaptation of Mr Eugene O'Neill's *All God's Chillun Got Wings*, a production of which in London, rendered memorable by the performance of Mr Paul Robeson and Miss Flora Robson, I had reviewed a few weeks before. The play is, of course, concerned with the Colour Bar.

I suppose that Soviet Russia has always suffered from persecution-mania. If you defy the world there is some justification for believing that the world's hand is against you. The consciousness of this inconvenient circumstance was very much alive when I was in Moscow; people were more sensitive to criticism, and much more sensitive to ridicule, than they had been two years ago. (This was particularly so in the case of the Metro-Vickers trial.) One could almost foresee the growth of an officially sponsored feeling of self-pity (this, of course, would not affect the outlook of the majority of the population who have lived on nothing else for years.) However that may be, it was to this growing sense of unjust oppression that I attributed the important place occupied by the Negro in Russia's cultural sympathies.

Negro had been an established favourite for several months; and I was told that attendance at a performance of *Uncle Tom's Cabin* formed part of the curriculum of Leningrad schoolchildren. As a play, *All God's Chillun* misses greatness; it is short, violent, staccato, and its execution lacks that measure of artistic detachment which would have enabled the author to do justice to his theme. The Russian production was interesting and effective; it was amusing to note the points on which it diverged, for ideological reasons, from the original.

The most noticeable difference was that in Moscow every scene was preceded by a song: or rather by two songs, sung respectively by a bourgeois (easily recognizable as such from his habit of wearing a tail coat, a straw hat, and a Leander tie) and by a Negro. They were popular songs, but so allotted, that, while the bourgeois always sang about the good time he was having, the Negro seemed to be concerned entirely with the tremendous amount of work he had on hand. Within the scenes themselves there were few important alterations, though the Negro's struggle to make good in spite of capitalist oppression was given a more specifically class-significance than the American author intended, and there were several interpolated hits at the Salvation Army, which, for some mysterious reason, was very unpopular in Russia at the time. For me, the most striking departure from precedent was that, when the Negro married the girl, they descended the church steps to the strains of *Annie Laurie*.

The chief actor, in Mr Paul Robeson's part (there were no Negroes in the cast), gave a very creditable performance in a quieter and more naturalistic key than is usually to be met with in the Russian theatre, where 'straight' acting too often betrays the fantasticating influence of the ballet. On the technical side Moscow had London beat; expressionistic devices vividly conveyed the jarring rhythm of the New York streets, where most of the action takes place, to heighten the emotional tension. The production was a very skilful and sensitive piece of work.

The audience struck me as being rather more restive than is usual in Moscow, and during one of the graver scenes there appeared to be a small animal, possibly a rat, at large in the dress circle. But as to that I could not say for certain.

My impressions of Moscow, as here set down, are fragmentary and superficial. They are not intended to be anything else. In the course of my life I have spent eight days in that city. I should do both you and myself a disservice by treating it otherwise than sketchily.

Besides, on my last visit I never really got to grips with Moscow. Between me and the numerous and fascinating problems of modern Russia there loomed the figure of a man I have never seen. For four days he dominated my life. His name was Jimmie Mattern, and he was engaged on a solo flight round the world.

He had landed at Moscow a day or two before I arrived, the wings of his plane under their coating of ice profusely speckled with the autographs of admirers. With the minimum of delay he had flown on eastward.

There is no one more inconsiderate than your spectacular aviator. The American correspondents, whose duty it was

31

to keep the world informed of Mr Mattern's progress, all agreed that he was a delightful man, but they wished fervently that it had never occurred to him to fly round the world alone. For them his inconvenient gallantry meant all-night sessions at the telephone, waiting for a call to announce his arrival at Omsk, his departure from Tomsk: it meant a constant *va et vient* between the hotel and the censor's office in the Narkomendal: it meant a perpetual angling, through distant and unreliable agents, for a Personal Statement from the young hero, who was a man of few words and seldom more than semi-conscious when he landed.

Living with the journalists in the hotel, I, too, became infected with the spirit of this vicarious chase. Perhaps out of an instinctive sympathy for my haggard and unshaven colleagues, I allowed the flier to corner my curiosities. The teeming millions of Russia were obscured by a single – or more properly a 'lone' – Texan, whose whereabouts were unpredictable and whose continued existence was constantly in doubt. My catechisms about the Five Year Plan and the food-supply were indefinitely shelved. I asked no questions about current ideology; no one would have had time to answer them if I had.

I escaped one afternoon from that atmosphere of tense but disillusioned expectancy to visit one of the Moscow broadcasting stations. It is housed in the Telegraph Bureau, a sufficiently impressive building, but the offices and studios have a slatternly and aimless air, in this respect contrasting unfavourably with the BBC, whose interior suggests a cross between a liner and a lunatic asylum, both very up to date. I was treated with the greatest kindness, a short fat girl translating for me in French while a female official explained the principles on which their programmes are constructed.

They sounded rather dreary programmes, beginning at six in the morning with physical jerks and continuing, all through the day, to try to do you good in one form or another. There is a children's hour, and an hour for the Red Army. The big men in the Government seldom broadcast. There are no licences, and no check on the number of receiving sets, though listeners are supposed to pay a nominal subscription. They receive thousands of letters, all of which are answered, the best verbally at the microphone . . . And what did my countrymen think of their broadcasts in English?

The question took me off my guard. I forgot how sensitive these earnest people were. I said I was afraid we didn't take their English broadcasts very seriously.

I was not forgiven.

5

TRANS-SIBERIAN EXPRESS

EVERY one is a romantic, though in some the romanticism is of a perverted and paradoxical kind. And for a romantic it is, after all, something to stand in the sunlight beside the Trans-Siberian Express with the casually proprietorial air of the passenger, and to reflect that that long raking chain of steel and wood and glass is to go swinging and clattering out of the West into the East, carrying you with it. The metals curve glinting into the distance, a slender bridge between two different worlds. In eight days you will be in Manchuria. Eight days of solid travel: none of these spectacular but unrevealing leaps and bounds which the aeroplane, that agent of superficiality, to-day makes possible. The arrogance of the hard-bitten descends on you. You recall your friends in England, whom only the prospect of shooting grouse can reconcile to eight hours in the train without complaint. Eight *hours* indeed . . . You smile contemptuously.

Besides, the dignity, or at least the glamour of trains has lately been enhanced. *Shanghai Express*, *Rome Express*, *Stamboul Train* – these and others have successfully exploited its potentialities as a setting for adventure and romance. In fiction, drama, and the films there has been a firmer tone in Wagons-Lits than ever since the early days of Oppenheim. Complacently you weigh your chances of a foreign countess, the secret emissary of a Certain Power, her corsage stuffed with documents of the first political importance. Will anyone mistake you for No. 37, whose real name no one knows, and who is practically always in a train, being 'whirled' somewhere? You have an intoxicating vision of drugged liqueurs, rifled dispatch-cases, lights suddenly extinguished, and door-handles turning slowly under the bright eye of an automatic. . . .

You have this vision, at least, if you have not been that way before. I had. For me there were no thrills of discovery and anticipation. One hears of time standing still; in my case it took two paces smartly to the rear. As I settled down in my compartment, and the train pulled out through shoddy suburbs into the country clothed in birch and fir, the unreal rhythm of train life was resumed as though it had never been broken. The nondescript smell of the upholstery, the unrelenting rattle of our progress, the tall glass of weak tea in its metal holder, the unshaven jowls and fatuous but friendly smile of the little attendant who brought it – all these unmemorable components of a former routine, suddenly resurrected, blotted out the interim between this journey and the last. The inconsequent comedy of two years, with the drab or coloured places, the cities and the forests, where it had been played, became for a moment as though it had never been. This small, timeless, moving cell I recognized as my home and my doom. I felt as if I had always been on the Trans-Siberian Express.

The dining-car was certainly unchanged. On each table there still ceremoniously stood two opulent black bottles of some unthinkable wine, false pledges of conviviality. They were never opened, and rarely dusted. They may contain ink, they may contain the elixir of life. I do not know. I doubt if anyone does.

Lavish but faded paper frills still clustered coyly round the pots of paper flowers, from whose sad petals the dust of two continents perpetually threatened the specific gravity of the soup. The lengthy and trilingual menu had not been revised; 75 per cent of the dishes were still apocryphal, all the prices were exorbitant. The cruet, as before, was of interest rather to the geologist than to the gourmet. Coal dust from the Donetz Basin, tiny flakes of granite from the Urals, sand whipped by the wind all the way from the Gobi Desert – what a fascinating story that salt-cellar could have told under the microscope! Nor was there anything different about the attendants. They still sat in huddled cabal at the far end of the car, conversing in low and disillusioned tones, while the *chef du train*, a potent gnome-like man, played on his abacus a slow significant tattoo. Their surliness went no deeper than the grime upon their faces; they were always ready to be amused by one's struggles with the language or the cooking. Sign-language they interpreted with more eagerness than apprehension: as when my desire for a hard-boiled egg – no easy request, when you come to think of it, to make in panto-mime – was fulfilled, three-quarters of an hour after it had been expressed, by the appearance of a whole roast fowl.

The only change of which I was aware was in my stable-companion. Two years ago it had been a young Australian, a man much preoccupied with the remoter contingencies of travel. 'Supposing,' he would muse, 'the train breaks down, will there be danger of attack by wolves?' When he un-dressed he panted fiercely, as though wrestling with the invisible Fiend; he had a plaintive voice, and on his lips the words 'nasal douche' (the mere sound of Siberia had given him a cold) had the saddest cadence you can imagine. This time it was a young Russian, about whom I remember nothing at all. Nor is this surprising, for I never found out anything about him. He spoke no English, and I spoke hardly any Russian. A phrase book bought in Moscow failed to bridge the gap between us. An admirable compilation in many ways, it did not, I discovered, equip one for casual con-versation with a stranger. There was a certain petulance, a touch of the imperious and exorbitant, about such observa-tions as: 'Show me the manager, the assistant manager, the water closet, Lenin's Tomb', and 'Please to bring me tea, coffee, beer, vodka, cognac, Caucasian red wine, Caucasian white wine'. Besides, a lot of the questions, like 'Can you direct me to the Palace of the Soviets?' and 'Why must I work for a World Revolution?' were not the sort of things I wanted to ask him; and most of the plain statements of fact – such as 'I am an American engineer who loves Russia' and 'I wish to study Architecture, Medicine, Banking under the best teachers, please' – would have been misleading. I did not want to mislead him.

So for two days we grinned and nodded and got out of

each other's way and watched each other incuriously, in silence. On the second day he left the train, and after that I had the compartment to myself.

There is a great deal to be said against trains, but it will not be said by me. I like the Trans-Siberian Railway. It is a confession of weakness, I know, but it is sincere.

You wake up in the morning. Your watch says it is eight o'clock; but you are travelling east, and you know that it is really nine, though you might be hard put to it to explain why this is so. Your berth is comfortable. There is no need to get up, and no incentive either. You have nothing to look forward to, nothing to avoid. No assets, no liabilities.

If you were on a ship there would be any number of both. A whacking great breakfast, sunny decks, the swimming bath, that brilliant short story you are going to write, the dazzling creature whose intuitive admiration for your writings you would be the last to undermine – these are among the assets. Liabilities include the ante-final of the deck quoits, the man who once landed on Easter Island, the ship's concert, dressing for dinner, and boat-drill.

At first the balance sheet strikes you as sound. But gradually, as the tedious days become interminable weeks, the traitorous assets insensibly change sides and swell the ranks of the liabilities. A time comes when there is nothing to look forward to, everything to avoid. That brilliant short story, stillborn, weighs upon your conscience, a succession of whacking great breakfasts upon your digestion; the sunny decks are now uncomfortably so, and even the swimming bath has been rendered for practical purposes inaccessible by that dazzling creature whose intuitive admiration for your writings you have been the first to undermine. At sea there is always a catch somewhere, as Columbus bitterly remarked on sighting America.

But on the Trans-Siberian Railway there are neither ups nor downs. You are a prisoner, narrowly confined. At sea you are a prisoner too, but a prisoner with just enough rope to strangle at birth the impulses of restlessness or inspiration. The prisoner sits down to write, then thinks it would be more pleasant on deck. On deck there is a wind; his papers are unmanageable. With a sigh he takes up a book, a heavy book, a book which it will do him good to read. After four pages there comes an invitation to deck-tennis. He cannot refuse. He goes below to change, comes up again, and desultorily plays. There follows conversation and a bath. The morning is over.

The morning is over. His typewriter is in the smoking-room, his book is on B deck, his coat is on A deck, and he has lost his pipe and broken a finger-nail. In everything he has attempted he has failed. All this peace and leisure has been sterile without being enjoyable. The afternoon will be the same.

Most men, though not the best men, are happiest when the question 'What shall I do?' is supererogatory. (Hence the common and usually just contention that 'My schooldays were the happiest days of my life'.) That is why I like the Trans-Siberian Railway. You lie in your berth, justifiably inert. Past the window plains crawl and forests flicker. The sun shines weakly on an empty land. The piles of birch logs by the permanent way – silver on the outside, black where the damp butts show – give the anomalous illusion that there has been a frost. There is always a magpie in sight.

You have nothing to look at, but no reason to stop looking. You are living in a vacuum, and at last you have to invent some absurdly artificial necessity for getting up: 'fifteen magpies from now', or 'next time the engine whistles'. For you are inwardly afraid that without some self-discipline to give it a pattern this long period of suspended animation will permanently affect your character for the worse.

So in the end you get up, washing perfunctorily in the little dark confessional which you share with the next compartment, and in the basin for which the experienced travel-ler brings his own plug, because the Russians, for some reason connected – strangely enough – with religion, omit to furnish these indispensable adjuncts to a careful toilet.

Then, grasping your private pot of marmalade, you lurch along to the dining-car. It is now eleven o'clock, and the dining-car is empty. You order tea and bread, and make without appetite a breakfast which is more than sufficient for your needs. The dining-car is almost certainly stuffy, but you have ceased to notice this. The windows are always shut, either because the weather is cold, or because it is warm and dry and therefore dusty. (Not, of course, that the shutting of them excludes the dust. Far from it. But it is at least a gesture: it is the best that can be done.)

After that you wander back to your compartment. The *provodnik* has transformed your bed into a seat, and perhaps you hold with him some foolish conversation, in which the rudiments of three languages are prostituted in an endeavour to compliment each other on their simultaneous mastery. Then you sit down and read. You read and read and read. There are no distractions, no interruptions, no temptations to get up and do something else; there is nothing else to do. You read as you have never read before.

And so the day passes. If you are wise you shun the regulation meal at three o'clock, which consists of five courses not easily to be identified, and during which the car is crowded and the windows blurred with steam. I had brought with me from London biscuits and potted meat and cheese; and he is a fool who does not take at least some victuals of his own. But as a matter of fact, what with the airless atmosphere and the lack of exercise, you don't feel hungry on the Trans-Siberian Railway. A pleasant lassitude, a sense almost of disembodiment, descends on you, and the food in the dining-car, which, though seldom really bad, is never appetizing and sometimes scarce, hardly attracts that vigorous criticism which it would on a shorter journey.

At the more westerly stations – there are perhaps three stops of twenty minutes every day – you pace the platforms vigorously, in a conscientious British way. But gradually this practice is abandoned. As you are drawn farther into Asia, old fetishes lose their power. It becomes harder and harder to persuade yourself that you feel a craving for exercise, and indeed you almost forget that you ought to feel this craving. At first you are alarmed, for this is the East, the notorious

East, where white men go to pieces; you fear that you are losing your grip, that you are going native. But you do nothing about it, and soon your conscience ceases to prick and it seems quite natural to stand limply in the sunlight, owlish, frowsty, and immobile, like everybody else.

At last evening comes. The sun is setting somewhere far back along the road that you have travelled. A slanting light always lends intimacy to a landscape, and this Siberia, flecked darkly by the tapering shadows of trees, seems a place at once more friendly and more mysterious than the naked non-committal flats of noon. Your eyes are tired, and you put down your book. Against the grey and creeping distances outside memory and imagination stage in their turn the struggles of the past and of the future. For the first time loneliness descends, and you sit examining its implications until you find Siberia vanished and the grimy window offering nothing save your own face, foolish, indistinct, and as likely as not unshaved. You adjourn to the dining-car, for eggs.

6

FLOREAT MONGOLIA

THAT is what a journey on the Trans-Siberian Railway is like, if you make it alone.

My own was mostly uneventful. The days seemed all the same; the hours shared with the horizon a quality of remote monotony. But of course every day was different, internally or externally. The first, for instance, was uncomfortably hot; but on the second morning the platform at Sverdlovsk, where they shot the Tsar, was whipped by a raw wind. For two days thereafter it was as if we had run into November over-night.

The Urals were left behind, and we crawled across the Black Soil Belt, where on the hedgeless and forlorn plains man and his beasts were dwarfed to the merest microscopic toys, and each little group of figures seemed a pathetic, un-availing protest against the tyrant solitude. The skies were dark. Rain lashed the streaky windows, and when we stopped at a station the wind made a desolate supplicating sound in the ventilators. In the villages very old, very hairy men, standing in thick black mud, stared up at us, from force of habit, without curiosity. Usually it is difficult to stop looking out of the windows of a train, however monotonous the landscape. You think 'I will read now', but for a long time you cannot take your eyes away from the window, just as for a long time you are reluctant to put back the telephone receiver when your number does not answer. Brrr-brrr . . . brrr-brrr . . . brrr-brrr . . . At any moment that aggravating sound may be superseded by a voice. At any moment those dull empty miles may show you something that it would be a pity to have missed. But here it was not like that; here there could be nothing worth waiting for. A grey cold blight had fallen on the world.

Nature when she is frankly hostile, when she is out to do

you down, I do not mind. There is stimulus in the challenge of her extremer moods. But when she is drab and indifferent, as though herself despairing, I am oppressed. On the second day of this anomalous November I was driven to seek sanctuary in the communal meal at three o'clock.

Ugly women and uninspiring men; children who squawled, as children have a right to squawl, and sitting on their mothers' laps put their tiny elbows in the tepid soup; Red Army Officers, dour men in blouse-like tunics of a dark khaki and high boots whose corrugated plasticity suggested Wardour Street; one seedy westernized Chinese from Moscow. . . .

We were all comrades: all equal: all brother-workers in the Five Year Plan: all actors (I reflected) in the most exciting drama of the modern world. . . . But none of this could have been deduced from our appearance. We sat and ate, with dull, heavy eyes. If you had been told to name the outstanding characteristic of this cross-section of the New Russia, you would have put it down as constipation. You would not have been far wrong.

I began to eat, without enthusiasm, synthetic caviar.

Then, all of a sudden, there he was, sitting opposite me; a tall, thin, pale youth, wearing horn-rimmed glasses and looking not unlike Mr Aldous Huxley. I smiled, and he immediately told me the story of his life in fluent though erratic English.

He was twenty-two. His home was in the south, in Baku, but he had run away from it four years ago to go on the stage in Moscow. He had studied the theatre (at the Government's expense) in one of the Dramatic Institutes, and now he was being sent by the Commissariat of Culture to found a National Theatre in Outer Mongolia. He had started as an actor, but now he was a *régisseur*: 'A – how do you call it? A conductor?' 'No. A producer.' Nowadays every one wanted to be a producer; the best producers got higher pay than the best engineers. Stanislavsky, for instance. . . . He told me about Stanislavsky.

He was extremely intelligent: he had an understanding of

the theatre, and a feeling for it. His mind was alert, receptive, and critical. 'Here,' I said to myself (for travellers are always tying labels on to things), 'is a representative of the younger intellectuals. It will be interesting to hear his criticisms of the Soviet regime.'

So it would have been. But he had none: not one. In an oration of some length he expounded to me the doctrines of Karl Marx, or most of them. His faith in them, his pride in the way in which modern Russia was giving them practical expression, were at once touching and impressive. He spoke of Marx as if Marx was the only man who had ever exercised the power of reason; other philosophers were dismissed, not as inferior in quality, but as different altogether in kind. He mentioned Kant as if Kant was a sewing-machine, or a slow bowler: something functioning on another plane altogether. Here was orthodoxy carried to the pitch of fanaticism. I asked him whether the majority of his fellow-students (he lived in the 'university town' in Moscow and presumably saw a lot of his own generation) accepted the present state of affairs as enthusiastically as he did.

'But, of course!' he cried. 'All the students, all the young people, are very, *very* . . . loyal.' His smile apologized for an epithet deriving from the bad old days of feudalism.

At first I was surprised. But gradually, as he talked, I saw that it was not only natural but inevitable that it should be so. The Soviet regime has not a few achievements to its credit, but also not a few failures; and in many, if not most of its aspects, the gap between ambition and achievement appears to the sophisticated mind rather comical than inspiring. The Mongolian impressario's contemporaries are potentially its best critics – young men of humour and perception who were too young to be transfigured by the wave of enthusiasm which launched the first Five Year Plan, and who have grown up to find that what was boomed as a crusade looks at times very like a rearguard action. But they will not criticize; they sincerely believe that the present order is ideal. And indeed it would be surprising if they believed anything else, seeing that under its dispensation they receive food, lodging, an elaborate education, full encouragement to pursue their special bent, as well as various privileges; all this gratis. No wonder that they are fanatically orthodox. It is not they dare not say 'Bo' to the goose that lays the golden eggs; they have not even recognized it as a goose.

I saw a lot of Assorgim (that was his name), and we discussed at length a number of subjects, among which Marxism played an increasingly unimportant part, for I early realized that it would be impossible to tolerate the society of this youth without simulating conversion to his creed. I liked him best when he talked of the theatre, which he did most of the time. The only news from abroad which reaches the average Russian concerns strikes, riots, mutinies, and other phenomena symptomatic of the movement towards a World Revolution; the largest country in the world is also by far the most insular. I found it typical that my friend, although familiar in some detail with conditions in the Elizabethan playhouses, was dumbfounded to hear that in England and America neither actors nor theatres are supported by the State, as they all are in Russia.

He had a profound reverence for, and some appreciation of Shakespeare, and he described to me at length the only two productions of what he called *Gamlet* that Moscow has seen since the Revolution. The first, by a nephew of Chehov's, was a fairly straightforward interpretation of the play, in which interest was centred on the conflict between the spiritual and the fleshy sides of Gamlet's nature. The second was a very different matter. The producer, a man called Akimov, saw in Shakespeare the upthrust of the New Bourgeoisie; he was not a court poet like Lyly, he was not a common man like Ben Jonson, he stood for the new middle class, the conquistadors who were destined to convert English society from feudalism to capitalism. And, naturally, he had put every ounce of his class-consciousness into Gamlet.

So *Gamlet* was played as comedy-melodrama, with a fat and merry actor in the lead, who usually came on to the stage on horseback, or at least surrounded by dogs. He was a gleeful upstart; his sole ambition was the throne, his only worry how to get it. The 'To be or not to be' speech he said while trying on a crown left on a restaurant table by the Player King. (I never quite understood about the restaurant.) As for the Ghost, that was simply a ruse on the part of Gamlet to terrify the ignorant soldiers into allegiance to himself, and to impress on them a belief in the King's iniquity; the Prince produced his father's voice by speaking into a flower pot. Ophelia was a girl more remarkable for her social ambitions than for her virtue; she would be queen, or know the reason why. Piqued at Gamlet's rejection of her advances, she got drunk, sang her mad song between hiccoughs, and went off on a necking party with the Fifth Gentleman. No one was surprised when she was found drowned. Claudius (or Clowdy, as we called him in Siberia) was drunk almost throughout the play.

One day Assorgim came into my compartment and wondered if he could ask me a favour? He meant to present a lot of different plays in Urga (which is the capital of Outer Mongolia), and some of them had English characters in them. He liked, when it was possible, to introduce songs into his plays; each group of characters ought to have a song of its own, it was nicer like that. In Moscow, unfortunately, they had only one song for the English characters to sing, and that was the song called 'Tipperary'. Frankly, he was tired of it. Besides, was it modern? Was it representative? Was it *correct*?

I could not altogether conceal from him my suspicion that – in civilian contexts, at any rate – it was none of these things. This was a mistake on my part, for he implored me to teach him another song. This put me in a very awkward position, because I cannot sing at all, being indeed so utterly unmusical that I quite often have to be nudged and hustled to my feet when they play 'God Save the King', which always seems to me practically indistinguishable, except of course by an expert, from 'Rule, Britannia'.

Putting, however, a bold face on it, I told him that the song he wanted was the Eton Boating Song, which is the only song I have ever sung more than once. After a painful half-hour he had mastered some sort of travesty of this immortal ditty, and was translating the first verse into Russian. He took it away to teach it to his friend, who was a little twinkling man like a clown; and as he went he said:

'I 'ave a play, and there are two Englishes in it. They are what you call clubmen. After long absence, much sorrow, great jobs of work, don't you know, they meet again. They shake hands, because they are clubmen. And then' (his voice grew anxious and wistful) 'and then – and then – they could sing this song? You 'ave such a custom? Yes!'

He was so eager, so anxious to use this little bit of local colour. 'Yes,' I said, 'we have.' After all it was better than 'Tipperary'.

He was a nice man, Assorgim. He was to leave the train at Verchne Udinsk, whence a motor road runs, or is believed to run, down to Urga. He asked me to go with him, and I very nearly did. But I knew the virtual impossibility of getting across that frontier into China, and not without an effort I allowed prudence to prevail. We parted with many expressions of mutual esteem, and I gave him all the biscuits I could spare. I often think of him, a distant gesticulating figure, teaching the Eton Boating Song to the inhabitants of Outer Mongolia.

7

CRASH

AND now the journey was almost over. To-morrow we should reach Manchuli. The train pulled out of Irkutsk, and ran along the river Angara until it debouched into Lake Baikal. At the mouth of the river men were fishing, each in a little coracle moored to a stake at which the current tugged. It was a clear and lovely evening.

Lake Baikal is said to be the deepest lake in the world. It is also said to be the size of Belgium. Its waters are cold and uncannily pellucid. The Russians call it 'The White-haired' because of the mist which always hangs about it. To-night the mist was limited to narrow decorative scarves which floated with a fantastic appearance of solidity far out above the unruffled waters. Out of the mist stood up the heads of distant mountains, dappled with snow. It was a peaceful, majestic place.

Contrary to general belief, the railway round the southern end of Lake Baikal is double-tracked, as indeed is the whole Trans-Siberian line from Chita westward to Omsk, and doubtless by now farther. This is, however, a very vulnerable section. The train crawls tortuously along the shore, at the foot of great cliffs. The old line passes through about forty short tunnels, each lackadaisically guarded by a sentry. The new line skirts round the outside of the tunnels, between the water and the rock. This is the weakest link in that long, tenuous, and somewhat rusty chain by which hangs the life of Russia's armies in the Far East. In 1933 her military establishments on the Amur Frontier totalled about a quarter of a million men, including reservists.

There is no more luxurious sensation than what may be described as the End of Term Feeling. The traditional scurrilities of

This time to-morrow where shall I be?
Not in this academee

have accompanied delights as keen and unqualified as any that most of us will ever know. As we left Baikal behind and went lurching through the operatic passes of Buriat Mongolia I felt very content. To-morrow we should reach the frontier. After to-morrow there would be no more of that black bread, in consistency and flavour suggesting rancid peat; no more of that equally alluvial tea: no more of a Trappist's existence, no more days entirely blank of action. It was true that I did not know what I was going to do, that I had nothing very specific to look forward to. But I knew what I was going to stop doing, and that, for the moment, was enough.

I undressed and got into bed. As I did so I noticed for the first time that the number of my berth was thirteen.

For a long time I could not go to sleep. I counted sheep, I counted weasels (I find them much more efficacious, as a rule. I don't know why). I recited in a loud, angry voice soporific passages from Shakespeare. I intoned the names of stations we had passed through since leaving Moscow: Bui, Perm, Omsk, Tomsk, Kansk, Krasnoyarsk. (At one a low-hung rookery in birch trees, at another the chattering of swifts against a pale evening sky, had made me home-sick for a moment.) I thought of all the most boring people I knew, imagining that they were in the compartment with me, and had brought their favourite subjects with them. It was no good. My mind became more and more active. Obviously I was never going to sleep. . . .

It was the Trooping of the Colour, and I was going to be late for it. There, outside, in the street below my window, was my horse; *but it was covered with thick yellow fur!* This was awful! Why hadn't it been clipped? What would they think of me, coming on parade like that? Inadequately dressed though I was, I dashed out of my room and down the moving staircase. And then (horror of horrors!) the moving staircase broke. It lurched, twisted, flung me off my feet. There was a frightful jarring, followed by a crash. . . .

I sat up in my berth. From the rack high above me my heaviest suitcase, metal-bound, was cannonaded down, catching me with fearful force on either knee-cap. I was somehow not particularly surprised. This is the end of the world, I thought, and in addition they have broken both my legs. I had a vague sense of injustice.

My little world was tilted drunkenly. The window showed me nothing except a few square yards of goodish grazing, of which it offered an oblique bird's-eye view. Larks were singing somewhere. It was six o'clock. I began to dress. I now felt very much annoyed.

But I climbed out of the carriage into a refreshingly spectacular world, and the annoyance passed. The Trans-Siberian Express sprawled foolishly down the embankment. The mail-van and the dining-car, which had been in front, lay on their sides at the bottom. Behind them the five sleeping-cars, headed by my own, were disposed in attitudes which became less and less grotesque until you got to the last, which had remained, primly, on the rails. Fifty yards down the line the engine, which had parted company with the train, was dug in, snorting, on top of the embankment. It had a truculent and naughty look; it was defiantly conscious of indiscretion.

It would be difficult to imagine a nicer sort of railway accident. The weather was ideal. No one was badly hurt. And the whole thing was done in just the right Drury Lane manner, with lots of twisted steel and splintered woodwork and turf scarred deeply with demoniac force. For once the Russians had carried something off.

The air was full of agonizing groans and the sound of breaking glass, the first supplied by two attendants who had been winded, the second by passengers escaping from a coach in which both the doors had jammed. The sun shone brightly. I began to take photographs as fast as I could. This is strictly forbidden on Soviet territory, but the officials had their hands full and were too upset to notice.

The staff of the train were scattered about the wreckage, writing contradictory reports with trembling hands. A charming German consul and his family – the only other foreigners on the train – had been in the last coach and were unscathed. Their small daughter, aged six, was delighted with the whole affair, which she regarded as having been arranged specially for her entertainment; I am afraid she will grow up to expect too much from trains.

Gradually I discovered what had happened, or at least what was thought to have happened. As a rule the Trans-Siberian Expresses have no great turn of speed, but ours, at the time when disaster overtook her, had been on top of her form. She had a long, steep hill behind her, and also a following wind; she was giving of her best. But, alas, at the bottom of that long, steep hill the signals were against her, a fact which the driver noticed in the course of time. He put on his brakes. Nothing happened. He put on his emergency brakes. Still nothing happened. Slightly less rapidly than before, but still at a very creditable speed, the train went charging down the long, steep hill.

The line at this point is single track, but at the foot of the hill there is a little halt, where a train may stand and let another pass. Our train, however, was in no mood for stopping: it looked as if she was going to ignore the signals and try conclusions with a west-bound train, head-on. In this she was thwarted by a pointsman at the little halt, who summed up the situation and switched the runaway neatly into a siding. It was a long, curved siding, and to my layman's eye appeared to have been designed for the sole purpose of receiving trains which got out of control on the hill above it. But for whatever purpose it was designed, it was designed a very long time ago. Its permanent way had a more precarious claim to that epithet than is usual even in Russia. We were altogether too much for the siding. We made matchwood of its rotten sleepers and flung ourselves dramatically down the embankment.

But it had been great fun: a comical and violent climax to an interlude in which comedy and violence had been altogether too lacking for my tastes. It was good to lie back in the long grass on a little knoll and meditate upon that sprawling scrap-heap, that study in perdition. There she lay, in the middle of a wide green plain: the crack train, the Trans-Siberian Luxury Express. For more than a week she had bullied us. She had knocked us about when we tried to clean our teeth, she had jogged our elbows when we wrote, and when we read she made the print dance tiresomely before our eyes. Her whistle had arbitrarily curtailed our frenzied excursions on the wayside platforms. Her windows we might not open on account of the dust, and when closed they had proved a perpetual attraction to small, sabotaging boys with stones. She had annoyed us in a hundred little ways: by spilling tea in our laps, by running out of butter, by regulating her life in accordance with Moscow time, now six hours behind the sun. She had been our prison, our Little Ease. We had not liked her.

Now she was down and out. We left her lying there, a broken buckled toy, a thick black worm without a head, awkwardly twisted, a thing of no use, above which larks sang in an empty plain.

If I know Russia, she is lying there still.

It was, as I say, an ideal railway accident. We suffered only four hours' delay. They found another engine. They dragged that last, that rather self-righteous coach back on to the main line. From the wrecked dining-car stale biscuits were considerately produced. In a sadly truncated train the Germans, a few important officials and myself proceeded on our way. Our fellow-passengers we left behind. They did not seem to care.

Two hours later we reached the Russian customs post, just short of the frontier. In 1931, I remembered, there had been some formality with regard to photographs. What was it? ... Oh, yes. Instructions had been passed along the train that we were to give up all films exposed on Russian soil. The young Australian had one in his camera, to which he instantly confessed. But there was an interval before the collection of films took place, and, not without trepidation, he adopted my suggestion that he should show up an unexposed film, rewound. This daring and elaborate

51

ruse was carried out successfully. The Australian kept his film.

It never occurred to me that the procedure might have been altered, the regulations tightened up. The proud possessor of (as far as I know) the only photographic record of a derailment on the Trans-Siberian line made by a foreigner, I took no steps at all to hide the two films in which it was embodied. They lay, side by side, plain to be seen by anyone who opened my dispatch case. I awaited the customs officials with composure.

They came on me suddenly: five large inquisitive men, commanding between them about as much English as I knew of Russian. It was instantly apparent that they meant business. My suitcases were systematically disembowelled. What was the number of my typewriter? Had I a permit for my field-glasses? Above all, had I any camera films?

But yes! I cried, I had indeed. I thrust into their hands a tiny Kodak, still rusted with the waters of the Amazon. I heaped upon them an assortment of unexposed films, whose virginity they tested by removing the tropical packing. I was playing for time.

Anyone can play for time with words, but my vocabulary was too limited for effective obstructionism. To decoy them into the subtler irrelevancies of debate was impossible, seeing that everything I said was either redundant or incomprehensible. This they quickly grasped. They were men of action. They ceased to listen to me. And all the time their search brought them nearer to that dispatch case, which lay on the end of the seat farthest from the door.

Words failing me, I fell back on inanimate objects. The train, I knew, must leave within a certain time. Every minute that I could delay them would make the closing stages of their search more perfunctory. So I showed them my shoes and my books. I made them all in turn sniff at my hair-oil. I pressed aspirins upon them, and potted meat. I demonstrated the utility of pipe-cleaners, and the principles on which sock-suspenders are designed. But the search went on. They were not to be fobbed off. Under the seat they had found the discarded packing of a film; they felt – and rightly – that they were on to a good thing.

It was very hot. My coat hung on a peg. And in the pocket of my coat (I suddenly remembered) was that photostat copy of Ian's letter from Stalin. I took the coat down and produced the letter.

It had no great success, though it checked them for a moment. A few polite exclamations, and the search was resumed. But in the meantime I, with an aggressively careless gesture, had flung down the coat upon the dispatch case, and the dispatch case was no longer in sight. Presently, with a great parade of exhaustion and impatience, I sat down heavily, sighing, upon the coat, the dispatch case, and the films.

Nothing would move me. Defiantly anchored, like a brooding hen, I watched the hounds draw blank. I signed the forms they gave me to sign. I handed over, protesting loudly, one partially exposed film containing photographs of my grandmother. The officials were puzzled, suspicious. They had seen everything there was to see? Yes, I said firmly, they had seen everything there was to see. Still puzzled, still suspicious, they withdrew. The train started. I had had them with me for three-quarters of an hour.

8

HARBIN

The train drew up in a station peopled by the ghosts of Mr Pickwick and his friends, and patrolled by scarcely more substantial little soldiers in grey uniforms. The labels on my luggage were out of date at last. We had reached Manchuli.

The flag of a brand-new kingdom, the flag of Manchukuo, flew above the station buildings. It was yellow, with a pleasant agglomeration of stripes in one corner. But the flag was the only outward sign of change. True, there was a little Japanese official who took the German consul and myself off to a remote part of the village, and there, when we had filled up forms the size of sagas, issued us with the new Manchukuo visas. (They take up a page in one's passport. They are recognized by only two other countries – Japan and Salvador.) But even this bureaucratic interlude had its typically Chinese side. We travelled to the passport office in a tiny decrepit droshky, pulled by a mouse-like pony. Crowded though it already was, we were saddled with a supercargo in the shape of an enormous coolie. He did nothing at all except slightly retard our progress, but his presence was clearly part of a recognized routine, and when it was all over he demanded a tip. He described himself as a 'visa-porter'.

The Chinese flair for creating employment is wonderfully quick. The passport office had only been open a month.

The train on the Chinese Eastern Railway had been held up for us. Soon we were rattling eastward across illimitable light-green plains, usually fringed by a formal jagged line of hills. There was not much of interest to be seen. Shaggy camels viewed our progress with phlegmatic scorn. A herdsman's pony lost its nerve and bolted. Duck in great numbers went wheeling up from marshes into an emptiness which found reflection on the earth. The interior decoration of the carriages, the portentous whiskers of the Russian guards, combined to lend a somehow late Victorian atmosphere to the train. Surrounded by plush and mirrors, we ran slowly across the wastes of North Manchuria.

Next morning we reached Harbin. It was fourteen days since I had left London. Ten of them had been spent in the train. I was glad to stretch my legs.

Harbin has been called the Paris of the Far East, but not, I think, by anyone who has stayed there for any length of time. It is a place with a great deal of not easily definable character. In outward things Russian influence is almost as strong as American influence is in Shanghai. But behind Harbin's hybrid façade it is to-day the Japanese, and the Japanese only, who count; this is true everywhere in Manchuria.

The Red engineer working on the Chinese Eastern Railway: the White Russian lady in exile, grown fat on the luxuries of nostalgia, for ever fantastically scheming the downfall of the Soviets: the Chinese coolie and the Chinese merchant: the British taipan on his way to lunch at the Yacht Club – all these form a shifting curious pattern in the crowded streets. But none of them are the masters of Harbin; few of them are the masters of their own destinies there. . . .

Athwart that shifting pattern, nosing its way through the crowd, comes a Japanese armoured car, on its way back from a police raid. You need look no farther for the masters of Harbin.

But the masters of Harbin have got their hands full. The city lives under a reign of terror, which in 1932, at the time of the shooting of Mrs Woodruff, had reached such a pitch of intensity that on the golf links a White Russian Guard, armed to the teeth, was much more indispensable than a caddy. Few foreigners dared to walk abroad at night, and none to walk unarmed. In 1933, when I was there, conditions were improving. Bandits still throve, but the Japanese saw to it that they throve, not on foreigners with sensitive governments behind them, but on the Chinese and the White Russians. Adequate protection was now available to all sympathizers with the new regime in Manchukuo.

But even the least adventurous still find it easy to live dangerously in Harbin. A Pole, the branch manager of an important British firm, entertained me in a compound of which the wall was crowned with electrified barbed-wire. There seemed to him nothing remarkable in this. A few weeks ago he had received the usual threat – a little paper figure of a man with a bullet-hole inked in red upon his forehead. This was accompanied by an exorbitant demand for dollars, and instructions as to how they should be delivered. The Pole went to the Japanese commissioner of police, and a young Samurai officer was detailed to protect him. For some time the officer slept every night at the foot of his staircase, his long sword ready to his hand. But now the danger was thought to have blown over, and the Pole observed only elementary precautions – the barbed wire, a White Russian guard at his gate, and plenty of revolvers in his car when he went out. The little paper figure of a murdered man joined lesser curios on his mantelpiece.

It was strange what an edge it gave to normal things, this faint but ever-present shadow of the bandit menace. Harbin is on the River Sungari, and in the hot summer months a brackish and fantastic Lido springs up along the mud banks opposite the Yacht Club. I bathed there one day, in company with that legendary figure, One-Arm Sutton, who helped to run the Mukden Arsenal for Chan Tso-lin, and is, I believe, the only Old Etonian claiming to hold the rank of General in the Chinese Army. Monstrous women sported like hippopotami in the shallows. The beauties from the night-clubs, heavily made up, minced beside their pot-bellied escorts in costumes which were hardly more than a figure of speech. A few slim Chinese, burnt copper by the sun, dived and laughed and splashed each other like children. The native boatmen, old-fashioned to the core, eyed with a scorn which had once been horror the modes and manners of the foreign women.

But what lent the scene its extra and redeeming touch of oddity was the presence, everywhere along this grotesquely decorated shore, of soldiers and police armed with rifles and automatics. Martyrs to boredom and to heat, they watched the bathers with a sullen envy. To the people I was with they were a normal and inevitable sight. Nobody mentioned bandits, except as a joke. But when the girls, who had withdrawn to undress behind some tombs, failed to reappear within the expected period, the jokes grew more and more perfunctory, and soon it was apparent that a nice problem for the chivalrous had been raised. But in the end our anxious whistles were answered and every one was reassured.

In Harbin I first began to pass myself off on people as a Special Correspondent of *The Times*. (For obvious reasons, I had kept quiet about this in Russia.) I immediately discovered that I had come all this way without ascertaining what exactly were the duties of a Special Correspondent, or how they should be discharged. The great thing, I decided, was to Preserve an Open Mind. This entailed the minimum of exertion on my part and was really very easy, because I started by knowing nothing, and everything people told me I forgot.

But to describe in detail the process of preserving an open mind might, I fear, alienate the sympathies of my readers. I will therefore pass over the subject of my professional activities in Harbin and go on to the next place, noting only in passing that in Harbin I entered for the first time the portals of an opium den. (We writers, as I dare say you have noticed, always describe the means of ingress to any haunt of vice as 'portals'.)

In my experience all opium dens are small, stuffy, and extremely disappointing to regular readers of fiction; in these respects, if in no others, they resemble the dressing-rooms of actresses. My first den was no exception to this rule. It was empty save for a facetious attendant and one very old man stretched out neatly on a wooden couch. He was asleep and, no doubt, dreaming. His features wore a look of the most profound boredom.

I refused a pipe and left the building.

9

PU YI

FROM Harbin I took the train to Hsingking, after mailing home those photographs of the Trans-Siberian smash whose publication would, I sincerely hoped, lead to some wholesale dismissals in the Russian customs service.

Hsingking is the new capital of Manchukuo, and incidentally the youngest capital city in the world. Capitals in China have always been highly movable, and the Japanese had plenty of precedent for shifting the seat of government from Mukden to a place which, in addition to being more geographically central, was uncontaminated by relics of the Young Marshal's evil influences. They chose Hsingking, formerly Chanchun, and in those days important only because it marked the junction of the Chinese Eastern Railway and the South Manchurian Railway. I had passed through Chanchun two years ago, when it was full of Japanese reinforcements for the invasion which had just been launched.

At the time of my second visit Hsingking had hardly adapted itself to the greatness so suddenly thrust upon it. It is a small town, of which the central part, focused round the railway station, has that symmetrical, sanitary, and entirely characterless appearance imposed by Japanese influence of all towns in the Railway Zone. The outskirts are more haphazard and Chinese. A sparse traffic of droshkies, rickshaws, and government officials' cars raises dense clouds of dust in streets which belong neither to the East nor to the West. There is a small hotel run by the South Manchurian Railway and, like everything Japanese, admirably clean and tidy. I was lucky to get a room there, for the place is full of homeless officials, and most visitors are exiled to the Railway Hotel.

The Railway Hotel is so-called for the best of reasons. It consists of a string of sleepers in a siding.

Hsingking was used to Special Correspondents. Members of that overrated profession had been indeed almost its only foreign visitors. Firmly but courteously I was launched upon a round of interviews. For three days I interviewed people without stopping.

The procedure was monotonous and unreal. You picked up an interpreter from the Foreign Office and drove round to keep your appointment. The Government departments were poorly housed as yet, and your Chinese Minister would be found lurking in the recesses of a former school or office buildings. He received you with the utmost courtesy, bowing ceremoniously in his long silk robe. Tea was produced, and cigarettes. In blackwood chairs you sat and smiled at each other.

He was the Minister of State for this or that. But in one corner of the room sat a clerk who took down a verbatim report of the interview, for submission presumably to the powers behind that throne of which the Minister was on paper, the representative. So it behoved the Minister to be guarded in his speech. And even if he was not – even if he forgot (or should it be remembered?) himself and was prompted by a lucky shot to indiscretion – it did not help you much. For there at your side was the interpreter, and he could ensure that whatever information reached you consisted only of official facts, garnished with the right official flavour. Quite soon I decided that interviews were a waste of time.

One of them, however, was not. I was granted an audience by His Excellency Henry Pu Yi, Chief Executive of the State of Manchukuo, and to-day its Emperor. Mr Pu Yi – as the newspapers, those harbingers of disenchantment, insist on calling him – is the heir to the Dragon Throne of the Manchu dynasty. He ascended it in 1908 at the age of three and at the wish of that fantastic character, the Empress Dowager. She died on the day after his enthronement. Two years later the Revolution broke out, and in 1912 the child was forced to abdicate. The last representative of the Manchu dynasty withdrew to Jehol.

In 1917 he was back on the throne, but only for a week; the restoration movement fizzled out. In 1924 his palace in Peking was invaded by the troops of Feng Yu-hsian, the 'Christian General', and the boy's life was only saved by the resource of Sir Reginald Johnston, his tutor, who smuggled him into the Legation Quarter. Most unfairly deprived, by now, of the privileges which had been granted him under the treaty of abdication, the ex-Emperor slipped out of Peking and took refuge in the Japanese Concession at Tientsin. Here he remained until a figure-head was required for the alleged autonomy movement in Manchuria. In 1932, nominally by the will of thirty million people, actually by a shrewd stroke of Japanese foreign policy, he became the titular ruler of Manchukuo. In 1934 they made him Emperor.

The temporary palace was the former offices of the Salt Gabelle. The Chinese soldiers on guard at the gate wore smarter uniforms than usual; they were armed with new Japanese service rifles, which are easily recognized because there is no outward and visible sign of a magazine. In the outer courtyard an aged general was wandering about. He had a straggling white beard and the air of an El Greco minor prophet. He seemed to be at a loose end.

I sent in my card and was presently ushered with an interpreter into an ante-room. This was full of Chinese officers of the Manchukuo* army, with a sprinkling of Japanese. One of these, an A.D.C., took over the duties of my interpreter during the audience.

While we waited, I asked him whether I ought to address the Chief Executive as Your Excellency or Your Majesty. He said he was not sure; Manchukuo was as yet without a

*This force, which numbered at that time about 120,000 men, must not be confused with the Kuantung Army, which is the Japanese army of occupation and consisted then of rather more than five divisions of regulars at peace strength (10,000 men to a division). The Japanese have no great faith in the Manchukuo troops, among whom an hereditary tendency to regard the bandits as allies rather than enemies has yet to be completely eliminated.

constitution, and its officials were often embarrassed by the questions of foreign visitors who, with their usual passion for labels, wanted to know whether it was a monarchy or a republic or an oligarchy or what? On the whole he thought Your Excellency would meet the present case.

Eventually we were summoned, and made our way up a narrow staircase into a large, parlour-like room, furnished in the European style, and having a markedly uninhabited air.

Mr Pu Yi received us alone. He is a tall young man of twenty-nine, much better-looking and more alert than you would suppose from his photographs, which invariably credit him with a dazed and rather tortoise-like appearance. He has very fine hands and a charming smile. He was wearing dark glasses, a well-cut frockcoat, a white waistcoat, and spats. All three of us bowed and smiled a great deal, and then sat down.

This time if there was anybody taking notes of the interview he was out of sight. His Excellency understands English, and I suspect speaks it as well; but he prefers to give audience through an interpreter. The audience began.

It lasted half an hour. I asked the inevitable questions, which it would have been unseemly to omit. They were beginning to sound pretty futile to me.

They were broad questions on political matters, and the answer to all of them turned out – not at all to my surprise – to be 'Wangtao'.

During the last few days the word had been often in my ears. Wangtao means the Principle of Benevolent Rule. It was found as a formula, and has remained as a gag. The more specific, the more awkward the questions you asked, the more · certain you were to get Wangtao for an answer. . . .

'Was it true that the Government, under the pretence of suppressing the cultivation and sale of opium, had in fact turned it into a profitable state monopoly?'

'Wangtao.'

'Had not the use of bombers on anti-bandit operations resulted in the destruction of much innocent life and property?'

'Wangtao.'

They answered, of course, at much greater length. It took a certain amount of circumlocution to lead you round the point. But the destination at which you finally arrived was always the same: Wangtao.

With His Excellency, needless to say, I raised no such uncomfortably controversial issues as the above. After a few Wangtaos had cleared the air we passed from high politics to the personal. Did His Excellency ever broadcast to his people, as our King had recently? Yes, he had, once; he would like to do it again. He had a great admiration for the King of England, who had once sent him a signed photograph. Did His Excellency contemplate becoming Emperor? (This was six months before the announcement was made.) His Excellency said that he would do whatever was thought best for his people.

I felt that we were slipping back to the Wangtao gambit. I tried a long shot, reasoning that even potential Emperors must like to talk about themselves. I asked His Excellency which had been the happiest time in his life – the old days in the Forbidden City in Peking, or his untroubled exile in the Foreign Concession at Tientsin, or the present, when he was back in the saddle again?

His Excellency, with a delightful smile, replied at length. The interpreter began to translate. 'His Excellency says that so long as you feel benevolent towards every one – so long as you practise the principle of Wangtao – happiness is surely only a question of. . . . ' He droned on.

The formula had been rediscovered. Very soon I took my leave.

I often think of Mr Pu Yi, that charming though reticent young man. He is surely the most romantic of the rulers of this world. The strong men in funny shirts; the dim presidents in top hats: Moscow's grubby Jews in 1910 Rolls-Royces: the rajahs and the emirs and the shahs, the big kings and the little kings – all these we have seen before. We have got used to them. They are no longer very remarkable. The relations between a man and his throne do not now excite in us that agonizing curiosity which they excited in Shakespeare. Perhaps democracy is to blame. We have found out how dull it is to rule ourselves; we are the less concerned to know what it feels like to rule others.

But Mr Pu Yi is a new line in rulers. Disinherited from an Empire, he now finds himself the nominal head of a new state which once formed part of that Empire. He is a figurehead, owing his position to an alien and – for most of his fellow-countrymen – a hated race. All round him they are busy working out the destinies of his people: little brown men in khaki, little brown men in frock-coats, very serious, very methodical, very energetic. Officially their actions are an expression of his will, officially he is the master. But actually he is at best no more than a privileged spectator. He cannot be unconscious of the fact.

What does he feel, as he watches them at work? What does he feel, as he signs state papers on the dotted line and lays foundation stones and speaks by rote on great occasions?

I often wonder.

I was not sorry to leave Hsingking. The atmosphere of that capital is too thick with humbug for comfort. The conscientious journalist will hardly escape that affliction which is now known among the correspondents in Manchuria as Fleming's Disease, or Propaganda Elbow. Every time you visit an official he gives you, on parting, a small ass-load of pamphlets, tracts, and proclamations. Propaganda Elbow is contracted from carrying this vast and unwieldy bundle back to your hotel. You cannot leave it in a taxi, for there are no taxis in Hsingking. You cannot drop it, unnoticed, in the street. You must lug it dutifully home.

It proves to be heavy stuff in more senses than one. The Japanese are not very good at propaganda, and they go in for it far too much. Few will be interested, none will be convinced by those interminable protestations of altruism, those laborious attempts to prove (for instance) that all the thirty million inhabitants of Manchukuo are really Manchus by birth, or that every individual who wrote an anti-Japanese letter to the Lytton Commission was in the pay of the Young Marshal.

After reading a few kilogrammes of the publications of the Ministry of Information and Publicity I lost patience with the stuff. The Japanese, I reflected, are doing what is, taken by and large, good work in Manchuria.* And even if it was not good work, no one is going to stop them from doing it. This being so, why this perpetual gilding of the lily? Why these everlasting and redundant attempts to pass off a policy of enlightened exploitation as a piece of disinterested rescue-work? This parading of non-existent virtues, this interminable process of self-vindication, breeds doubt and scepticism in the foreign observer. His reactions are the obvious ones. 'Why,' he says, 'are these chaps so terribly anxious to appear, not merely reasonably decent, but extravagantly quixotic? I don't like all this eyewash.' And next time he meets an official, full of the usual evasions and the usual overstatements, he decides that the Japanese are a race of liars and not to be trusted a yard.

The truth is, I think, that this frantic and misguided insistence on propaganda has its roots in an inferiority complex. The unsubtle Western methods of propaganda are a game to which, like many other games, the Japanese are new. Behind their sturdy bluster they are shy and uncertain of themselves. Their lack of inner confidence is expressed in the usual way. They play the new game too hard and too seriously. They overdo it. They protest too much.

Looking through those pamphlets and proclamations, with their stiff portentous phraseology, I wished for a moment that the rulers of Manchukuo had broken with the hackneyed technique of modern diplomacy – that they had ceased to 'view with grave concern', to 'confess themselves at a loss to understand'; I wished it was not typical of the new state that her genesis – the military invasion of Manchuria – was still invariably referred to as The Incident. In the old days

* They have, for instance, stabilized the currency; an inestimable blessing to a country formerly flooded with worthless paper money by the warlords.

the rulers of the world were not so mealy-mouthed; they did quite often say what they meant. And they sometimes said it with humour. They knew the power of a joke. The French Dauphin sent tennis balls to the English King; and it is significant that the scene in which they are delivered is the only one in Shakespeare's play in which Henry V appears, for a moment, at a disadvantage.

Laughter is a strong weapon, because it is incalculable and there is no defence against it. But in diplomacy the weapon has long been voluntarily discarded. It is a sad pity; a Strong Note would be all the stronger for the infusion of a little mockery. But no: we must be slavishly formal, we must go on rumbling at each other in the old pompous jargon of which every phrase has the polished stiffness, the bulky complacence, of Victorian furniture.

It is too late, now, for us to escape from those conventions. But Manchukuo need never have submitted to them. The other nations cold-shouldered her, ignored her existence. She had every excuse for taking a line of her own, and humour is a line worth trying. When called to order she should have cocked a snook. She should have conducted her correspondence with foreign powers on picture postcards, or in verse, or not at all. If she had sent (say) an enormous sturgeon to the Secretary General of the League every day for a month he would, I think, have become uneasy in his mind, and Manchukuo might have stood a better chance at Geneva.

But the rulers of the new state are the Japanese. They toed the line. They stuck to long and disingenuous communications, couched in frock-coated prose.

They threw away a big chance, I think.

10

WINGS OVER MUKDEN

FROM Hsingking I went on to Mukden.

Before leaving Hsingking I should have liked to say something about a man I met there. He was a young Chinese. The work he was doing there was as difficult and dangerous as you could wish. I have met, I suppose, few braver men, and no greater patriots. His patriotism, a rare quality in China, was magnificent but futile. To write about it would be to make it more futile still and perhaps – if he still survives – to endanger his life.

So from Hsingking we go on to Mukden.

Mukden is nondescript and suburban. Here again an unhappy compromise between East and West drains the place of character. Within its walls the Chinese city seethes almost unnoticed, as separate and isolated as a zoo. The broad streets, the fine buildings, of the Japanese Concession are neither here nor there. Synthetic and transplanted, they fail to commend themselves even by incongruity. There is – outwardly – something lack-lustre and half-baked about the place.

The night after I arrived in Mukden they had an anti-aircraft practice. Japan, like other nations, is terribly afraid of attack from the air. At Vladivostok, and westwards along the Amur frontier, Russia (and who shall blame her?) maintains powerful air bases, said to be well-equipped. In the event of hostilities, the crowded and combustible cities of Japan would be within the cruising range of the biggest bombers, while the towns of Manchuria and Korea would be still more easily vulnerable. In all three countries, therefore, sham air-raids are periodically staged, and the civilian population is put through its paces against the day of wrath.

A charming Japanese official invited me to see the fun as his guest on the roof of the Yamato Hotel. There were two other guests, both American: a lady, white-haired but indefatigable, who described herself – repeatedly – as a freelance journalist, and a seraphic gentleman, prematurely bald and said to be a lecturer ('interested' as the lady said with a touch of superiority, 'primarily in the Older Things'. Her, she implied, for the New, the Vital, the Significant). Both were delightful people, but the lady, with her highbrow jargon and her morbid interest in hygiene and the Status of Women, was a familiar transatlantic type. The lecturer interested me more.

You could have sold that man anything. He was so innocent, so eager to please and to be pleased. He had looked for so long on the bright side of things that I doubt if he was aware that there was another side. He was a gift to the Japanese, who are desperately anxious to impress foreigners favourably. Everything that they told him he believed. Several of his articles, he confided to me with pride, had already been incorporated in the official publications of the Manchukuo Government. He was a man whom it was impossible not to like.

During dinner a Japanese official's wife, an attractive lady very well dressed in the Western style, confessed her nostalgia for Washington, where her husband had formerly held a post. Life in Manchuria, she said, was dull. The civil officials there were back numbers; it was the army that counted. The Consulate-General at Mukden had formerly ranked almost as high as an Embassy; now it was of minor importance, both internally and externally, compared with military Headquarters. She wished she was back in Washington.

After dinner we went up to the roof. It was Midsummer Night. The stars looked down on a city lying like a dark plaque on which the lighted streets cut cubist hieroglyphics. The sound of an unceasing and slightly petulant turmoil, which is the very breath of urban life in China, rose through the sweet air, a little blurred and mellowed by the height. It is one of those unintermittent noises, like the grilling of cicadas, of which you soon become entirely unaware.

The roof was crowded. Access to it was possible only for those holding an invitation from divisional headquarters. Khaki predominated. Japanese officers, trailing their long swords musically across the concrete, clicked and bowed and smiled and chattered in little shifting groups. Consular parties, ripped untimely from the dinner-table, rattled the small change of gossip and awaited developments with an unserious and slightly condescending air. Goldfish swam aimlessly in a little fountain.

Suddenly a siren cried, intolerably shrill. All over the city lights went out. Darkness seemed to well up out of the bottom of the streets, levelling the roofs; the features of the place were flattened out. When the siren's voice dwindled to a moody whine only one light was left. It was in the window of a room over a Chinese shop near the hotel. The whole weight of public disapproval was focused on that impenitently yellow square of blind. I felt sorry for whoever was behind it, gambling or making love. At last, with a startled suddenness, the light was extinguished.

Now, in the night, could be heard the hum of engines. The fingers of two searchlights beckoned in the sky. Presently a plane, two planes, appeared. They flew slowly and at no great height. Their under-sides, pinned by the beams, shone a deathly pale green, the phosphorescent colour of decay. As they approached sham bombs were exploded in the city; they made a heavy, apologetic sound. Loudspeakers on the roof began to bellow regulations and advice in the Chinese language. An anti-aircraft gun chattered in the suburbs, and as the planes passed overhead, dropping an occasional streamer on the city's vitals, a machine-gun on the roof beside us opened spasmodic fire. The faces of the crew, fierce and intent, sprang out of the darkness in the flash of the blanks. Presently the planes disappeared, leaving the searchlights to wave inquisitive antennae in an empty sky.

Soon they were back. This time a huge stack of sleepers, piled in front of the hotel and soaked in kerosene, went up suddenly in flames. Nobody had been expecting this; a rush was made to the parapet which overlooked this inexplicable and indeed alarming conflagration. From the square below us – the centre of the town – the crowd, curious and unquiet, was being cleared by the police. A fire-engine came roaring down an empty avenue between packed pavements. Working like demons in a hellish light the firemen went into action. The long flat hose trailing in the dust behind them swelled, rounded, grew purposeful, like the body of a snake. A jet of water leapt like a spear upon the flames and killed them with a disconcerting abruptness, creating an unpleasant smell. The Chinese crowd cheered loudly – not for the firemen, but for a little mongrel dog which defied police regulations, eluded the cordon, and comically shared the centre of the stage reserved for the firemen alone. Overhead the planes still droned.

They continued to drone for some time. It was an hour before the lights went on again, and then, after a brief interim of peace, the siren sounded and the process was repeated. In military circles on the roof repetition failed to dull the edge of enthusiasm; with pride and excitement the officers continued to point, to gasp, and to applaud, like the fireworks crowd at an Eton Fourth of June. There was something childlike and primitive in the pleasure they took in a pantomime with such lethal implications. 'A barbarian's Midsummer Night's Dream'; notes my diary, perhaps rather rudely.

The detached observer, that insufferable person, is always difficult to please. An element of repetition in the spectacle combined with a crick in the spectator's neck to produce, quite early on, a sense of surfeit. Nor, as a matter of fact, were the manoeuvres as a whole particularly impressive. No great demands were made on the searchlight crews, for the attacking planes carried lights on their wings, kept within easy range, and appeared to seek rather than to shun exposure in the tell-tale beams. Only the most perfunctory attempts were made to sight the machine-gun on the hotel roof, which did very little firing, presumably to spare the rifling from the effect of blanks. Bombing practice by the attackers was, judging by the streamers picked up in the most irrelevant places next day, of a disappointingly low standard.

On the roof, however, a good time was had by all.

There are two nice things about the foreign communities in China.

One is that they are always glad to see you no matter how repulsive or insignificant you may be. In England you may be shunned or ignored. But in China you are a stranger, your face, however unattractive, is a new face; in short, you have scarcity-value. You are made welcome for your own sake.

The other nice thing is that none of the foreign residents in China is a bore. Few of them, I admit, would endorse this statement; but I am speaking from the point of view of the traveller, and from the point of view of the traveller it is true. In China, as elsewhere, he will meet men and women with all the deadly attributes of the King or Queen Bore: people with narrow minds and no imagination, people full of prejudice and empty of humour, people from whom he would run a mile at home. But in China he meets them only fleetingly; and in China transplantation has raised their value. Men who would be intolerable in their native suburb become, by virtue of their very limitations, fascinating subjects for study in the compounds of Cathay. To see how they adapt themselves to the subtle and exotic background against which their lives must now be led, to gauge their reactions to the charms and deceits of China, to examine their technique in exile – all these are preoccupations of the first interest. Most of the foreigners, of course, are interesting and amusing in their own right; but in a way it is the others – the transplanted nonentities – who are the most intriguing.

In Mukden everyone was nice, but there was very little doing. The swimming-bath, the squash court, the ponies – these were not the serious business of a Special Correspondent, even when one of the last-named carried him out to the magpie-haunted tranquillity of the Pei Ling tombs, which the following notice doubtless does much to preserve:

NOTICE

1. No fowling piece allowed
2. No plucking allowed
3. No fishing or hunting allowed
4. No clamour or quarrel allowed
5. No burning allowed
6. No throwing from the elevated allowed
7. No nakedness allowed
8. No urine outside the w.c. allowed

BY ORDER.

For my purposes, the fourth regulation was being observed too faithfully all over Manchuria. When I had signed on for this journey the Japanese were hurling their mechanized columns down through the frozen passes of Jehol against the Great Wall; the prospect of some form of fighting had been reasonably bright. But the Chinese defence – let down, as ever, by the High Command – had melted; the Japanese had made good a line which they ought by rights to have found impregnably held against them. Long before I reached the frontier the Jehol situation had been liquidated, leaving the Japanese unchallenged masters of an extra province.

All over the country, however, anti-bandit operations were in progress, and from the moment of entering Manchukuo I had been angling assiduously for permission to accompany a punitive expedition. In Mukden, thanks to the courtesy of Lt.-Gen. Koiso, the Chief of Staff of the Kuantung Army and in effect the ruler of Manchukuo, I achieved my object. A small flying column of the Independent Railway Guard – one unit in a big encircling movement – was leaving, secretly, in a week's time for the mountainous district east of Mukden. I could go with them if I liked.

The intervening week I filled in with visits to Newchwang and Jehol. Newchwang is a small, decaying port, of no particular interest in itself. But in the marshes outside Newchwang (which was the scene in 1932 of the capture of Mrs Pawley and Mr Corkran) three officers of the British coasting vessel s.s. *Nanchang* had for three months been held captive by pirates. So the place was in the news.

71

M. and I went down by train. We were welcomed with the greatest kindness by Mr Denzil Clarke, whose successful conduct of the Pawley case had won for him the doubtful privilege of negotiating the release of the *Nanchang* captives. With the local agent of the *Nanchang*'s owners and a language officer from our Legation in Peking, Mr Clarke had endured for three months uncertainty and tedium in their acutest forms; he was to endure them for another two.

Bandits are sticklers for tradition. There is a certain due course which negotiations for ransom must pursue; in no circumstances can their progress be accelerated. To and fro the emissaries pass: slipping out of the city at night, meeting the pirates' agents in a distant creek, after a few days returning with the next development in the interminable (and to all Chinese delightful) process of bargaining. A maddening sense of impotence oppresses the would-be ransomer. There, only a few miles away, are the bandits, a puny though exorbitant rabble, subjecting their prisoners to hardship certainly, perhaps to cruelty. Direct action, attack, revenge, are out of the question; any attempt to implement a threat may cost the captives their lives. The only chance – a chance which seems often to dwindle to vanishing-point – of securing their release is by a correspondence as tortuous, as leisurely, as improbably successful as any on the files of a government department. I did not envy Mr Clarke.

Some sort of official fête was in progress at Newchwang. It celebrated, I think, the anniversary of the opening of the Manchukuo Customs. I have confused recollections of a cheerless compound decked with bunting, in the centre of which four geishas mopped and mowed upon a windswept stage. Trestle tables groaned under a quantity of cold unappetizing food; Japanese beer flowed freely. The local Chinese general wore a straw hat. An English lady pined for the amenities of her husband's last post in Upper Burma (nostalgia in one form or another is very prevalent in China). Japanese in frock-coats bowed repeatedly and smiled. M., the traitor, had somehow foreseen this function and was correctly resplendent in tropical whites, against which my ancient flannels seemed a solecism. But a gust of wind suddenly possessed the hat of the German consul, and this, in its insensate career, upset a bottle of beer over those irreproachable legs. So much for forethought.

We returned, via the hospitable ward-room of a British destroyer, to the shipping company's mess where Mr Clarke had his headquarters. Here, among sporting prints which bore, in addition to the honoured signature of Thorburn, agreeably sentimental dedications by previous tenants, we dined and exchanged chimerical solutions of the *impasse* which was uppermost in everybody's mind. Of these perhaps the most original and the best was the suggestion that one of the captives should feign madness. The Chinese are more afraid of madness than of anything else; judicious raving might secure release, or at any rate a good chance of escape. But the British Merchant Service is presumably not over-stocked with Hamlets, and the discussion, though animated, remained rather academic.

We left early next morning. Negotiations had just broken down for the third or fourth time on the eve of success. The military were now going to take over the situation; the desperate remedy of direct attack was to be tried. The captives' chances of survival seemed slender indeed.

That winter I met two of them in London. They had been ransomed at last, after five and a half months' captivity in circumstances of the greatest discomfort and danger. Since they have told their story elsewhere* I shall not repeat it here.

Pirate Junk: by Clifford Johnson.

I I

GEISHA PARTY

HE wore a thick black suit, a stiff collar, and a felt hat. He was a short, sturdy man, and there was a sort of sulkiness about his face which made it rather attractive. This sulkiness, or truculence, was borne out in the aggressive set of his shoulders and his rather rolling gait. The general effect, however, was disarming rather than formidable. He looked less like a bully than a shy suspicious little boy who cultivated a defensive swagger. You could not help liking him.

He was Mr H., a prominent Japanese official in Manchukuo. He had announced his intention of accompanying me to Jehol. The Government was displaying a benevolent interest in my activities as a Special Correspondent.

We stood, side by side, in the early sunlight on the Mukden airfield. A military aeroplane, with room for four passengers, stood glittering on the baked and dusty earth. Mr H. eyed it with a certain apprehension.

'Before now, I never fly,' he said. There was a wistful note in his voice.

I was feeling rather unkind. Mr H., fanatically methodical, had got me out of bed an hour earlier than was necessary. Now I told him that before leaving London I had consulted a fortune-teller; the only one of her predictions which I could remember at all distinctly had been to the effect that I would be involved in a flying accident.

'Yes?' said Mr H. He gave a hollow laugh.

Soon we were on board, piled into the stuffy cabin with two Japanese officers, their swords, and their kit. Mr H. clutched to his bosom, with a slightly desperate air, a bottle of whisky which he was bringing for his colleague, the Japanese consul in Jehol City. The engines roared. We bumped away across the airfield.

Our pace quickened. The tempo of the bumps merged into a steady, an almost imperceptible jarring. Then, as the plane prepared to rise, her stride seemed to lengthen. In a series of bounds, each bigger than the last, her wheels spurned the earth. At last she left it altogether. Banking, we circled over the Young Marshal's gigantic arsenal, which lies on the outskirts of Mukden, and made off southwards.

How neat the Chinese are! The country below us was patterned intricately and with affection, like a patchwork quilt. Here, in the North, the fields are mostly larger than in the rice-growing South. The country is less crowded; there is more elbow-room. Even so, none of it is wasted. Symmetry and economy of space ruled in that meticulously quartered land. The different greens of the different crops were partitioned by paths and dykes which might have been drawn with a ruler. Their nice pattern was a natural growth, the gradual but spontaneous product of many years and long traditions; it did not bore or repel, as does the tailor-made, the rather parvenu regularity of English garden suburbs and small American towns. It lent the land dignity, and made you think of its people with respect.

For three hours we flew South, and presently came in sight of a big, dark-grey, sprawling city. This was Chinchow, and here we landed. The second and longer stage of the flight to Jehol would be completed in another plane.

It was almost immediately apparent that it would not be completed by us on that day. A telegram had gone astray; no reservations had been made. We watched with mortification the second plane make its departure, bursting with officers.

The big aerodrome was a military aerodrome. Chinchow was a garrison-town. Mr H., though a person of importance, was a civilian. The event of that day gave me a fleeting insight into the cleavage which exists between the civil and the military authorities in Manchukuo.

I am by nature very bad at enduring delay, and Chinchow was in any case a poor place to endure it in. Politely but firmly I pestered Mr H.; I wanted to ensure – what at the

moment was by no means certain – that we should leave for
Jehol to-morrow. Together we visited a succession of officers.
His shoulders defiantly hunched, his felt hat pulled down
over one eye like a gangster's, Mr H. grew more and more to
resemble a sulky little boy. I longed to comfort him.

Nobody else did. The officers were indeed extremely polite.
Several firkins of tea were consumed. But they could promise
nothing. All the seats in to-morrow's plane were booked; we
must live in hopes of an eleventh-hour cancellation.

Poor Mr. H.; it was painfully evident that he cut no ice.
He was losing face, and he was worried. If only, he said, they
had sent an officer from Headquarters with me a special
plane would have been forthcoming at once. ... We departed sorrowfully in quest of lodging for the night.

This was not easily come by. Chinchow is a purely Chinese
city, with no foreign concession. Two Japanese hotels have
sprung up there since the occupation of Manchuria, but the
larger and more commodious was already full. At the other,
a tiny inn in a narrow street, we did, however, get a room. It
was a building of one storey, run by a Japanese lady of exquisite affability. We took off our shoes at the door and put
on slippers. These in turn were discarded when we came to
the threshold of our room. It was a tiny, flimsy room, with
matting on the floor but no window. The furniture consisted
of two fans, two fly-swatters (very badly needed), and a low
table; no chairs. There was a roll of bedding in the corner,
ready to be spread out at night. Everything was very bare
and clean and close. I felt rather like a beetle in a matchbox.

We took off our coats and squatted on the floor. Like most
Europeans I was not very good at squatting. Presently a meal
was served by a very pretty girl who knelt and bowed as she
offered each dish. There was a kind of intimate formality
about her manners which was most agreeable; but the strain
of keeping a straight face in my presence was clearly almost
unendurable, and I felt sorry for her. The first dish was a
bowl of thin soup in which balefully floated the eye of a fish
called Tai. Mr H., consuming his with relish in its entirety,
assured me that the eyeball was peculiarly delicious; this was

one of the few statements emanating from a Japanese official source which I did not feel called upon to verify. The rest of the meal consisted of more fish (happily represented by those parts of their anatomy which we are accustomed to associate with the table), some sinewy mushrooms, assorted vegetables, and bean curd. We washed it down with beer. I was glad to find that my pristine skill with the chopsticks had not entirely deserted me, though I was far from expert.

In the afternoon I wandered round Chinchow. A Chinese city is seldom a very beautiful place. The streets are tortuous, narrow, irregular, and dirty. If there are fine houses they are concealed behind walls, and you cannot see into their court-yards through the gateways, because the gates are masked, on the inside, by another short section of wall, designed to prevent the ingress of evil spirits which (as everybody knows) can only fly in a straight line. In the streets, which in summer are partially roofed over with mat awnings called *pengs*, the shop-fronts are thickly hung with the long vertical banners and the lacquer signs of the tradesmen. There is always a great noise and a great smell. The shops all open into the streets, and in their dim interiors you can see the owner and his family at work. You get the paradoxical impression of infinite labour and infinite leisure. The Chinese, though they work from dawn to dusk, work as individualists, and in units very rarely bigger than the family. They wisely disdain the clock-punching technique of capitalist industry; there is no lunch hour, no overtime, no single symptom of rationaliza-tion or indeed of any conscious method. They live not only for their work, but in it: lunching on the counter, sleeping on the work-bench, stopping to talk and drink tea when they feel inclined.

So, as a picture in the grand manner, the Chinese city is a disappointment. As a series of curious and intimate sketches it is unforgettable – the fierce argument between an old woman and a coolie with a pig slung from either end of the carrying-pole across his shoulder: a tortoise suspended on a string, spinning as aimlessly as a planet above the counter of a fishmonger's stall: the click of coppers on the matting tables of the gamblers' booths: a very old man with a foolish face caressing the smooth wooden flank of a coffin at the under-taker's: a stout lady with many silver pins in her black hair admiring unreservedly a dreadful American oleograph of Moses in the Bullrushes, late nineteenth century: the little ineffectual, domineering policeman, with his thin legs and his shamefully dirty Mauser: the beggars and the poultry and the children and the fierce, cowardly dogs. . . .

Cities in the West may cast on you the same kind of spell that a mountain casts. In China they have the fascination of an ant-heap.

That night a party was given for us by the Japanese Consul. The Japanese are highly insular; temperamentally they are the worst – by which I mean the most reluctant – colonists in the world, the French not excepted. Though the figure has risen by 50 per cent since the invasion of 1931, there are still only 300,000 Japanese residents in Manchuria, of which the total population is over thirty millions.* This neglect on the part of an overcrowded island to make use of a rich and only partially developed country, lying next door to it, as an outlet for its alarming surplus of population is largely attributable to two basic causes. One is the climate, which in winter is too severe for the Japanese; the other is the fact that Japanese labour cannot compete with the low standard of living set by Chinese labour.

But even if these cogent considerations did not exist a 'Come to Manchuria' movement would not attract the average Japanese. He likes his own place and his own things, and when he finds himself perforce stationed in Manchuria he is more assiduous than any of the other foreigners in trans-planting his own amenities and some of his own atmosphere. Exile in the West is more easily endurable, for the West is one of his two spiritual homes. But in Manchuria (unless I am much mistaken) he is afflicted by a sense of superiority amounting almost to disgust. The people he regards as

*Seven hundred thousand Koreans bring the total number of registered Japanese subjects in Manchuria up to a million.

backward to the point of barbarism. The gods which he has learnt to adore with such auspicious results in the last eighty years mean nothing to them, save occasionally as a cue for laughter or a source of profit. He – the representative of a higher type of civilization (but not, remember, its best representative; and remember also that you cannot judge an Empire by her colonial officials) – virtually ignores the barbarians. He mixes with them not much more than he must, though he acquires, at second-hand, a working knowledge of their psychology. He finds it hard to learn their language, though they pick up his very quickly. In their temples and their customs, in their doubts and their beliefs, he rarely displays more than a tourist's curiosity. Turning his back (except for business purposes) on his thirty million neighbours, he does his best to make Manchuria a Home From Home.

All this, or some of it, explains why there are geisha houses in Chinchow. To the best of these we drove in the car of the Japanese Consul, blasting the inhabitants and their livestock out of our path with a powerful horn. Three young officials made up the party. We turned up a narrow lane into a courtyard, shed our shoes, and presently were squatting on cushions round two sides of a large airy room of which the floor was matting and the walls movable partitions. One side of the room, opening on to a verandah, let in the rays of the setting sun and the faintly melancholy notes of a bugle.

It was a good party, though very hard work. Mr H. and I were implored to take off our coats and ties, and this we did, for it is a matter of etiquette that the guests should appear as informal and as much at their ease as possible, in order to please the host. The others were all wearing the kimono.

My command of the Japanese language began and ended with the word for Thank You, the word for Bandit, and the expression Hullo. It was in the circumstances fortunate that most of those present could speak some English. The Japanese, though lacking in a sense of humour, are a people very easily merry, and ice was quickly broken by the exchange of rather elementary badinage.

Dinner, a much more elaborate version of the midday meal, but having the same sort of dishes as its basis, was served, and under the influence of *saki* the atmosphere became rapidly convivial. Saki is a wine made of rice, tasting rather like sherry; it is served warm in little bowls smaller than a coffee cup. On me its effect as an intoxicant was always negligible however much of it I drank. But the Japanese have weak heads. Every one toasted each other repeatedly with a cry of 'Kan pei', which means in English 'No heeltaps' and in American 'Bottoms up'; and pretty soon even the staid Mr H. could not have honestly described himself as sober.

Meanwhile I observed with interest the activities of the geishas. Their name has a glamorous (to say the least of it) connotation which gives a rather false impression of their function. A geisha falls somewhere midway between a waitress and an American night-club 'hostess'; though sometimes venal, she is not a professional prostitute. Her duty is to minister to the guests at table and to amuse them. Her face is less likely to be her fortune than a gift for repartee, and the best geishas are not necessarily the youngest and most attractive girls. They wear an elaborate but not, in my opinion, a very becoming costume. Their equally elaborate coiffure is also, to most Western eyes, remarkable rather for ingenuity than for beauty.

I imagine that the best type of geisha is rarely found in Manchukuo. The ones in Chinchow, though amiable, seemed to me pudding-faced and foolish. But they had a sort of sparrow-like perkiness, an apparently inexhaustible fund of spontaneous high spirits, which was disarming and enviable. In waiting they showed an unobtrusive solicitude for one's needs. After dinner they sang and did a static formal dance, partly to a gramophone and partly to an instrument suggesting an elongated banjo, of which the strings were plucked with what looked to me like a shoehorn. The dance was a traditional one, based on a tragic theme; it was amusing to see their faces, religious and intent during its execution, break into broad smiles and shrill ribald repartee the moment it was over.

After that there was some haphazard dancing in the Western style and various childish games. Every one shouted and shone with sweat. A keenly contested egg-race took place, the eggs being propelled across the matting floor by blowing on them. The only form of contest in which I showed the least proficiency was that in which the competitors had to balance a saki bottle on their heads, lower themselves into a prone position, drink without handling it a cup of wine placed on the floor, and then stand up again without up-setting the bottle. I beat everybody at this, and acquired a lot of 'face'.

Presently one of my hosts, a delightfully Falstaffian man, showed signs of giving way to that one of Falstaff's appetites with which his apologists make the least play. The geishas protested, and, since it was now late, the party broke up.

We went on to a café, pronounced 'coffee' by the Japanese in Manchuria. This was a dingy place with a gramophone, a few Chinese girls, and some tipsy Japanese. Before I knew what was happening I found myself provided with an enor-mous beef-steak, a glass of whisky, a glass of brandy, and a lady claiming the proud title (so they assured me) of 'Miss Chinchow'. At the moment I had no use at all for any of these. Miss Chinchow, however, though unable to speak English, turned out to be very hungry. While my hosts were absent on the dancing floor I surreptitiously fed her almost the whole of the beef-steak, thus escaping a charge of grave discourtesy. I remember that girl with affection.

It was very late when Mr H. and I lay down on the floor of our little stifling room. Several scores of house-flies, which had been waiting for this moment, settled on us with a contented buzz. If they had been vultures they would not have kept me awake.

12

JEHOL

At dawn we were awakened. An extra plane had been put on the Jehol service; there would be room for us in it. We breakfasted lightly off seaweed and hurried out to the airfield.

Here there was a slight hitch. My luggage was overweight. It consisted of a light suitcase, a dispatch case, and a typewriter.

My experience as a traveller has been of a kind to give me a curiously keen nose for delay. I find that I can very often foresee, if not the nature of a setback, at any rate its result; this, in nine cases out of ten, is a period of enforced idleness under aggravating conditions. I felt in my bones that something of the kind was in store for us in Jehol. So I stuck to my papers and the typewriter and left the suitcase. It is better to have nothing to wear than nothing to do.

We roared up into the hot blue sky and flew west into the mountains. There was no longer below us a curious pattern stamped by men upon the earth. Sprawling, rearing, falling away, the hills ruled turbulently. There seemed no end to them, no boundary to their kingdom. Wave upon wave of reinforcements marched up over the horizon to meet us. Our shadow, which had glided so serenely with us on the plains, now had to scramble wildly, racing up screes to meet us as we skirted a cliff face, then plunging down the shoulder of a mountain to switch-back, diminished, across the gullies at the bottom of a valley. The plane, which before had lorded it unchallenged in the void, now seemed a puny, vulgar intruder, a little quivering minnow among immobile Tritons.

We flew mostly at 3,000 feet. But when we crossed a range the pilot was tempted by the passes as a diver is tempted by a penny at the bottom of the bath. They were a challenge to his skill, and we would swoop roaring through the steep defiles while herds of small, black cattle went streaming fan-wise down the nearer slopes, stricken with panic. Once a little fighting plane overhauled us; she seemed unaccount-ably suspended in mid air, for the noise of her engines was drowned by ours. Once we passed a convoy of military lorries, crawling like beetles out to Jehol along the bottom of a valley, where ran the dirt road which – unless clogged by the rains or cut by the bandits – links Jehol to railhead at Peipiao. We landed once, at Chaoyang, to deliver mails. The ground was ominously soft. If any more rain fell the airfield at Jehol would be out of commission and I should be exiled indefinitely.

We flew on through the sharp, fantastic mountains, ancient, ribbed, and horny, like folded dragons' wings. At last, ahead of us, we saw a cliff crowned with an unnatural club-shaped rock, far bigger at the top than at the base. The finger of the altimeter began to fall. We dipped steeply through a pass and discovered the City of Jehol.

It lay beside a river, a teeming, undecipherable pattern in grey. Temples stood outpost to it in the encircling foothills, and round each temple ran a sinuous embattled wall, climb-ing the steep slopes gracefully. They looked like great coloured citadels. They had rose-red walls, and the blue and green and yellow tiles of their roofs flashed in the sunlight. Their courtyards were crowded with the dark meditative heads of trees. We circled over them, leaning sharply at an angle, and the valley, thus set spinning beneath us, seemed like a place of magic in a book.

We landed in the river-bed, under a black cliff. The silver plane, toy-like and anomalous, glittered with a certain effrontery in the sudden silence. We stood on the caked mud, stretching our limbs. The two Japanese officers who had flown with us were being greeted by a group of their colleagues; all clicked and bowed and smiled, impervious to magic. Everyone began to walk – slowly, on account of the heat – up the river-bed towards the city, which had rather unfairly receded to a surprising distance.

It was very hot. Mr H. seemed in low spirits. 'Very amusing', was his only comment on the temples. In this strange valley under the blazing sun he trod suspiciously. He was on the defensive.

The river (which is called Lwan) was in flood and had swept away the bridge. It was, nevertheless, quite shallow, and while we waited for a ferry we watched naked Chinese fording it with bundles on their heads, some dragging donkeys behind them, and all behaving with that disproportionate animation – those bursts of ephemeral rage, those murderous gestures, and those sudden fits of laughter – which make the Chinese scene at once so absorbing and so tiring to behold. At last a cumbrous hulk was poled across to fetch us. The Japanese, their Wellington boots projecting comically, their swords held carefully out of the water, were carried out to it on the backs of coolies. I had no hat, and when I came on board an octogenarian Chinese unfurled with infinite courtesy his umbrella and held it over my head against the sun. We were poled back slowly athwart the current. From the huddled houses on the bank a powerful smell drifted out across the tumbling yellow waters. The peacock temples could not be seen from here.

In the capital of Jehol (which, strictly speaking, ought to be called Cheng-teh) Mr H. and I had planned to stay for one day. We were marooned there for three.

Thrice we prepared for departure (an almost purely psychological process in my case, since I had no luggage). Thrice we were turned back. Either there were wounded, who had prior claims to the accommodation in the plane; or else no plane could land, because the rains had made the ground too soft; or else it landed but could not take off again for the same reason. In Jehol Romance, though overpoweringly present, brings up no 9.15.

But delay was easily bearable in Jehol. The place had the double interest of the tropical and the historical; it was like staying in Windsor in 1919, supposing that the Germans had won the War.

It was a garrison town. Divisional Headquarters were in

the palace of the late Governor, which had once been the hunting-box of Emperors from Peking. The late Governor's name was Tang Yu Lin. He was a man – to judge by his record – of exquisite iniquity: though I have little doubt that if you or I had met him we should have found him charming. A former bandit, he oppressed his people vilely. When the Japanese threatened his province, he announced to the world his unquenchable determination to resist them to the last man and the last round. For perhaps a week the telegrams of the news agencies portrayed him in the sympathetic posture of a patriot fighting for his home against odds; he looked, at a distance, like the King Albert of the Far East.

But he never fought. His armies melted from their impregnable positions in the north-eastern passes; the confidence of his men in their commanders may be gauged by the fact that they did not even go through the formality of digging themselves in. Tang Yu Lin, poorly attended, rode out of Jehol in flight a few hours before the triumphal entry of the Japanese; the townspeople welcomed the invaders unreservedly. A few months later Tang Yu Lin was in Japanese pay. I should say that that man might have acquired, and did in fact lose, more sympathy and prestige for China than any other living Chinese.

His palace stood on the outskirts of the city, in a magnificent park. A wall ran round it, enclosing – with that careless, thorough ostentation which is typical of China – several fairly considerable hills. Hawks and pigeons and magpies flitted or circled round the splendid trees, shrewd though unconscious observers of history in the making. A herd of spotted deer, incuriously aloof, nibbled sweet grass on which was stamped the faint oval of a race-track where Tang Yu Lin's wives, eight in number, had been capriciously obliged to take equestrian exercise every morning. (They were also required to learn to read.) A long, low building in a corner of the wall now housed a Japanese sanitary squad; formerly it had been the place where Tang Yu Lin manufactured morphine, for sale to his army and his subjects. Japanese soldiers, their short legs dangling from the formal lovely bridges, fished unfruitfully in the lily ponds.

One day manoeuvres were staged for my benefit in the park. The unit engaged corresponded to a half company in the British Army. Their objective was a pagoda on the top of a steep knoll; it contained a hypothetical machine-gun and would, in practice, have been impregnable. The attack was launched from under cover, and from a distance of about half a mile. Between their jumping-off point and the pagoda the ground was broken by four sharp banks, two of them separated by a shallow canal. Dominating though the position of the machine-gun was, the attackers had plenty of dead ground of which to take advantage.

They did not, however, take advantage of it. Instead of leaving their Lewis gun* sections in position on the nearest bank to cover the advance of the riflemen they launched the attack pell-mell. Attempts to correlate fire and movement were unscientific to a degree. But their dash was terrifyingly impressive. The men, though acting under perfect discipline, uttered bloodcurdling yells as they advanced. The canal, waist-deep, was forded as though it had been the final obstacle in a cross-country race. And the ultimate assault on the pagoda was carried out with a deadly seriousness which was as far removed as possible from the spirit of strenuous burlesque which distinguishes the climax of mock warfare in this country. Where the British private, coming at last to close quarters, goes all out to make his opponent laugh, the Japanese does his best to freeze the other's blood.

It was a most instructive demonstration.

*I do not know the name of the Japanese army's equivalent to a Lewis gun.

13

PRAYERS

WE sat down four to breakfast: Mr and Mrs Panter, young Mr Titherton, and myself. They were American missionaries.

Mr Panter was a very tall, very doleful man. His voice was the voice of Doom, slow and terrible; it seemed to come from a very long way away. He never smiled. He had an aloof and absent-minded manner. For thirty years he had struggled in a remote place to convert heathens to Christianity and (harder still) to make the converts Christians in something more than name; you had the feeling that this had bred in him a bitterness of soul which once it had been difficult to suppress. Now he had the mastery of it; but the inner super-added to the outer conflicts had left him worn out. He had no longer any interest or energy left for anything outside the duties which he so indomitably carried out. He was more nearly a ghost than anyone I have ever met.

His wife had, and needed to have, both feet on the earth. Her manner was not nearly so sepulchral as Mr Panter's. Though almost ostentatiously narrow in her sympathies, she was a person of great kindliness. She was accessible. She reflected her husband's austerity and his controlled fanatic-ism, but she remained nevertheless an ordinary human being, capable of laughter and willing to admit vulnerability.

Young Mr Titherton was the most interesting of the three. He was out there, I gathered, on probation; he was a kind of apprentice missionary. Although he had lived with the Panters for a year, and although for hundreds of miles round there were not more than half a dozen other white people, he was still addressed as 'Mr Titherton'. He was not, I think, entirely approved of. He was about twenty-five. His bland, slightly unctuous face became, when he was amused, all of a sudden facetious in a curiously disreputable way; you would almost have said that he leered. He quite often was amused. He had a natural leaning towards controversy, and at meal times would gratuitously stir up trouble for himself by defending the use of the word 'damn' in moments of ungovernable annoyance, or by putting in a word for Confucianism, or by partially condoning the less respectable aspects of Chinese life. Mr Panter, reproving him with a vehemence which he clearly found it difficult to curb, would become for a moment almost human.

However sternly reproved, Mr Titherton was irrepressible. A supremely tactless man, he would both make and withdraw his heretical statements in such a way as to give the maximum of offence. 'Well, well,' he would chirp, when enfiladed by a withering fire of orthodoxy from either end of the table, 'I dare say you know best. Let's say no more about it.' Then he would wink at me in a very sophisticated way. This put me in a false and embarrassing position.

Breakfast was at 7.30. We sat down, and then Mr Panter said a grace. But he never said it quite soon enough for me.

Try as I would I could *not* remember about that grace. The opening words always caught me with a spoon or a sugar-bowl poised guiltily over my porridge, while the others all had their hands folded devoutly on their laps. This made me appear both greedy and irreligious.

After breakfast, prayers.

Mr Titherton distributes little red books, entitled *Redemption Songs: for Choir, Solo, or The Home*. Mrs Panter seats herself at an instrument distantly related to the harmonium and strikes a wheezy chord.

'Number 275!' announces Mr Panter in an awful voice.

Mrs Panter rolls up the sleeves of her dress. We are off. . . .

The Redemption Songs do not seem to be very good songs. Their composer often expresses himself in so turgid and involved a style as to be practically incomprehensible. His syntax is occasionally weak, and even at its strongest is over-richly encrusted with allusions and invocations ('Oh Tsidkenu!' is a favourite one) which mean nothing to me. Nor is Mrs Panter, at the harmonium, particularly adept at glossing over his frequent metrical inconsistencies; her lively but straightforward attack is based on the assumption – too often unjustifiable – that both lines in a couplet will contain roughly the same number of syllables.

However, save for some daring experiments in the third verse, this morning's Song is fairly plain sailing. Each verse ends with the lilting refrain 'Wonderful Man of Calvaree-ee!' and we usually manage that bit rather well.

On the whole, though, the singing is ragged. Mr Panter's voice, though not lacking in vigour, ploughs a lonely furrow just where we most needed co-operation. Mr Titherton flutes away modestly and, as far as I can judge, in tune; but he stands no chance against Mr Panter, who produces a consistently formidable volume of sound and makes a point of shouting all the holier words at the top of his voice. In all this uproar I myself am a mere cipher, for I well know that I cannot sing, and it is better that I should not try. I go, nevertheless, through the motions, opening and shutting my mouth with a rapt air, and occasionally emitting a little sort of mew.

At last the Song is over.

A passage from the Bible is now read aloud, either by Mr Panter or Mr Titherton, and afterwards extracts from a commentary upon it. This is an extraordinary compilation, thunderously phrased but somewhat bigoted in conception. Yesterday the commentator launched a furious attack upon witches. It was ridiculous, he warned us, to assert that these creatures were either harmless or non-existent. On the contrary, they represented a very real peril to Church and State alike, and when encountered should be severely dealt with.

To-day he is in milder mood. Sternly, but in temperate terms, he animadverts on the folly of attaching undue importance to some popular prejudice or superstition.

He must have been a remarkable man.

After that we pray for fellow-missionaries belonging to the Panters' denomination. A little pamphlet is produced – the Army List, as it were, of the Church Militant – and all the names and addresses on one page are read out as being those to which on this day we especially wish to call Divine attention. Yesterday they were all in Spain, and Mr Panter, who is not too good at foreign words and when reading the commentary gets terribly tied up over Latin phrases like *vox populi, vox dei*, had considerable difficulty with the Spanish place-names.

But to-day it is Mr Titherton's turn, and Mr Titherton is much more nimble-tongued. Also, he has the pleasing custom of annotating the list, wherever possible, from personal knowledge of the people whose names are on it. His manner towards the Deity is friendly and informal. He reads out something like this:

'ADDIS ABABA – Reverend Macintyre. . . . MEDINA – Miss Tackle, Miss P. Flint (*I know these two ladies, Our Father. Please look on them to-day. They're two of the very best. I can tell you*). . . . ALEPPO – Reverend and Mrs Gow. . . . MOSUL – Miss Gondering, Miss J. Gondering. (*Now, that printing-press they've rigged up, Our Father! That's a splendid bit of work. I do hope you'll help them to make a success of it, Our Father.*) . . . DAMASCUS – Reverend Pretty, Reverend Polkinghorne, Miss O'Brien . . . ' and so on, ending up with a swift and delightful transition from the Near Eastern deserts to 'ICE-LAND – Reverend Gook.'

Now we kneel down, and either Mr Panter or Mr Titherton embarks on a long impromptu prayer. Here again I prefer Mr Titherton's technique. Mr Panter is apt to be stilted and ponderous; he thanks God for 'the bright weather which obtains'. Mr Titherton is very different. Nothing stilted about him. He has a straight talk to God. He is confidential, almost racy. 'Stop me if you've heard this one, Our Father', you expect to hear him say at any moment.

I much admire his ingenuity – far greater than Mr Panter's – in finding things to give thanks for. Mr Panter has to rack his brains to recall a blessing; his struggles are indeed a sad comment on human felicity. But Mr Titherton is never at a loss. It rained yesterday. Mr Panter would have thanked God for the rain and left it at that. But Mr Titherton examines every aspect of the shower. Its timeliness; its cooling propensities; its value to both the flora and fauna of the district; the damage it inflicted on the graceless poppy-fields; and last of all, just when it seemed that Mr Titherton must have exhausted all the potential cues for thanksgiving, its effectiveness, in falling on good and evil alike, as a reminder of God's impartiality. Mr Titherton's pious courtesy is Oriental in more than its setting.

After this there are more prayers, of a general nature, at the end of which I am suddenly shaken out of a stupor by the discovery that I myself am being prayed for. The experience, however salutary, is embarrassing. The prayee – his mind flashing back to the ritual of after-dinner toasts – has an uncomfortable feeling that he ought to stand up, or at any rate adopt some posture other than the kneeling. There is also the haunting fear that he may have to – and certainly ought to – reply.

Mr Titherton's position, however, is almost equally awkward. Aware, like the rest of that tiny congregation, that my prime desire is to leave Jehol with the minimum of delay, he leads off with a request for Divine intervention to accelerate my departure. Then something – perhaps a cough from Mr Panter – tells him that this was not the happiest of beginnings, and in the end the difficulty of reconciling the purpose of his prayer with the laws of hospitality is overcome only by a great deal of circumlocution, qualification, and parenthesis. His voice becomes halting and apologetic. For the first time uncertainty has reared its ugly head in that comical but gallant little community.

In several ways Prayers were rather a strain.

14

AN AFTERNOON WITH THE GODS

FROM the moment when our journey was conceived Mr H. had professed an almost ungovernable curiosity with regard to the famous lama temples of Jehol. This was, however, to some extent quenched by propinquity, and our visit to them was mysteriously deferred whenever I suggested it. But at last we set off, in the Japanese Consul's car. We took with us a gendarme from the Consulate, for it was alleged that a guard was necessary.

On the outskirts of the city, under the palace wall, the car stuck; the rains had made a quagmire of the road. But I was pleased, because I needed exercise, and the nearest of the temples was less than two miles away. Mr H. – *splendide mendax* – maintained that he, too, was passionately fond of walking, and as we strode off briskly through the blazing midsummer noon regaled me with highly statistical accounts of the pedestrian exploits of his youth. The gendarme followed behind us, carrying some *kiaoliang* cakes wrapped up in a coloured handkerchief and wearing an amused expression.

It was a lovely day. The hills shimmered in the heat. A patrol of Japanese cavalry clattered along a causeway under the palace wall and disappeared through the city gate. Peasants with wide hats and copper-coloured torsos were working in the sparse fields of the river valley along which we walked. The poppy fields, rather surprisingly, were patches of white and mauve; I hardly saw a scarlet poppy all the time I was in Manchuria. Along the crest of the very steep hill on our left ran the machicolated wall surrounding Tang Yu Lin's park. On our right was the river.

We started in good order, but Mr H's enthusiasm for our mode of progress had waned perceptibly within the first half mile, and when we reached the first temple he was showing signs of distress. The gendarme had some more than tepid water in his water-bottle, and I suggested that we should supplement this by getting tea from the monks. The idea was greeted by the Japanese with surprise and a certain repugnance, but thirst overcame their qualms, and soon we found ourselves seated in a small room within the purlieus of the temple walls. Our hosts were two Buddhist monks, dingily habited but full of a charming courtesy. We talked to them through the gendarme, who knew Chinese.

It was pleasant, sitting there in the little bare room and drinking tea. The cakes which the gendarme had bought from a stall in the streets of Jehol were excellent, and even Mr H. so far overcame his suspicions of Chinese cooking as to eat the insides of them, leaving the potentially contaminated crust. The monks had a little terrapin in a China bowl, and at the expense of this creature several obscure jokes were cracked. The tortoise and its kindred are, I believe, regarded with the gravest disapproval by the Chinese, who call them 'Forgetting Eight', meaning the eight ethical principles. In the light of a belief that all specimens of this genus belong to the male sex, it is inevitable that their habits should appear at times indefensible. A similar suspicion of sodomy clouds the reputation of the hare.

The roof of the monks' room was papered with, among other things, several pages from a San Francisco newspaper. 'Chair for Love Nest Slayer', 'Booze Probe Slated' – through these and other not less heartening legends the light of Western civilization faintly irradiated a corner of the farthest East.

Fortified by the tea we set out to view the temples. But Mr H's heart was no longer in the expedition. He became more and more inwardly subdued, more and more outwardly truculent. A growing tendency on his part to sit down on things for several minutes at a time gave to our progress the semblance of a subtle and peculiar variant of Musical Chairs, in which I was for ever delicately riding him off all vacant seating accommodation. At last, after about an hour, he threw up the sponge and went home. He and the gendarme disappeared down the road towards the city, walking very slowly. I was left to my own devices.

I have not the knowledge to tell you anything worth knowing about these temples, nor the skill in writing to convey their charm. Imagine a chain of huge, brightly coloured forts, set dispersedly in a waste of jagged and spectacular hills. They are deserted save by a shy handful of monks, who can less justly be called caretakers than the impotent spectators of decay. In their dark halls the gods gesticulate in silence; a thin filament of smoke, rising from a bowl full of the grey dust of joss-sticks, is their only certificate against complete oblivion. Their gold faces scowl importantly among the heavy shadows; their swords are furiously brandished. There are hundreds of them standing there in the half-darkness, fantastic, taut, tremendous. Yet all the tribute they will get in a week is a few paper 'cash' burnt by a peasant.

When you penetrate these courtyards you ought by rights to feel oppressed. The place is empty and silent. Above you curl the sweeping and bedragoned eaves of the great yellow roof which so enchanted your eyes from a distance. But the ground at your feet is thick with the tarnished golden fragments of its tiles, and you are forced to wonder how much longer that roof will shine so bravely in the sun. The walls are breached: a turret has dissolved into a pile of stones: a staircase leads up the side of an overhanging terrace into thin air. Decay is seeping through the structure of the temple. Decay pervades its atmosphere.

You ought by rights to feel oppressed, but I did not. It did not seem to me to matter that these peacock monuments to a faith had become its tombs. Nor did I care that they were neglected. Pomp and a formal impressiveness do not appeal to me even in buildings. I could not believe that these courtyards would have been a nicer place to spend an afternoon in if they had been well kept. A few goats, a mongrel, a pair of magpies, and a visitant kestrel were better company than a throng of worshippers. Give me the lion and lizard in preference to the personally conducted tour and the postcard vendor. I wandered contentedly, without even the rudiments

of historical knowledge to guide and interpret for me. Blissfully ignorant, I was under no distracting compulsion to
identify influences and correlate periods. It was like – if the
analogy is not too strained – it was like spending Christmas
Day alone: a great occasion, with none of a great occasion's
responsibilities.

There was a god which stood 120 feet high and had eighteen pairs of arms. I climbed musty and untrodden wooden
staircases in which, when I went up, one step in three was
missing and which I left still further demolished. The face of
the image, viewed at disconcertingly short range from a
balcony among the roof beams, wore a complacent expression. In another temple there were obscene images, discreetly
covered with a cloth. Then there was a blue-tiled roof on
which complex golden dragons raced furiously. One is missing and is said to have flown away, an action betraying, in
my view, a lack of sagacity. It was a lovely place.

The Potala is the biggest and most impressive of the
temples. It was completed, like the rest of them, by the Emperor Ch'ien-lung in the late eighteenth century, and is in
many respects a copy of the Tibetan Potala. It forms one of a
line which faces, across a narrow valley, the sharply ascend-
ing spur of hills crowned by Tang Yu Lin's palace wall. I had
it on good authority that the best place from which to photograph the Potala was this wall which confronted and from a
great height overlooked it. Mr H. and the gendarme, to
whom I had confided this information, had forbidden me to
attempt the ascent. The outward portions of the palace wall,
they said, were patrolled by Manchukuo troops, and these
would be liable to shoot on sight any stranger seen scaling
the semi-precipitous, thousand-foot face whose crest they
guarded.

But the crenellated sky-line was empty; if sentries were
posted they were asleep in the shade on the inside of the wall.
Mr H's solicitude, and his flattering estimate of Manchurian
marksmanship, were no longer factors in the situation. So
I climbed, sweating, to the base of the wall, following the
vertical line of a gully which offered cover in the unlikely

event of the Manchukuo patrols taking their duties seriously. Scattered below me – each as self-contained and as markedly individual as the farms in the bottom of an English valley – the temples seemed even more attractive than before. They were like curious jewels cast up by the sea of hills indefinitely tumbling behind them. I sat for a long time, at the base of thirty unscalable feet of stone, looking out over a desolation exquisitely picketed.

My aesthetic raptures, I am sorry to say, are rare and never last for long. Thirst, a very sublunary incentive, brought my thoughts from the skies and my feet once more down into the valley. I reached it safely, though I admit that, now my back was to the wall, the misguided but withering volleys of Mr H's imagination seemed a less unlikely phenomenon than they had an hour ago. An enemy you cannot see is always to some extent terrible, even if non-existent.

In the outer courtyards of the Potala I found a very small, very pock-marked Mongol and explained to him, by signs, my need for tea. When it was ready I drank it sitting on the *k'ang* in his tiny dwelling, on the walls of which hung temple keys, an old gun, a horn, some bridles, and other small things. Through a dense cloud in which wood-smoke and flies played equally obscurantist parts we grinned and nodded to each other. He was a charming man. I overpaid him and went my way.

15

GARRISON TOWN

WHEN I got back to Jehol the thirst was on me again. It was a hot day, and I had spent it strenuously. I had an insensate craving for beer, and the Panters' was an aggressively teetotal household.

In the street I met Mr Titherton, and to him disclosed my need. Would he show me where I could buy some beer? Mr Titherton rather apprehensively said he would. We made for the centre of the city.

Jehol was a garrison town. Though its capture was recent and its position remote, it was yet not wholly without the amenities usually associated with a place of its kind. I have never found the adage Trade Follows The Flag more strikingly illustrated than by the fact that the first civilians to enter Jehol on the heels of the Japanese army were twenty lorry-loads of Korean girls. In the main street a number of garish 'coffees' had sprung up, and in the shops the Japanese talent for mimicry was reflected — not perhaps to the best advantage — by bottles alluringly labelled Queen George Old Scotch Whisky, Buckingum Whisky, and Real Old Toe Gin. At dusk a drunken Japanese soldier was a common sight, and also an anomalous one, for in China it is extremely rare to see a man drunk in public. Mr Panter, after thirty years' experience, could remember only two occasions on which he had known Chinese the worse for drink.

Mr Titherton and I inspected with a judicious air the outsides of the 'coffees' and at last selected one which looked a shade less repellent than the rest. Outside its portals (yes, I am afraid that it was that sort of a place) Mr Titherton left me. It was not, he said, that he disapproved of my drinking beer. He had observed that there was a great deal of variety in human nature, and he could not expect everyone to share

97

his own strong views on alcohol. No, it was simply a question of keeping up his reputation with the local Chinese; if he was seen going into a place like that he would lose it. He wished me luck and hurried away.

Muttering under my breath the Chinese and the Japanese words for beer, I stepped over the threshold, pushed aside a curtain, and found myself in a large, dark, dirty room with an earth floor. Wooden tables stood round the wall, and at these, ministered to by battered-looking girls in what had once been geisha dresses, sat a number of Japanese soldiers, drinking beer and sweating and making a noise.

I had no time to observe more than this before I found myself involved in a brawl with one of them. Extremely drunk, he was steering an erratic course towards the door through which I had just entered. He regarded me, I am convinced, more as an anchorage than as an enemy. Still, however amicable his motives, his hands he laid on me were violent. I thrust him, no less violently, away, and he fell over the end of a bench and sat down backwards. He got up looking baleful.

Now you could write the next bit of this narrative far better than I shall. You know the form. An ugly rush: a straight left to the jaw: pandemonium: more ugly rushes, more straight lefts (in your hands I should have been almost certain of my half-Blue): the flash of a knife: a warning scream from some flower-like chit in the shadows: and the whole desperate situation suddenly liquidated by the appearance of an urbane but sinister mandarin (Harrow and Balliol), full of a well-informed curiosity about the last National and the next Ballet Season.

You could do it, you see, on your head; but the consequences would be on mine. And I have – I don't know why, for nobody expects a traveller to tell the truth – some scruples in the matter of veracity. They constitute the gravest possible handicap to a man in my *métier*, but I cannot for the life of me get rid of them. You would have thought – at least I know I often think – that there ought to be some compensation, that life should offer to one who reports it with such pious and boring fidelity an occasional good-conduct prize in the shape of an authentically Strong Situation, a ready-to-wear adventure off the peg. But life apparently thinks otherwise. Colourless experience continues to be delivered in plain vans. I get no credit for my quixotry.

That is why your version of what happened is far superior to mine. Life let me down once more, and I must give you anti-climax where you have a right to crisis.

Although the Japanese soldier showed unmistakable signs of disgruntlement, and although he advanced on me in a manner which might be interpreted as menacing, and although I stood my ground as an Englishman should, hostilities were destined not to be resumed. Their averting had an element of bathos. A Japanese lady of advanced age bobbed up suddenly between us. She was clearly the proprietress of the place, and her motto was 'Peace With Honour'. She addressed the soldier in shrill, angry tones. The soldier stood still and looked sheepish. Pressing her advantage home the old lady stamped imperiously on the ground and pointed to the doorway; her voice almost rose to a scream. The soldier began to weep. The old lady took him by the sleeve and led him out into the street.

I sat down at a table and succeeded in ordering some beer, of which I now stood in urgent need. It was brought by a Korean girl. When she had poured it out she sat down opposite me. I took a prodigious draught and said, with some feeling, 'Thank you'. The girl smiled. It was a dreadful smile, so completely perfunctory, so flatly denied by her eyes, that I felt awkward, as one might in the presence of a corpse.

She looked about seventeen. She had a small, plain face. The thick, formal finery of her dress was soiled and worn. She showed no curiosity in me, though she had never seen a white man in that place before. She had that heavy listlessness which is commonly born of some deep disgust or pain. Her actions were as mechanical as those of a doll set dancing by a penny in the slot. Whenever I put down my glass she pushed across to me a little dish of sunflower seeds, moving it ever nearer, when I did not take some at once, like a child coaxing an animal to eat; but she did all this with a tranced detachment which produced in me a feeling of horror and pity that it is quite impossible to explain. Though it may only have been that she was tired or ill, she seemed to me a tragic figure. I tried to make up for things by saying 'Thank you' a great many times.

The beer was warm and expensive, but welcome. When I had finished it I got up. The Korean girl bowed. As I went out the old lady was sending her over to a Japanese soldier at another table.

On my way back I made a detour past the palace. The palace was the Headquarters of the 8th Division, and there was a sentry on the gate. A convoy of lorries had arrived at the farther bank of the river, and coolies were bringing stores from them into the palace on wheelbarrows. As each one entered he had to set down the shafts and take off his hat to the sentry.

These men belonged to a race which has for centuries ranked the military profession lower than any other. The spectacle had accordingly a certain irony: and not, I suspect, for me alone.

16

REUNION IN CHINCHOW

NEXT day Mr H. and I departed in an aeroplane.

It was about time. Equipped only with a toothbrush and a typewriter, I found myself, long before the end of our stay, in a grave sartorial predicament. I had arrived wearing shorts. In China, as at Wimbledon, these sensible garments are gradually establishing themselves. But only gradually. The old-fashioned people in the interior regard them as not only fantastic, but vulgar. To call on a provincial governor thus attired is the worst kind of solecism. It was a solecism which I was forced to commit.

Nor are shorts suitable for riding in the company of Japanese officers. I felt my position acutely, in more senses than one, as we clattered through the streets on the big, very decorative light-weight chargers which Japan started breeding as soon as she noted the superiority of the enemy cavalry in the Russo-Japanese War. As a matter of fact, the mare they lent me had such perfect manners and such equable paces that the discomfort I suffered was almost entirely psychological.

Still, it was hot weather and I badly needed a change of clothes. As Mr H. and I walked slowly out to the airfield across the scorching surface of the river-bed I was not sorry to be leaving. There was, however, one person besides the kindly Panters and the disarming Mr Titherton whom I regretted that I should not see again. This was Père Conard. He was a Catholic missionary, Belgian by race and probably about seventy years old: a majestic, patriarchal figure, with a flowing beard, a whimsical outlook, and a profound understanding of the Chinese which had grafted upon him a pleasant blend of cynicism and tolerance. He had come out to China as a very young man and had never been home since. To the Japanese he was an object of suspicion. When the town was in panic at the time of the invasion the Protestant mission gave shelter to refugees but not to their belongings; the Catholics on the other hand let them bring into the compound whatever they had with them, and this led Headquarters to believe that Père Conard's cellar was bursting with Tang Yu Lin's ill-gotten dollars. They tried to enforce a search, but their emissaries handled the affair with too palpable a lack of courtesy, so that the old priest had a grievance which he used skilfully and with success to thwart their purpose. He was, I suspect, a born politician; it appeared most of all when he gleefully recounted to me his manoeuvres to obtain military protection for an outlying station of his mission where the church had been sacked by bandits.

He was a delightful man. He gave me tobacco and grenadine, and some beer which, lapsing into English, he rather aptly described as 'self-made'. One night, as we sat talking, we became aware of a man spying on us in the compound. Père Conard was delighted. He abandoned French, which was Greek to the spy, for Chinese, and embarked on a long, impassioned speech, in which the Japanese received alternately the warmest praise and the most virulent abuse. The spy, who believed himself unobserved in the shadows, soon disappeared. '*Il faut surtout les déconcerter, ces petits Japonais,*' explained the holy man, shaking with laughter. '*Ce n'est pas très difficile, enfin.*'

We parted with regret.

The aeroplane was four hours late. We spent them exposed to considerable heat and not a little doubt on that naked stretch of baked mud. But at last it came, and we swung up over the city, while the great temples which had dwarfed us yesterday shrunk to small cheerful toys set among mountains which were now mere major corrugations, holding no secrets from us. The flight back to Chinchow was uneventful, though there were no seats in the aeroplane and no fastening on the door, so that as we took off all four passengers slid violently aft and I, being nearest the door, was very nearly forced out into space.

But at Chinchow the vicissitudes of travel crowded in upon us again. They came in a familiar guise. Once more a telegram had gone astray, and there was no room in the Mukden plane. Once more Mr H's shoulders hunched aggressively, once more he became a small, proud, thwarted boy. . . .

Was there a train? Yes, there was. If we commandeered a car and made straight for the station we should just catch it. But the cars were military cars, and I saw that Mr H. did not like to ask for the loan of one. The car from the Consulate, he said, was already on its way. He had telephoned. . . .

Precious minutes slipped by. At last the car arrived. We leapt into it and fled honking over the frightful road which led from the airfield to the city. All kinds of livestock and their owners sprang into safety at the eleventh hour. We drew up at the station in a cloud of dust. It cleared to reveal the tail of the train disappearing round a bend.

I had no love for Chinchow, but at least, I consoled myself, it contained my suitcase and a change of clothes. Perhaps the consulate could raise a bath-tub? I felt very dirty.

I continued to feel very dirty. My suitcase had been sent back to Mukden on the strength of a report in the local press that Mr H. and I had returned there some days ago. We went off disconsolately to our former inn and drowned our sorrows in beer.

That night another party was given in our honour by the Japanese Consul. It was identically the same as the last one. Once more we balanced saki bottles on our heads, once more blew eggs – perhaps the same eggs – across the floor. Once more the evening was crowned with an introduction to Miss Chinchow. . . . But here at last came a break with precedent. Miss Chinchow was a different girl. The title had changed hands.

Next morning we flew on to Mukden in a Puss Moth. Our landlady, that estimable creature, came out to the airfield to see us off. She bowed when we got into the plane. She bowed when the engines roared. She bowed as we taxied across the ground, and she went on bowing and bowing and bowing until she was only a tiny black speck on a biscuit-coloured background, so small that you could not tell whether she was still bowing or not.

But I expect she was.

17

PAX JAPONICA

Two days later came the successful climax of some weeks of intrigue. I left Mukden with a flying column of Japanese troops engaged on the task of bandit-suppression. The chapters which follow give an account of that expedition. It is an accurate account, but dull. It would be duller still if the reader had no understanding of the general situation with regard to banditry in Manchuria. Accordingly I append an estimate of that situation here.

Banditry is the biggest problem which the Japanese are facing in Manchukuo. Contrary to the general belief, which is based on information issued by Japanese sources, the pacification of the country – which covers an area greater than those of Germany and France combined, and is mostly mountainous, thickly wooded, and inadequately served by communications – is far from complete. Banditry is endemic in Manchuria. Until the Japanese came in 1931 Manchurian banditry differed in kind from most of the banditry of China proper, which was in great part a phenomenon of despair, the by-product of civil wars, famines, floods, and plague. Since 1931 Japanese propaganda has blinded the world to the fact that Manchuria under Chan Tso-lin, and in a lesser degree under his son, was a region not only naturally richer, but actually better administered and no more over-militarized than any area of corresponding size south of the Wall. The bandits who troubled it were for the most part professional desperadoes, not men made desperate by necessity. Because pay in the Old Marshal's armies was both higher and more regular than in the ephemeral levies of China proper, the soldier-bandit – shifting from one walk of life to the other as the chances of civil and military loot varied – was not a serious menace.

The typical Manchurian bandit was a racketeer, an enterprising and old-established parasite; he operated in small groups, stuck to a certain district, and worked in strict accordance with ancient and universally recognized conventions. Under normal conditions he was not so much a threat to the peace of the community as a permanent and carefully regulated drain on its finances. He probably bulked in the eyes of the peasant much as the income-tax collector bulks in the eyes of the British *rentier* – as an iniquitous but inevitable consequence of the way his country's affairs have been mismanaged. He kept the peace in return for a form of Danegeld, paid partly in cash and partly in kind. To travellers and merchandise passing through his territory he issued an expensive but usually inviolable safe-conduct. His relations with the local defence force were friendly. He was rarely suppressed, but could sometimes be 'reclaimed' by a punitive expedition, whose ranks he was probably glad to join under favourable conditions. He was, in fine, a scandal rather than a peril.

His numbers were, however, augmented and his irresponsibility increased by the Japanese occupation of Manchuria. The bandit problem changed its complexion. Large bodies of soldiers, without leaders and without pay – the rabble of the broken armies which had attempted resistance – increased the feeling of insecurity and alarm in the country which, while they plundered, they said they meant – one day – to save. Lawlessness in Manchuria reached a pitch unparalleled before. Travel, hitherto safer than in any other part of post-revolutionary China, became an impossibility, and no railway, with the exception of the main line of the South Manchurian Railway, dared to run night trains. For the foreign community the year 1932 was darkened by such outrages as the murder of Mrs Woodruff and the kidnapping of Mrs Pawley and Mr Corkran. For all their good intentions the Japanese forces in Manchuria were powerless to prevent the establishment of a reign of terror.

In the autumn of that turbulent year the total number of bandits active in Manchukuo was officially computed by the

Japanese military authorities at 212,000. They were classified as follows:

(1) The pseudo-patriotic 'political' forces, mostly remnants of the Young Marshal's armies – 69,000.
(2) Bands of religious fanatics like the 'Red Spears' – 16,000.
(3) The old-style bandit, whose technique I have analysed above – 62,000.
(4) The bandits of despair – peasants forced into crime by the pressure of circumstances – 65,000.

Towards the close of the year a drive was launched on a big scale against these lawless elements. (In official circles the annexation of Jehol is still carefully referred to as the culminating stage in this campaign of pacification.) Its results, though admittedly a disappointment to the military, were by no means negligible. The large, semi-organized forces were broken up; it was a picnic for the Japanese troops.

In the summer of 1933, when I was there, the number of bandits at large was officially given as 60,000, in my opinion an extravagantly conservative estimate. I should, however, explain that banditry in Manchuria is in some measure a seasonal problem, which reaches its maximum gravity in the months from July to October. During this period the kiaoliang, or millet, a staple crop all over the country, stands ten feet high and more, so that even in the plains each village is surrounded by a belt of good cover. In July, also, the raw opium is brought in from the poppy fields, and, since most habitual bandits are addicted to the drug, it provides an added incentive for marauding activities. The official estimate may therefore be taken as representing only the whole-time bandits; the Japanese themselves confessed that they expected to see it trebled in the autumn.

To sum up, the effects of the Japanese invasion on lawlessness in Manchuria have been two: one good, and one bad. The good one was, not to restore order, but to make available, at certain points, the effective agents of order – troops who could neither be bought nor defied (though they could be evaded) by the bandits. This meant, roughly, that every town with a Japanese garrison in it was safe, and that major outrages in the interior stood a good chance of being avenged, if not averted.

The bad effect was enormously to increase the number of bandits, while at the same time breaking down the harmonious relations between the criminal classes and the agents of the law – relations which, however deplorable in theory, at any rate secured a *modus vivendi* for a substantial proportion of the community.

Fundamentally, the problem of eliminating the bandits is economic. As the prosperity of the country increases discontent will die, and banditry with it. Yet the bandits themselves are the chief obstacles to economic progress. The immediate primary needs are better communications and education, the former for obvious reasons of strategy, the latter to undermine the apathy with which the peasants endure the depredations of bandits as they endured the corruption of officials. Both these will be forthcoming in time. Some progress has, of course, already been made. Since 1932 the problem has been reduced to its original dimensions. But as its scope has contracted its difficulties have increased. The military now have to deal with small groups of criminals, operating for the most part in difficult country full of good cover. They are protected by a network of spies. In appearance they are indistinguishable from their law-abiding fellow-citizens, for they seldom wear uniforms; on the approach of a punitive expedition they can bury their rifles and revert to those innocent agricultural pursuits which are, in fact, for many of them, a part-time occupation. Fighting the bandits is, as a Japanese officer disgustedly said to me, 'like swatting flies'.

It will be a long time – at the very least, I should say, five years – before that thankless task has been completed and the flies reduced to a negligible pest.

18

FLYING COLUMN

M. AND I stood on the platform of Mukden station.

The scene, outwardly, was a gay one. The Japanese ladies (and these predominated) were wearing their best clothes. So were their children. Commemorative fans, specially manufactured for this occasion, fluttered ubiquitously. At the windows of the troop train the soldiers lolled and were facetious. Another flying column was leaving Mukden on anti-bandit operations.

It was a normal occurrence. There was nothing in the history of these recurrent expeditions to suggest that there would be a firm tone in either death or glory. I was rather surprised to see how tragically, behind their gaily agitated fans, the seers-off were taking it. Beside me a Japanese lady wept silently, and with a touching dignity. All up and down the platform there was a deeper undercurrent of emotion than seemed to me warranted.

A whistle went. M. and I took our places. The train pulled out.

All that we knew of the plan of campaign was this: The worst bandit country in Manchuria was in the mountains east of Mukden. On this area a number of small, swiftly moving units were about to converge. Each had as its first objective a village inside the area, on reaching which it would go into garrison for a time and carry out intensive pacification measures in the district. The second stage of the campaign depended on developments and had not yet been formulated.

The unit to which M. and I were attached was a mixed force of Japanese and Manchukuo troops, under the command of a Japanese major. The Japanese, who numbered about 175, were men of the Independent Railway Guard, which is a force roughly equivalent to a division, with its Headquarters at Mukden. (Officially, as its name suggests, it does not count as part of the regular army. This was one of its most useful characteristics in the days when Japan's forces in Manchuria were limited by treaty.) There were also about 400 Manchukuo troops, controlled, though not nominally commanded, by a Japanese captain. We saw very little of these, for they marched always in the rear, and accompanied the column, I think, as much for training as for anything else.

Our jumping-off point was Fushun, which for the benefit of those who like to think in household words may be called the Sheffield of Manchuria. The men were detrained and marched off to barracks on the outskirts of the town. M. and I and our interpreter were directed to a Japanese inn.

Our interpreter was a private soldier called Takani. To those not familiar with the Japanese system of conscription it may seem incongruous that a private soldier should also be a graduate of the Massachusetts Institute of Technology. This was the case with Takani. He came of a good middle-class family and had returned from America to take up an excellent engineering job in Tokyo for which he was qualified by his foreign training. But he, like every other young man who was not debarred from doing so by physical or moral disability, had to serve his two years in the army. He had been nine months in Manchuria, and he did not much care for it.

His was rather a special case. He was twenty-six years old. Every recruit had to submit to the rigorous discipline, the monotony, and the minimum allowance of leave which are the lot of the Japanese soldier. But most of them begin their term of service before the age of twenty, and the two years involved are no serious loss to their career. Takani, however, brought into barracks a mind to some extent emancipated from the simple unquestioning traditions of his contemporaries and moreover the necessity of putting in his period of conscription had lost him a good job, hardly won. Besides which, he found that after his life abroad he had little

in common with the comparatively callow boys who were
now his companions. So, although he made an admirable
soldier, being quick-witted and handy, he was a little dis-
contented. To us he was invaluable.

We were an odd trio. M. was – and still is, as far as I know
– a member of the House of Lords. He was twenty-nine years
old and tall for his age. He had some sort of journalistic pre-
text for his presence in Manchukuo, but it was a thin one,
for during a prolonged stay in the Far East he was never
known to put pen to paper. Really it was the hope of adventure that had brought him. As a companion he had numerous
advantages besides his native charm: among them a capacity
for enduring discomfort without complaint, an inexhaustible
fund of conversation on a variety of topics, and a courtesy
towards the Japanese which was more flowery and more
appropriate than anything which I – a rather boorish individual – could hope to sustain for long. Also he was well
equipped.

How well equipped I only realized when we made an
inventory of our belongings in the inn at Fushun. I had interpreted literally our instructions to travel light by putting
into a rucksack a shirt, shorts, two pairs of socks, a bottle of
whisky, Boswell's *Life of Johnson*, and half a pound of cheese,
the sole, indomitable survivor of my Trans-Siberian victuals.
This, with blanket, camera, films, field-glasses, and water-
bottle, made a load which in case of necessity could be
carried on foot.

M. was far better provided. A large suitcase and a haver-
sack were found to contain, amongst other things, twenty-
three different sorts of medicine, the *Concise Oxford Dictionary*,
a prismatic compass, a solar topee, eight pencils, a ground
sheet, pyjamas, a pair of goggles, a cummerbund, and a slide-
rule. M. was armoured against almost every contingency,
from leprosy to long division.

We had been issued by the Japanese Consulate-General
with automatic pistols, but these we had left behind, partly
on the principle that it never rains if you wear a macintosh,
and partly because these weapons are – except as local colour

— more trouble than they are worth to those not expert in their use.

Horses, we had been told, would be provided. We were to move off at dawn. The inn was a pleasant place, cooler and more commodious than the one at Chinchow, and we went to sleep early. I felt very content. This expedition was an opportunity which it had taken several weeks and much cunning to wangle. Previous dabblings in what other people insist on calling adventure had forewarned me that the yield in excitement would probably not be high; but at the least we could rely on plenty of fresh air and exercise, commodities to the pursuit of which our fellow-countrymen devote so much of their spare time and money.

Next day, before it was light, a car whirled us out to the barracks through a still sleeping town. Our headlights flicked the irregular flanks of the Manchukuo column, which was already on the move from its more distant quarters: a soft-footed river of little slouching men in grey, the officers barking shrill commands from the backs of shaggy and recalcitrant ponies. The darkness was full of a stimulating last-minute bustle. As usual in China, bugle calls were almost incessant. The intoxicating effect of our preconceptions had not had time to wear off, and the atmosphere seemed to me pleasantly theatrical.

Outside the barracks we found our mounts. Huge, gaunt, and apathetic, two Siberian chargers of uncertain age contemplated with ill-disguised foreboding the preparations for a forced march. There was a Russian in charge of them, an attractive figure in a black blouse and a flamboyant slouch hat made of straw. While M. and Takani went off to stow our belongings on one of the transport wagons I inspected the horses dubiously. They did not look as if they were up to hard work, and I felt that they would be clumsy and uncertain in the hills, where the cat-footed Mongolian ponies are at home. But the Japanese, knowing the gigantic stature of foreigners, had thought that we would prefer horses; and these Rosinantine ghosts were the only horses available. I asked the Russian how old they were.

'The mare is ten years old.'

'And the other?'

'Twenty-one.'

M., being half as heavy again as I am, had to have the *ingénue*. I started out on her elderly companion, but at the first half changed mounts with the Russian, who had a little white pony, a very pretty, wise, and completely tireless animal. She carried me wonderfully, and I grew very fond of her. The horses, as a matter of fact, instead of collapsing as I had expected, did extraordinarily well, though they were tiring, lifeless creatures to ride.

Presently M. reappeared with Takani, and we mounted. (Takani had no horse, and in any case could not ride. He alternately marched or rode on the carts with the transport.) The column was moving off.

Through the gates they came, feet and hoofs and wheels: an intricate and perplexing rabble which was to sort itself out during the next few days into a pattern as familiar and significant as a pack of cards. Now, as they strung out down the road in the grey light before dawn, one had no framework to fit them into and grasped only here and there some striking detail – the carrier-pigeons in cages strapped to the backs of men, the two little mountain guns on pack mules, the Major's big dapple-grey pony with its ugly head.

M. and I fell in behind Headquarters, the Russian's Chinese wife waved to her husband from the roadside, and the march began.

19

THE FIRST DAY'S MARCH

THE sun rose as we moved off down the road. There was no breath of wind, and above the tall chimneys and the slag-heaps of the steel-works smoke from the furnaces hung in curious horizontal layers. Cooking-fires began to glimmer through the doorways of mean houses. Women, bucket in hand, paused to stare on their way to the wells. Feet and hoofs made hardly any noise at all in the thick dust, which sprang up and hung around us in a grey cloud and lent the marching men a ghostly air as they wound eastwards through the outskirts of Fushun. Nobody talked. Only, from the tail of the column, came the screaming of the transport-wagons' axles, the faint crepitation of their drivers' whips.

At six o'clock we halted. The men breakfasted off cold rice and pickles, issued in neat, flimsy little baskets. Already the officers with whom we rode began to stand out as individuals. The Major, an unsmiling, laconic little man, rather bow-legged; the Adjutant (whose duties Takani aptly defined by calling him 'the Major's wife'), a full-bodied forceful warrior, who looked alternately very fierce and very merry: the Doctor, slim, handsome, bespectacled, the only man except for M. and me whose head was not cropped. None of them spoke English, but they were very good to us in an off-hand way. If they looked on our presence as a nuisance they did not show it. Rather they regarded us with a certain perplexity. They felt that we were a joke, but they could never be quite certain that they saw what that joke was.

After breakfast we rode on to a village which marked the eastern boundary of that patch of civilization of which Fushun was the centre. The column, winding its way through the narrow streets, would have filmed well. Smoke rising from the cooking-shops mingled with our dust to form a haze, athwart which the shafts of sunlight came down between the houses to pick out our banners and the bobbing coolie hats which all the men wore as a protection against the heat. The inhabitants gaped and quickly raised their prices.

After a brief halt we marched out of the village, forded a river, and found ourselves in a shallow valley innocent of habitations. At the end of this the hills stood up like a wall. The road had dwindled to a track. The sun was high now, and the heat intense. We moved slowly along the floor of the valley and up into the mountains, a long disjointed file of men and animals and carts. Cuckoos called from the wooded slopes above us. The country was very beautiful.

About noon we passed through a tiny scattered village. I had waited behind to photograph the transport crossing a river; when I had finished I found a hiatus in the column, so I was making up for lost ground and came on the little village at full gallop. I had my eyes on the ground, which was broken and needed watching, and I was only dimly aware of the cluster of poor houses ahead of me. I was accordingly startled to find myself greeted with an ovation.

The entire village was lined up in a single rank beside the track, cheering wildly. Children waved flags. The local militia (a proverbial force of two men and a boy) presented arms. I was given a civic welcome.

It was an embarrassing moment. Clearly they took me for one of the more eminent of their country's saviours. There would perhaps have been no harm in this had I only been able to keep a straight face. Alas, I was not. Roaring with laughter, I made a vague and ludicrous gesture of appreciation and, giving my pony her head, was carried for ever out of the lives of that demonstrative community.

In the afternoon we came to another village and camped there. We had been going since three o'clock in the morning, and the men's uniforms were dark with sweat. Headquarters were established in the *yamen*, the seat of justice and a centre of insect life. A wireless section installed its transmitter in a corner of the courtyard and got into touch with Mukden; the next most modern object in the courtyard was a pair of blunderbusses ten feet long, the backbone of the local defence organization.

M. and I did rather less than justice to a meal of boiled rice, pickled mushrooms, and tinned fish, washed down with a local tea-substitute of kiaoliang. (Practically everything in Manchuria is made of kiaoliang. It serves as raw material for many manufactured articles, from hats to houses; also as fodder and fuel. Men eat it as a form of flour, and drink a spirit distilled from it. Its political significance as a stimulus to banditry in the summer and autumn I have already indicated.)

Japanese army rations are the same for officers and men (and special correspondents, too, for that matter). Their Spartan simplicity is one of the secrets behind the amazing mobility of the Japanese army; it thrives on a few bowls of rice and a piece of sorry-looking fish, a menu in comparison to which the British soldier's minimum needs seem Lucullian. The stomach on which the Japanese marches requires no field kitchens to fill it.

I found the rations adequate if unappetizing. Rice is not a bad thing to live on, but it is difficult without practice to get into the habit of eating the large quantities which the body needs. It is still more difficult if the rice is not boiled with some fat in it, which for some reason makes a lot of difference. M. had a thin time of it, being unable to stomach the rice. It was something of a mystery to me how he kept himself alive at all. His dietetic difficulties were increased by his courageous insistence on the use of chopsticks. I had basely brought with me a spoon and fork, knowing that we might have sometimes to eat in a hurry, and also that when it required an effort to eat at all it was better not to increase that effort by complicating the processes involved. But M. stuck gallantly to his belief that in Rome one should do as the Romans do, and I think the Japanese admired him for it. I certainly did.

Although the rations were the same for all, the officers displayed none of that solicitude for their men's welfare which in the British army prevents an officer from having his meal until he has seen that his men have got theirs. The Japanese officer is by tradition much more aloof than the British. He does not mix with the men in sports or in anything else, and rarely speaks to them except, so to speak, in the way of business. There is more of formality – and therefore, to my mind, of artificiality – in their relations than there is in this country; the assumption, implied by most forms of military discipline, that officers and men are two different sorts of animal is interpreted both more consistently and more literally in Japan. Whether the fabric of their relationship is designed in the best possible way to withstand the stress of emergency I do not know; but it certainly produces faultless discipline in times of peace.

Towards evening I went out in quest of a bath, and presently found a shallow stream of water which, though it ran swiftly, had acquired a startling degree of warmth from the sun. Here I wallowed for an hour in company with Takani and the Russian (whose name was Davidoff) and the Japanese captain who was the power behind the throne of the Manchukuo contingent. He was a pleasant, effective-looking man; his independent command made him freer in his speech and less constrained in his manner than any of the officers with Headquarters. He had been campaigning up in the north, near the Mongolian border, and told us wild stories of men there who ride down hares and shoot them from the saddle with a revolver. He also said that we were certain to see fighting before we reached Sinpin (our objective). The hills were stiff with bandits; we were marching by a route never before followed by troops, and our departure had been kept so successfully secret that the bandits would have no time to decamp into another area. It was pleasant to lie on one's back in the shallows, staring up at the small, but jagged peaks which overlooked our valley, and listen to this warlike talk.

We scrounged two eggs for dinner and ate them raw in rice. M. and Takani and I had a little room in the yamen to ourselves, and as soon as it was dark we spread our blankets on the boards of the k'ang and courted sleep. The moon, nearly full, rode high up over the mountains, making the dusty courtyard silver and stamping on it the horned black shadows of Chinese eaves. On the outskirts of the village a dog was howling. Ponies stamped and jerked their head-ropes under the compound wall; mule-bells jingled softly. The thick-wheeled wagons stood loaded for an early start; we should be off again in five hours' time.

The officers were talking in the next room, and I noticed as I have often noticed before the strange effect of going to sleep to the sound of foreign words. You do not know the language. You are not listening. But perhaps a speaker raises his voice, and your mind, sliding luxuriously into uncon-sciousness, involuntarily catches a sequence of sounds and, dragging you back from the happy frontiers of oblivion, translates them automatically into some fantastic English sentence with a corresponding cadence. So you are suddenly awake again, and there is ringing urgently in your ears some such altogether unaccountable phrase as 'John said all my sea-lions were glass', or 'Why go to Crewe, Barabbas?' The tone, the vowel-sounds of the speaker who disturbed you are exactly reproduced; but your fuddled mind has adapted them, with great rapidity and a kind of wild ingenuity, to the word-medium in which it works.

But perhaps it is only I who am cursed with this automatic gift. Sometimes, when you are tired, its involuntary exercise has an infuriating effect. You long to go to sleep. Yet you are perpetually being woken up by the challenge of words which were never spoken. It is as though your mind were making a series of apple-pie beds for your body, to deny it rest. You feel a fool.

20

GETTING WARMER

NEXT morning we were off soon after three. We followed the winding course of a little river. The track was deep in white dust, and the column moved in it so quietly that while it was still dark we could hear, far above our heads, the wing-beats of wild duck on the dawn flight to their feeding-grounds.

The track was always narrow, and we moved without a screen of scouts, the throwing out of which would have cut our speed in half, for they would have had to scramble through dense scrub on slopes which were often semi-precipitous. I had often heard the Japanese anti-bandit operations compared by foreigners to our own campaigns against the Boers; but I reflected, as the column plunged blindly into steep defiles from the lip of which a handful of reasonably armed men could have cut it to pieces with impunity, that the analogy was only partially applicable. The bandits were vermin who, in nine cases out of ten, would show no fight unless they were cornered. They had neither the wit, the courage, nor the weapons to put up that formidable resistance for which the terrain offered golden opportunities. Against an organized force they embarked on guerrilla warfare only at the last moment and from necessity; though there have been cases – mostly hushed up – of Japanese expeditions meeting with complete disaster, these have been exceptions due to the presence in the bandits' ranks of someone with the gift of leadership. So we marched without qualms through a series of death-traps which no one had taken the trouble to set.

Davidoff was an admirable man, and very good with his horses. He was one of eight brothers. Seven of them had been killed in the Revolution, and Davidoff, who was then a young officer with Tsarist sympathies, thought it prudent to visit China. Here he joined the armies of the Old Marshal, Chan Tso-lin, and rose to the rank of major. When Chan Tso-lin was blown up by the Japanese, Davidoff drifted desultorily into civilian life and married a Chinese woman. Now he kept a stable in Fushun. He had a small, handsome head, a charming smile, unlimited powers of endurance, and a philosophical outlook.

The most entertaining figure in the rather stolid atmosphere at Headquarters was Kaku. He was a diminutive Korean boy of fifteen. His home was in the district towards which we were marching, but his family had been dispossessed and some of them murdered by the bandits. Kaku had made a hit with a punitive expedition as an interpreter, and since then had lost no opportunity of seeing active service, for he held strong views on the subject of bandits.

His first appearance was unforgettable. As we passed through the outskirts of Fushun we had been hailed by a loud, facetious cry. A tiny figure bursting out of a still tinier military uniform was seen pricking towards us along the top of a bank separating two paddy fields. His pony was the smallest imaginable, and bore every appearance of being a rodent. As he came up Kaku gave an exaggerated parody of a military salute, and instantly disappeared from sight, pony and all, into an unforeseen ditch. He emerged quite unruffled, and from then onwards kept up a running fire of badinage, mostly directed against the Adjutant, whose large chestnut stallion was a perpetual menace to march discipline.

When we halted in a village the Japanese would subside limply in the nearest patch of shade while the officers retired to the magistrate's house for tea and a rest. But Kaku was indefatigable. He would scamper off up the street on his farcical pony, fling himself into a house, and start cross-questioning the inhabitants for news of the bandits. I can see him now, his small, aggressive head thrust forward, his switch imperiously tapping his absurd Wellington boots, bullying some respectable citizen old enough to be his grandfather with a series of shrill domineering yaps. Kaku and I got on very well together. He always saw to it that I had a leafy branch to keep the horse-flies from my pony's belly, and sometimes he gave me eggs, for whose whereabouts in professedly foodless households he had an uncanny flair.

In the middle of the morning we debouched into a biggish valley, and found ourselves looking across rice fields to a village on the farther side. The track split up into a number of narrow paths running along the tops of the dykes, so the transport had to make a detour round the bottom of the valley. The troops also divided, each unit taking a different path through the paddy.

We made a splendid sight, in the early D. W. Griffith manner. The detachments marched in single file along the high banks, paced by their reflections in the water of the paddy fields. At the head of the advance-guard fluttered the banner of the Rising Sun. Behind us, grey and compact, the Manchukuo contingent was just entering the valley, led by a standard bearer with a yellow flag. The transport, making its way along the shale of a river bed far out on our left flank, moved slowly in a cloud of bright dust under the shadow of steep cliffs; each wagon had its little banner – yellow, or red and white – and the whole equipage wore a markedly romantic air.

The transport was a wonderful thing of its kind. The little stocky wagons with two enormous iron-studded wheels, often spokeless, were drawn by mixed teams of two ponies and a mule, or two mules and a pony. They looked impossibly clumsy, but they were up to anything. We had before us some steep passes, climbed by a track often indistinguishable from the dried-up bed of a stream. The wagons took them in their stride. Yelling like demons and using their long whips with refined cruelty the Chinese drivers kept their teams scrambling like cats at the rough brittle surface. They were always up with us a few minutes after we had halted; they were never a drag on the column.

We were due for a rest in the village on the other side of the valley. We had been going for a long time and it was very hot. The men took off their packs and sprawled in the shade. The Chinese inhabitants, pathetically anxious to please, trotted to and fro among them, bringing well-water in the inevitable kerosene tins. Scrofulous dogs cringed in the offing, torn between greed and fear. Naked children wondered. From behind the tattered paper windows of mean houses very old men and very old women looked out on these alien campaigners with only bemusement in their eyes. Like all the villages we passed, it was a place of almost inconceivable poverty.

Of such poverty that in the chief house they could offer us (this was often, indeed almost always the case) only boiling water to drink. They had no tea, and the lovely ice-cold water from the wells was considered, except by me, unsafe for anyone above the rank of private to drink. But Head-quarters, when I reached it, had forgotten its thirst. The Major, cross-legged and impassive as ever, sat in a low room full of the buzzing of innumerable flies. His staff were stand-ing to attention in front of the k'ang. There was a certain tension in the atmosphere. In whispers I got Takani to diagnose it.

We were on the bandits' trail, and the scent was breast high. A small detachment of the gang we were after had visited this village the night before, departing into the hills with sixteen captives, for whose ransom they demanded half the season's crop of opium and a quantity of miscellaneous provisions. Their retreat, the headquarters of the main body, was known; we should find them in a valley fifteen miles away. This sounded promising. I prepared to cancel my precautions against disillusionment.

When he had fully questioned the elders of the village the Major began to issue his orders. His level voice droned on, drowning the importunate flies. The senior non-commissioned officers took down notes of what he said and afterwards – parrot-like but extremely accurate – repeated their instruc-tions. The meeting broke up, and everyone gave their attention to the (in this temperature) difficult problem of consuming enough boiling water to see them through to the next halt, which was not potentially remote.

The plan of campaign was roughly as follows: The

Manchukuo contingent and more than half the Japanese force were to march by separate routes and take up positions covering the passes on the far side of the valley. The small remainder of the Japanese was to carry on by the shortest route, and deliver a frontal attack on the bandits' headquarters at dawn, thus driving such as they failed to annihilate into one of two ambushes. Headquarters would ride with the smallest contingent. M. and I were pleased, for it sounded as if these were the people who would see most of the fun.

We set out almost immediately. The dusty little street was a cacophonous tangle of wagons and unwilling mules and soldiers struggling hastily into their kit; the simultaneous departure of three units in three different directions had tied the column temporarily into a knot. But at last we were free, and I found myself with a little force of fifty men pushing slowly up a valley which seemed to have risen to the occasion and appeared more savage and picturesque than any we had passed as yet. The track was certainly worse.

That was the hardest day we had. At the end of the valley, in the heat of noon, we climbed a pass so steep that it was a miracle the wagons managed it. Two men fell out with heatstroke. (They were all young soldiers. That is inevitable in a conscript army with a two-year term of service. But on the whole they stood the heat less well than I had expected.) At last we reached the top and found a breeze and a little broken shrine to rest by. We looked down in luxurious self-esteem on the track we had so lately left, writhing ignominiously along the floor of the valley.

The descent on the farther side was almost equally hard work. But at the bottom there was a poor house by a stream, and everyone cheered up at the thought of lunch and began to unbuckle their equipment. A family of peasants welcomed us unreservedly. The officers were ushered into their miserable dwelling and encouraged to make themselves at home on the filthy fly-blown k'ang. Everyone sprawled about and waited for water to be boiled.

But from a rafter in the middle of the room hung a little hammock covered with a cloth on which the flies crawled two deep. Presently something stirred beneath it; the flies rose with a buzz, then settled again. But now there was a child's hand sticking out, a small, hot, wretched hand, of which the wrist was pitted deeply. Everybody was asleep, or nearly asleep, except the Adjutant. I called his attention to the hand, and we pulled back the cloth. In the hammock lay a child dying of the smallpox.

Five minutes later we were on the march again.

A mile farther on we found another house where we had some food and such rest as the flies would allow us. In the afternoon it grew uncomfortably hot, and two more men fell out. We struggled up another pass, the highest yet, and dropped down into a valley, in one corner of which there was a cluster of decrepit houses. It was getting late, and we stopped here for a meal and a few hours' sleep.

I bathed, upstream of the mules, in four inches of running water, and came back to find that beer had been issued with the rations. Davidoff and Takani and M. and I had two bottles between us. It was heavenly. The worst of travel in the interior of China during the hot weather is that you can seldom (and never with complete safety) get anything cold to drink. It is only a minor hardship, but it has a disproportionate effect on anyone who, like myself, has a freakish but violent aversion from tea. The European is so used to quenching his thirst with cold liquid that his system does not at first recognize the advantages of the opposite method, which is, I believe, theoretically superior.

As we sat on the grass in front of the principal compound, drinking the excellent beer, there suddenly appeared on the sky-line across the valley the figure of a man. When he came in sight of us he stopped dead in his tracks, then went quickly back over the ridge. He may, or he may not, have been responsible for what happened next day.

The flues of the cooking-fire ran under the k'ang in the farmhouse where Headquarters were billeted; the small and very dirty room was unbearably hot, so I took my blanket and spread it on a low mound of turf in the compound. When M. joined me I told him, I don't know why, that we were sleeping over a sealed-up cess-pit. He prepared immediately to decamp.

'It's all right, M.' I said (in vain). 'It was only a joke. It's not true.'

Later, however, I discovered that it was.

21

CUCKOO!

IT was two o'clock the next morning. A brilliant moon over-romanticized the huge and shaggy hills. In the courtyard before Headquarters the wagons were being loaded hastily. There was a feeling of excitement in the air. It was shared, to the common danger, by the mules, and the curses of the drivers, vitriolic but subdued, rose like the hissing of a pit of snakes. I edged my way cautiously between malicious teeth and hoofs to find my kit and fill my water-bottle. I had a little fever that morning, and life seemed more than usually fantastic.

Inside the farm everyone was scrambling methodically for their things by the inadequate light of a candle. When we came out the courtyard was clearing. My white pony was waiting for me by the gate, a patient little ghost. I strapped my belongings on to her back and mounted We had ten miles to go before dawn.

We moved off at 2.30. At the head of the column the banner of the Rising Sun went forward, flickering like a spectre. The track showed grey before us. The feet of men and ponies made little sound in the thick dust. The small, plodding infantrymen still wore their coolie hats, and the steel helmets slung across their backs were humps below their shoulders. These things, and the silence of their march, made them grotesque and eerie; I felt that I was riding with a goblin army.

An order came down the column, and bolts rattled as the men loaded their rifles. With a certain surprise (for I was leading the kind of life that suits me, and it had lulled me into a peaceful and unreflecting state of mind) I reminded myself that presently, if all went well, we should be doing our best to kill a lot of other people, and they would be doing their best to kill us. The prospect of whistling bullets was mildly exciting; but only mildly, for the chances of their whistling in anything uncomfortably like the right direction I took to be remote. A posse of opium-addicts armed with rusty Mausers did not, however lavishly they might be decorated with paper charms conferring invulnerability, constitute a very redoubtable foe. Besides, I strongly suspected that they would scratch the fixture altogether.

In campaigning of this sort intelligence is more than half the battle, for without intelligence no battle can take place; and I did not doubt that in this respect the bandits were better served than we were. In every village of the district they harried they were reputed to have the wealth of the principal families so exactly assessed that they knew, not only which people to capture, but how much to demand for their ransom. (Except when dealing with foreigners, the Manchurian bandit is too good a business man to be impossibly exorbitant.)

It was in short virtually certain that we had been brushing all the time against an unseen web of spies; and news travels fast in the East, in fact as well as in sensational fiction. That man on the sky-line last night had been only one – the most spectacular – of a thousand potential sources of warning to the bandits. I looked at the intricate moonlit pattern of the mountains and reflected drowsily that for a small force escape should be an easy matter, however well we blocked the passes in their rear. I resigned myself to disillusionment and presently fell asleep in the saddle.

Two hours later the sky was paling and the stars were almost gone. Now you could see the bats as they flew. In a little it would be dawn. The head of the column debouched suddenly from the wide, irregular gorge down which we had been marching, and our objective was in sight: a big jagged mountain, which thrust forward shoulders to enclose a valley. The bandits' place was in the valley, which was perhaps a mile away, and of which little could as yet be seen. Our other two contingents were presumably in position on the other side of the mountain. The battlefield was before us.

So far I had ridden in an agreeable torpor, shot with

momentary flashes of anticipation and conjecture. Now things began to happen.

They were the wrong things, but they happened in such a baffling and enigmatic way that it took us some time to realize this. First of all, from the inside of the valley, which was half hidden from us by a spur, there rolled up with great deliberation a thick cloud of pallid smoke; someone had fired a house, or houses. (But, who? And why? We had neither the time nor the data to answer these questions.) Then more smoke was seen, coming this time from a little corrie in the hill just above us, quite close; it rose slowly in the still air, a slim and deprecating column. (How long had that signal fire been burning? Had it evoked the other, or the other it?) The officers, sitting squatly on their ponies, looked with disapproval at these portents.

The Major issued an order. Kaku and two other mounted men went clattering up an old path and disappeared into the corrie above, from which the smoke continued to ascend in a bland, rather self-conscious way. The column was halted, but very few of the tired men lay down. It was just beginning to get light.

In five minutes the horsemen reappeared bringing with them one prisoner. He was a tall, facetious-looking youth, who seemed in no doubt of his ability to pass the situation off with a laugh. But Kaku went at him like a terrier, threatening fearful things in a series of staccato yaps, while the officers stood round, majestic but uninitiated, eagerly absorbing what few scraps of Japanese the little boy flung them over his shoulder. Meanwhile the smoke-cloud above the bandits' valley thickened and slowly spread in sumptuous, bulging convolutions.

The prisoner's facetiousness drained slowly from him. At last he gave way altogether: indicated which of the three paths before us led to our objective, and was ordered to guide us down it. The horsemen scrambled into their saddles. The bandits' ally, grinning in a sickly way, was given the colours to carry and a stirrup-leather to hold on to. An advance guard on ponies, half a dozen strong, set off down the winding path. M. and I went with them, expecting to be called back at any moment. The infantrymen followed as fast as they could.

That scrambling charge, though unprofitable, was exhilarating. It was the hour of dawn – that instant in the day's long life when everything seems still and poised and has a quality of surprise, like unexpectedly good scenery disclosed by the rise of the curtain. We rode circuitously between a succession of little bluffs which rose like tree-crowned islands from the valley's floor; and all the time we dipped in and out of dead ground, so that our goal was not continuously in sight. The chance of an ambush, though it seemed to be remote, lent to the landscape, already picturesque, an added interest; no geologist could have eyed the crags, no botanist the tangled scrub, more keenly or judiciously than we did. Or more in vain.

For nothing happened. We trotted forward, important and intrepid; and were ignored. Only, as we drew near it, the original column of smoke was joined by others. Clouds less well established but as dense began to plume the whole area in which our imaginations were busy reconstructing the bandits' stronghold. A petulant and unaccountable incendiarism was clearly the order of the day.

We came to a place where the path forked and halted for a moment. On the very noticeable silence thus created there fell, with an air of premeditation, the hollow sound of an explosion, some way distant. This increased our perplexity; nobody could guess what it meant. Later we learnt that it was a random shot – such a shot as one fires into reeds to see if they hold duck – from the mountain gun of the Manchukuo contingent. That, I am ashamed to say, is the nearest I have ever come to hearing a shot fired in anger.

The sound, though inexplicable, was exciting. Everyone put their ponies into a gallop. We went clattering down the path, past a clump of trees, round the corner of a deserted hut, and slap into the bandits' stronghold. Stronghold, indeed! It looked like the early stages of a heath fire in what house-agents call the Surrey Highlands.

From the never very desirable sites of half a dozen huts flames leapt noisily into the air. A mean hamlet was going up in smoke before our eyes. Three or four houses had not been fired: an omission which we lost no time in making good. This seemed to me more like co-operation than revenge, but there was nothing else that we could do, even by way of a gesture. The bandits' village stood in a clearing at the foot of a slope; behind it the face of the mountain rose steeply, clothed with a forest of almost sub-tropical density and to all appearances trackless. The last of the bandits could not have left the clearing more than ten minutes ago, but they were as far beyond the reach of pursuit as if they had had an hour's start. It was hopeless country.

Of their captives there was no sign. For some reason nobody seemed to bother their heads very much about the fate of those sixteen unfortunate people. Alas for the theorists, who pretend that in these internationally minded days all members of the human race are fast becoming as equal in each other's own eyes as in the eyes of God. . . . I could not help reflecting that if those sixteen Chinese had been one English spinster I might have had a different tale to tell of our abortive expedition.

The fires burned briskly in an empty valley. We left them crackling irresponsibly and rode sadly back to meet the main body, feeling that we had been scored off. (Though how exactly that wanton destruction of their own property could be interpreted as one up to the bandits, I am to this day far from clear.) Still, we felt that we had been sold, where we had prepared to sell our lives. The steam rising from our ponies stank of anti-climax.

Where would we be without the pleasures of anticipation? Life is like (among other things) a child's money-box. The process of hoarding, whether it be hopes or pennies, affords a delight which, though mild, is continuous and never turns sour. When at last we spend what we have saved up, we purchase almost always disappointment. 'This isn't at all what I wanted,' we grumble. 'This isn't up to expectation.' And in our chagrin (against which experience should have taught us to forearm ourselves) we forgot what pleasure expectation gave us before it was cheated.

In this matter I am at once a defeatist and an opportunist. I allow myself to entertain high hopes, not because I expect them for a moment to be realized, but because I enjoy entertaining them. I am a connoisseur, a rather unscrupulous connoisseur, of the delights of anticipation. I promise myself great things purely for the fun of making the promises. In this way I had got the maximum enjoyment from this expedition which had just ended in fiasco. No optimist could have more keenly or more consciously relished its excitements in advance; no sceptic could have accepted their non-fulfilment with more impregnable equanimity. This capacity for making the best of both worlds – the present and the future – I attribute to my Scottish blood.

Even now, in this moment of deflation, anticipation was at hand to buoy us up again. There is always something to look forward to. In this case it was breakfast. We had been on the move for some hours, and as we sprawled beside a pleasant little stream the prospect of putting something in our empty bellies made failure seem, for the moment, much less bitter. Soon we were eating cold rice and pickles and making, with a judicious air, chimerical surmises about the bandits' flight. The hills looked very lovely. A cuckoo called from a copse of oak. Huge clouds of smoke drifted and hung and rose to catch the early sunlight above a valley which was still a bowl of shadows. There was a smell of burning thatch in the air.

On a spur above us three signallers were heliographing to one of the other contingents on a ridge across the valley. How very up to date we were, I reflected: so modern, so mobile, so well disciplined. We ought to be a match for any bandits. . . .

'Cuckoo! Cuckoo! Cuckoo!' called that aggravating bird, in what seemed to me a very pointed manner.

22

OVATION

THAT day we did another long march, eating our midday meal in a farm through which some of the bandits had passed only three hours before us. After that we never picked up their trail again, and indeed in these labyrinthine hills it would have been surprising if we had.

In the late afternoon we joined forces with the other two contingents where two valleys forked, and camped there in a little village. The mayor of this place made a speech of welcome in the course of which he was sick twice; done in the offhand, matter-of-fact way in which he did it, this struck me as rather an effective oratorical trick.

The other contingents had been no luckier than we. The Manchukuo troops had (so they said) fired at long range on a party of bandits as they disappeared into a wood; the volley, it was claimed, had wrought great havoc, but unfortunately there had been no time to verify any casualties. They had, on the other hand, captured a man who was carrying a written warning of our approach to the bandits, and also some of the charms which guaranteed invulnerability.

These were thin, yellowish strips of paper on which was washily portrayed in red the face of a man (or demon) in the grip of some powerful but not easily definable emotion. I have heard various accounts of the ways in which these charms are used. The fanatical, politico-religious bandits – the Red Spears, the Big Swords, and such like – are the most addicted to them. Sometimes the charms are merely pinned to the breast, or fastened to the rifle, sword, or spear. More often they are taken internally – either chewed or swallowed, or burnt and their ashes dissolved in water, which is drunk. As a form of Dutch courage they can be extraordinarily effective. I know of cases where bandits, naked to the waist, have faced the machine-guns of an armoured train and suffered annihilation, sooner than repulse. The regular, dyed-in-the-wool fanatics are dominated by priests of a Rasputinian denomination, and it is these priests who issue the charms. Superstition alone can hardly account for the stimulus which they lend to the tactics of a race given neither to doing nor dying; there is a theory, which seems to me plausible, that these little slips of paper contain some kind of drug. I verified the case of a Polish schoolboy from Harbin, who was held for ransom by a gang of Red Spears. In the course of his captivity he noticed that the bandits always ate these charms before going into action, and was amazed by the uncharacteristic daring which they then displayed. One day he stole and ate a charm. Its effect, he said, was to make him feel 'like a king' for half an hour, after which he became dizzy, lost consciousness, and went into a deep and lengthy sleep.

I must admit, however, that in the charms I saw there appeared to be no traces of narcotics; not that I should have been able to recognize them if they had been there.

We marched for three more days after we had missed the bandits. They were uneventful but not uninteresting. In the village where two valleys forked and the mayor was queasy we left behind us a hundred men to clear up – '(sic)' notes my uncharitable diary – the gang which we had failed so signally to exterminate.

I should have mentioned before now the propaganda unit which was attached to the column. Its personnel consisted of a Japanese, a Chinese, and a Korean – all young men – and its equipment of a gramophone, an unlimited quantity of pamphlets, and a lot of medical supplies. When the column halted for the night the propagandists set about getting an audience. This was where the gramophone came in, for the peasants had never seen its like before. The children were usually the first in whom curiosity conquered their instinctive distrust of this new magic; they were easily entranced, and would cluster round, sucking their fingers and mechanically scratching, while the plangent Chinese music repeated itself in the dusk. After a bit they would be sent to fetch their elders, and the concert continued until a decent audience had been collected.

There followed a brief medical interlude. Purges were administered, cuts bandaged, and the sores which at least half the children had on their eyelids treated with ointment. This won the audience over decisively and the time was ripe for speech-making. The burden of this was usually borne by the young Chinese, a university graduate from Peking. In what seemed to me a very impressive way he explained to the gaping villagers that they now belonged to a new and independent state (this was news to most of them) to which the Japanese were lending a helping hand. He outlined the principles on which the state were founded, and the benefits they would derive from its existence if they pulled themselves together and took a strong line with the bandits. He ended with the inevitable little piece about Wangtao.

The villagers listened with a sheepish but respectful air. It was sufficiently clear that the new government of Manchukuo was an institution almost as remote from their comprehension as the London County Council; they were not interested in Wangtao. But they were unmistakably glad to see the Japanese, not because they stood for autonomy or any other abstraction, but because they had rifles and plenty of ammunition, and when they came the bandits, if only for a time, departed. The vast bulk of the thirty-odd million inhabitants of Manchukuo are not, and do not want to be, politically conscious; and it is worth bearing in mind the fact that a very large proportion of them have never seen a Japanese out of khaki, for there are few parts of Manchuria where a Japanese civilian can travel without military protection.

I remember one incident which I think gives a fair idea of what Manchukuo means to its subjects in the interior. I went with the propaganda men (all of whom seemed to me to be both able and sincere, and to have more elasticity of mind than the regular soldiers) to a school where they were to give a lecture. The children, solemn and scrofulous, sang the national anthem of Manchukuo at a funeral pace. The lecture was delivered. Then the chief pupil, a boy of about eighteen, made a speech of thanks. He had obviously been coached by the master, and everyone obviously thought that he was saying the right things. But he never mentioned Wangtao, or autonomy, or any of the other high-sounding things on which the lecturer had concentrated. He talked about the Japanese soldiers, and nothing else: what fine fellows they were, how good it was of them to come and clean up the bandits, how glad the village was to see them. The Chinese are realists.

And there could be no doubt that we were welcome. Chinese discretion and Chinese hospitality would, of course, have combined to prevent the display of any marked coldness; but there were incidents – the gift of three puny but precious chickens, the women's readiness to let their children fraternize – which substantiated external impressions. Of these last the most memorable was our reception at Sinpin.

Sinpin, you will remember, was our first objective, the place where the column would go into garrison for a time. We had been marching since dawn up a valley on which a thin but none the less depressing veneer of civilization had been laid; for Sinpin is a place of some local importance, where the agricultural produce of a big district is marketed. A road was being constructed, and the sudden appearance of a patrolling lorry full of soldiers sent my pony scrambling like a lizard up the rocky face of a bluff. My sympathy with her reactionary attitude to the march of progress had almost evaporated by the time I got her down.

Just before noon we realized that our destination was at hand. A cloud of dust on the road before us resolved itself into a detachment of Manchukuo cavalry. This was headed by a civil official, a tall, sad young man uneasily astride a pony which bore a startling resemblance to a tapir; he was dressed in a black coat, white flannel trousers, and a straw hat. Courtesies were exchanged, the cavalry fell in behind Headquarters, and the march continued.

A mile farther on we came to a bend in the track. Here were

symmetrically arranged in order of height the entire student body from the various schools in Sinpin. They awaïted our approach in silent immobility, expressing (I imagined) a tacit sympathy with our failure in the field. But I was wrong. That prelude of silence was a carefully rehearsed stage effect. As we drew level with the line some well-intentioned cheer-leader uttered a low, urgent cry. It was answered by a deafening ovation. Hats were waved wildly in the air; flags, hitherto concealed, were agitated to and fro; cheer upon cheer crashed upon our unsuspecting ears at point-blank range.

The effects were immediate and far-reaching. The Major's pony bolted. The Adjutant's stallion bounded sideways into a ditch. An orderly was bucked off into the dust. The head of the column was thrown into complete confusion.

The student body, going slowly black in the face, continued to bellow its loyalty and to wave its banners.

When Headquarters had passed it grew quiet again, waiting for the next detachment. These were infantrymen, who bore the disconcerting outburst with a solemn composure. But soon, I knew, the transport must arrive; so I stayed behind to watch its advent from a distance.

The trick worked better than ever. Mute and motionless, the carefully tapered rank of boys and girls gave the drivers no indication of what was in store for them. Not until the leading teams were well abreast did they release their pent-up gratitude. Then, with shattering effect, they once more blasted the column sideways with a salvo of cheers, frantically flapping their banners to complete the mules' alarm. The animals jibbed and shied; some bolted. The drivers leapt from their seats on the shafts to the heads of their teams, with piercing cries of irritation and dismay. A great cloud of dust rolled up above the stamping and confusion. The student body went on cheering.

23

TWO MEN TIED UP

At the gates of the town, and all along the principal street, the crowds, though dense, were happily less demonstrative. It was a queer feeling, this riding in triumph through a sea of yellow faces: particularly queer for M. and me, who were doubly impostors, for not only had no victory taken place to justify those cheers, but it would have been nothing to do with us if it had. We aroused a disproportionate curiosity – disproportionate because the townspeople had experience of missionaries and knew what white men looked like. But M's enormous stature drew many subdued cries of 'Ai-ai-ai-yah', which is Chinese for 'Coo-er!' and I was still more overtly exclaimed at. The reason, I heard afterwards, was that I was thought to be the representative of an entirely new race. I had worn no hat on the march, to the amazement of the Japanese, and now my face was a kind of chestnut colour which put me in a different ethnological category from the pale-faced missionaries. The more educated onlookers inclined to the belief that I was an Indian, but most put me down as a devil.

We were assigned our quarters, which centred round a big courtyard. (It was astonishing how quickly, in the room which was being used as a kitchen, the Japanese killed all the flies and covered the torn paper windows with gauze against a further invasion.) A company of Japanese troops had been garrisoned in the town for the last six months, and M. and I were invited to accompany our officers to lunch at their Headquarters.

It was here, in the courtyard outside their mess, that I saw my first bandit. He was tied to a post – a net-ball post, to be exact. A few feet away, lashed to a smaller stake, was one of his spies, a man who, posing as a respectable citizen, had been caught sending out information to the bandits from Sinpin. They were both going to be shot that night.

They were not an attractive pair. The bandit was a youth of nineteen; he had commanded a gang of forty men. He was poorly dressed in peasant's clothes, and he had a large, round, moon-like face. It gave you the impression of being unnaturally swollen, and this impression was heightened by a generous black eye which embossed one cheek – the legacy presumably of Third Degree methods after his capture. The face wore an expression of surly and bestial resignation. His pig-like eyes betrayed little interest in his captors, who for their part betrayed little interest in him. They treated him as if he were a permanent, inanimate, and only slightly out of the ordinary fixture in their temporary home. (*'Oh, that? Yes, it is rather a curious old sundial. Perhaps you'd like to go and have a look at it after lunch?'*)

If there was something brutish and remote about the bandit, his spy was a Caliban, beyond all question hag-born. He was a big ape-like man, with a forehead villainously low and a jaw which at once jutted and sagged. He had a battered look about him, not recently acquired. His pose conveyed despair, but in his heavy, bloodshot eyes, eternally scrutinizing the dust, there was only a kind of dull, incurious brooding. He was like a beast which has been too long in a trap.

I photographed them both, without compunction, but not without a vague feeling of embarrassment. They had only a few more hours to live; but the little I had seen and learnt of the effects of banditry was enough to dull all pity. Still, the conventional part of me found something queer and awkward in the thought that those two trussed bodies would be food for worms long before some chemist in a dark-room brought to light the figures they had cut on the threshold of death and dissolution. It was a situation which would have put Donne's muse on her mettle.

As we went in to lunch a light rain began to fall, which was perhaps just as well, for the July sun dancing on those two unprotected bodies outside the window might have impaired one's appetite.

Lunch was the best meal we had made for some days. Beer flowed freely, and M. made a speech. I conversed, through Takani, with a young Japanese officer wearing Chinese dress. He was doing intelligence work, and what he said crystallized and confirmed the impressions I had formed about the bandit problem. These impressions may be roughly summarized as a belief that all the bandits had to do to escape a just retribution was to walk up the nearest hill and stand behind the nearest tree.

This is what the intelligence officer said: His company had been in Sinpin for six months. They now had maps (which he showed me) on which were indicated the position and strength of the various gangs frequenting the district under their control. Hardly any of these gangs mustered more than a hundred men; the average was about sixty. Many of them were within one day's march of the town, none more than three days away. Of the principal men in each gang exact and comprehensive dossiers had been compiled, and the details of their armaments, supply of ammunition, and morale were also known. On paper, the Japanese had the bandits taped.

But only on paper. Over that period of six months operations in the field had been rarely, and never more than partially, successful. The bandits owed their salvation to a superior intelligence system. Whenever the garrison moved, no matter how secretly, against them, the bandits knew of it in advance; and it was no difficult matter for a small gang to vanish into thin air, since most of them were in dress and demeanour indistinguishable from the law-abiding peasants. The leaders hid, the rank and file buried their Mausers and picked up a hoe, and the punitive expedition returned empty-handed.

This was a thing which the bandits themselves very seldom did. In Sinpin, for all that it contained an energetic and well-equipped garrison, two thousand farmers and their families were at that moment taking refuge, leaving their crops unharvested. The bandits beggared the countryside and grew rich on ransoms. The intelligence officer told me that out of every three captives taken one (on an average) escaped, one was ransomed, and one – the ransom not appearing – was murdered. The time-honoured custom of gingering up the market by enclosing, with the penultimate demand for dollars, a finger or an ear was still adhered to. It looked as if peace and order would be a long time on the way in that part of the country.

At first it was said that our column would send out without further delay punitive expeditions operating with Sinpin as their base. But the lapse of two days found Headquarters still waiting for reports from spies; everything depended on intelligence work carried out through distant and unreliable agents. At last the Major admitted that he had no idea when they would be able to move; it might not be for another fortnight. So I decided to go back to Mukden.

There was nothing to keep us in Sinpin, which was a flat, nondescript town altogether lacking in charm, and it was impossible to go outside it without a military escort. Besides which, both M. and Takani were in poor health. For some days M. had had very little food and very little sleep, and it was lucky in the circumstances that there were two charming American Catholic missionaries in Sinpin. (The Catholics, unlike most of the other denominations, stay at their posts throughout the hot weather.) These two treated us with the utmost kindness, and M. was comfortably installed in a bed at the Mission. I set about inquiring how to get home.

This, it turned out, was an easy matter. A newly built road ran down to the railway, and the journey took only four hours by lorry. I said good-bye to the officers, who still regarded me with a kind of puzzled amusement; but they had, I think, found us less trouble than they expected, and said kind things about our performance on the march. Davidoff had already departed for Fushun with the transport, riding my pony and leading the horses. I was really sorry to see the last of the pony and her master; they were both good creatures.

Very early in the morning we carried our kit down to the end of the town and took our seats in the lorry. Travel in any form of public conveyance in China is almost always

instructive, amusing, and uncomfortable. We shared the
lorry, which was open and devoid of seats, with a large and
varied assortment of peasantry and small tradesmen, on
whose faces in the course of the journey the whole gamut of
human emotions was reflected. Takani and M., heavily doped
with a liberal though arbitrary selection from our twenty-
three different kinds of medicine, and to all appearances
inanimate, sprawled on our kit. A light rain fell – too light to
lay the dense clouds of dust which blotted out the rearward
horizon. The road was very bad, and from time to time the
whole contents of the lorry, human and otherwise, would be
thrown a short distance into the air, so that for a mile or so
everybody would be busy sorting themselves out again.

I had often heard from the Japanese that road-construction
was to be one of the chief agencies in the elimination of the
bandits – that any area could be quickly pacified once it had
been opened up by strategic communications. This particular
road was a new one and had been specifically built for military
purposes. I was accordingly surprised to find that its only
apparent effect had been to simplify the bandits' task by
canalizing all lootable traffic. It was impossible for the Sinpin
garrison to patrol it continuously, and only yesterday the
daily lorry had been wrecked and its eleven passengers
robbed. To-day our four Manchukuo guards showed more
signs of alertness and determination than are commonly to be
detected in Chinese soldiery. Whenever we approached, as
we often did, a sharp bend, or a gully, or some patch of dense
cover which looked like a potential ambush, they stood to
their rifles and flipped back their safety catches in a way
which would have been most reassuring had their foothold
in the lorry been rather more secure.

But I would appear to be a kind of Jonah on these occasions,
a charm against bandits. No party of which I have been a
member has ever established even the most indirect contact
with the lawless elements in the population. And so it was on
this journey. No volleys rang out, no agglomeration of
boulders suddenly barred our way on a steep gradient; our
progress was as uneventful as progress ever can be in China.

Once, it is true, we came sharply round a corner and found a solitary house beside the road blazing merrily though enigmatically. But at the sight of it the driver trod unhesitatingly upon his accelerator, so I can give you no details of an atrocity which may, after all, have been an Act of God.

The little railway station where M. and Takani and I waited for four hours for the train to Mukden had also recently been burnt. The rain, now much heavier, dripped through holes in the roof on to the indispensable pages of Boswell. A wounded Japanese soldier arrived in a Ford car and was carried groaning into the stationmaster's office. Otherwise the place was deserted. We lay in some straw, eating boiled eggs and scratching honourable and by now fairly numerous bites. Our little excursion was over. If it had not been so exciting as we hoped, it was not as dull as I have made it sound. When at last we heard a train whistle in the distance I remember thinking – what I now know to be true – that I shall always recall with the keenest pleasure those silent early hours as we filed along the bottom of a valley, and the breeze which met us when we climbed a pass under the fierce eye of noon, and the muffled sound of men marching in dust, broken by the discreet clink of accoutrements, and my white pony standing in the moonlight, and many other things as well.

Then the train arrived, and as we boarded it a curtain seemed to fall; we were back in the humdrum audience, no longer actors on an outlandish stage. Already the faithful Takani was reviewing despondently his imminent return to duty; already M. and I discussed with animation the prospect of a bath.

The interlude was over.

24

AND SO SOUTH

Two days later I left Mukden for Dairen. Dairen is a sort of Japanese Hongkong, very orderly and hygienic and up to date. You can drink the water from the taps without fear of poisoning. All the cab-horses are stabled at night in a depot outside the town, so as to minimize the insect menace. There are any number of large schools and hospitals, though it is true that these might be fewer were Dairen less potentially important as a strategic base where extra barracks may one day be needed. The general atmosphere of the place is suggestive of a garden suburb.

From Dairen I went by boat to Taku, and thence, in a slow, hot train, to Peking. I stayed in Peking for ten days, writing dispatches and enjoying the hospitality of people too numerous to mention. To describe Peking you must be something of an artist and something of a scholar; I, who am nothing of either, prefer not to attempt it. You will be spared the pen-picture which you had good reason to dread; the charm of the place is incommunicable.

For all its curious beauty, I would not like to live there. An atmosphere of unreality pervades the Legation Quarter. The diplomats drift to and fro with the slow, stately, and mysterious grace of fish in an aquarium. Yes, that is what Peking is like: an aquarium. Round and round they go, serene and glassy-eyed. Their natural surroundings have been artfully reconstructed in a confined space, behind glass. Round and round, round and round. ... How imperturbably they move! Are they contented! Have they forgotten the sea? I doubt it.

Feng Yu-hsian, the 'Christian General', was creating a diversion at Kalgan. Nanking had rushed 60,000 troops up the short line which reaches the marches of Inner Mongolia.

I was planning to follow them when the line was cut; to travel that way was impossible, and the situation seemed suddenly on the point of being liquidated. So I went south from Peking.

I took away at least one memory which will always give me pleasure. It is a picture of one of the many courtyards in the beautiful house in which I was staying. I used to have breakfast there. The boy would bring the coffee and the scrambled eggs and the local paper and go away. While I ate and read, an old, brown, wrinkled man would come shuffling down a narrow flagged path between the shrubs to the pool in the centre of the courtyard; very meticulously, muttering to himself, he would feed ants' eggs to the frilled elaborate goldfish in the pool. His face was terribly serious. From the lane outside came the shriek of a wheelbarrow axle, or the plaintive, mechanical cry of a hawker. Sparrows chirped among the demons and dragons on the eaves. Overhead, against the blue sky, a flashing cloud of pigeons wheeled in formation; there were tiny bamboo tubes fastened to their wings, and these made a kind of piping drone, a queer music which rose and fell and was unlike any other sound. It was very peaceful.

I broke the two-day train journey to Shanghai at Tsinanfu, the capital of Shantung. The governor of this province, Han Fu Chu, is in a quiet way one of the strongest men in China. Nominally subservient to Nanking, he is in fact semi-independent and does not embroil himself in Kuomintang politics. He gave me an interview which lasted two hours. A square, bull-like man, he began his career in the armies of Feng Yu-hsian, the 'Christian General'; the democratic influence of his former leader is apparent in the Shantung troops, whose officers dress as plainly as their men and renounce most of the privileges of rank.

Han Fu Chu compels all his ministers to rise early and take violent exercise before breakfast. Punctuality, which is regarded in China rather as an eccentricity than as a virtue, is rigidly enforced in all government departments, and public morality is safeguarded by edicts restricting the spread of

Western fashions among the women; all shingled heads are shaved by the police. In himself, Han Fu Chu impressed me chiefly by his modesty; he would accept no credit for running his province well and strenuously urged the claims of other governors who ran theirs better. He insisted that he was by birth a coolie, and had had no education. I liked him.

And so at last to Shanghai, a city belonging to no country. You have all read before of the overbearing skyscrapers which line the Bund: of the Chinese City, which hardly a foreigner visits: of the meditative Sikh policemen, with their short carbines tucked under their arms, like men out shooting rabbits: of the shipping on the wide, dirty river which, ranging from the sampan to the C.P.R. liner, reflects the whole history of commercial navigation: of the Shanghai Club, which has the longest bar in the world: of the unnumbered night clubs, where the slim, slick Chinese girls are on the whole more popular than their Russian colleagues: of the rich Chinese, whose big cars are packed with guards against the kidnappers: of the trams, and the electric lights, and the incessant noise, and the crowds for ever promenading, capriciously suicidal (a traffic sense is not one of the lessons which the West has been able to teach the East): of the strange cosmopolitan atmosphere, in which an American flavour predominates. . . . You have all, I say, heard these things fully described before.

If you hear them fully described again, it will not be my fault.

Part Two

RED CHINA

I

HAMMER AND SICKLE

THE chapters that follow are an account of a long journey undertaken with the object of investigating the Communist situation in South China. Unless the reader understands more or less what that situation is, the narrative will lose such interest as it may have for him. Accordingly, I will summarize at the beginning of the journey the conclusions which I reached at the end of it. Much of the information comprised in this survey was known at any rate in its general outline, in British official quarters in Peking and Shanghai: outside official quarters few foreigners in China, and almost none elsewhere, were familiar with the realities of a movement which now completely dominates half one large province and about a third of the next, and intermittently ravages others. So far as I know, no previous journey had been made to the anti-Communist front by a foreigner. I cannot claim that the new information which I was able to obtain, or the old information which I was able to confirm or modify, was of a nature to revolutionize the best theories already current about the situation; but perhaps it gave them a sounder basis, and I think it was worth collecting.

Neither the theory nor the practice of Communism is indigenous to China. The Chinese are individualists, and their unit of community is the family. It is their strength as a people that they think in terms of this unit, their weakness as a nation that they cannot think in terms of a larger – cannot effectively subordinate the interests of the clan to the interests of the province or the Republic. What hold Communism has on China to-day is therefore traceable to outside influence, and some survey of its brief history must necessarily precede an analysis of the present situation.

In 1926, when the Northern Expedition set out for the Yangtse Valley from Canton, the influence of Borodin and the Russian advisers was strong, and threatened to become paramount. The armies were preceded on their northward march by small, effective, Russian-trained parties of propagandists, whose roseate promises sowed the seeds of the present Red menace. Then came the break with the Russians. Borodin fled, and the elixir of Communism was officially labelled 'Poison'. Chiang Kai-Shek had the Yangtse Valley; but behind him on his line of march the ideas of Moscow, specially prepared for Far Eastern consumption, had taken root in a soil made fertile by agrarian discontent, and many of Moscow's apostles, proscribed elsewhere, filtered back to an area which Chiang's preoccupations farther north made safe for their activities.

A Communist state was set up, with its headquarters in Kiangsi, and the desertion of two Nationalist divisions provided it with the nucleus of what has now become perhaps the most formidable fighting force in China. Russia continued to play the Fairy Godmother, though of necessity from a distance. The Chinese Communists received moral and financial support through the Far Eastern Bureau of the Comintern, an organization with a small European staff which worked secretly in the International Concession at Shanghai. With the arrest of its head, Hilaire Noulens,* in 1931, this organization was broken up, and subsidies from Moscow – which were at that time coming into Shanghai at the rate of more than £140,000 a year – were cut off. If they have been resumed since, it is on a negligible scale.

By 1931 Communism had assumed the status of a national problem in China; attempts by the Nanking Government to solve it were becoming annually more serious, though not more successful. A Chinese Soviet Republic had proclaimed itself and controlled – as it controls to-day – an area of which central and southern Kiangsi and western Fukien are the permanent nucleus, but which has at one time or another

*Noulens and his wife are now in gaol at either Nanking or Soochow.

been expanded to include part of Hunan, Kwantung, and Hupeh.

I found that most foreigners in China maintain that Communism in this instance is merely a courtesy title for the familiar phenomena of banditry, discontent, and unemployment. The following observations, based on the journey which I am going to describe, may provide the material for a truer and less reassuring interpretation.

The curse of China is ineffectiveness; the Chinese Communists are not ineffective. The Red Areas are controlled, and rigidly controlled, by a central government with headquarters at the 'capital', Shuikin. Theoretically, the policy of this government is directed by the Chinese Communist Party from Shanghai; in practice, it would appear to be independent while remaining open to suggestions. The form of government is modelled on the Russian; the 'Party', guided by a small Central Executive Committee, is paramount. The territory under its control is subdivided into areas, each of which is ruled by a local Soviet with a 'Party' man at its head.

All land is common. When they came into the villages the first thing the Communists did was to kill all the landlords, burn all the title-deeds, and tear up all the landmarks. The land (even including temple lands and burial grounds) was then redistributed. All marketing of produce is done through a central government agency, and to-day the peasant inside the Red Areas is buying his rice and pork cheaper than the peasant outside them. One central and at least two local banks have been established, and notes and silver coins have been issued, the former bearing the head of Lenin and the latter the hammer and sickle. A 'progressive' tax is levied in proportion to income. Marriage, religion, and the hereditary system have been abolished. All capital above a certain very small amount is confiscated, and the prosperous are relentlessly proscribed.

In the autumn of 1933 the fighting strength of the Red Armies was about 70,000 rifles; it fluctuates widely, but rarely falls below 50,000. The nucleus of this force is the

First, Third, and Fifth Army Corps. These are hard, well-disciplined and very mobile troops with a formidable reputation. Nominally every citizen, male or female, of this ruthlessly improvised republic is conscripted for service in or with the Red Armies between the ages of fifteen or forty, while boys below fifteen, must join the 'Youth Vanguard'. A number of semi-independent units, mostly bandits, act in co-operation with the organized main body, and during a campaign the first wave of the Communist attack usually comprises a screen of these guerrillas, supplemented by boys – occasionally women – armed with spears, on whom the enemy expends much of his never very plentiful ammunition. An arsenal has been established in which rifles can be repaired, bullets cast, and old cartridge-cases reloaded; but hitherto the main supply of arms and ammunition has come, voluntarily or involuntarily, from the Nationalist armies.

When, as not infrequently happens, a detachment of Government troops surrenders, the officers are shot, the rifles and bandoliers collected, and the men sent home with a dollar or two in their pockets, for as allies in the ranks they are less valuable to the Reds than as parasites living on the surrounding country, where their unwelcome presence breeds an atmosphere favourable to Communism.

The Red Armies are commanded by Chu Teh, a general of experience and resource, said to have had some German training. His political adviser is Mao Dsu Tung, a gifted and fanatical young man of thirty-five suffering from an incurable disease. This pair have made themselves into something of a legend, and the Communist High Command is invariably referred to as Chumao. In addition to the Red Armies in Kiangsi, there is a Communist force of some 5,000 rifles in southern Hupeh, and a large roving army which has found its way up to the borders of Szechwan after being dislodged from Hupeh in the autumn of 1932. The former of these is in reasonably close touch with headquarters in Kiangsi; the latter is presumably not. All the Red Armies are equipped with wireless.

The novelty of the Chinese Communist movement lies in

the fact that – in a country where the man with the big stick has always hitherto had the last word – the army does not, and cannot, rule the roost, as it would if the movement represented no more than that chance agglomeration of malcontents and freebooters which optimists see in it. The control of the Central Government (in other words, of the 'Party') is absolute, because the 'Party' percolates, in the Russian manner, into every branch of military and civil life. There is, as it were, a 'Party' man at the hub of every wheel. The mutiny of a division, the rebellion of a district, is impossible as long as there are officers and officials to see it coming, report it to the 'Party', and have it nipped in the bud.

Moreover – again in the Russian manner – every one belongs to various overlapping organizations all under 'Party' control and supervision. As a member of (say) the League of Youth, the Farmers' Union, the Peasants' Revolutionary Society, and the nth Red Army Group, you are caught in a cat's cradle of obligations and threatened with a cloud of penalties. Even the 'Party' members themselves are supervised by 'Control Commissions', working incognito and reporting to the Central Executive Committee. The peasants may find this harness of terrorism galling, but they cannot kick over the traces.

It will be seen that a great deal depends on the quality of the leaders. These would seem to be for the most part young Chinese students (throughout the movement there is a tremendous emphasis on youth), many of them trained in the Lenin University in Moscow or in a similar institution at Habarovsk. It is freely alleged by the most reliable authorities that the Reds have several foreign advisers with them in Kiangsi; my conclusions on this point are indicated in a later chapter. There can be no doubt that the standard of ability among the leaders is high and unquestionably most of them are sincere. There is probably less corruption in the Red districts than in any other area of equal size in China.

Communism is like platonic love. It is all right as a theory, it is all right as an experiment, but after that it too often fails to maintain its original nature. Communism in Kiangsi is probably not much further removed from orthodox Communism than the adulterated brand now practised in Russia. It is, of course, very much simplified. The principal tenets to which the peasant is called on to subscribe (or perish) are broadly indicated by the two slogans, 'The Land For The People', and 'Down With Imperialism'. The first is simple and makes pleasant hearing. The second can hardly be so easy to expound to people who have never seen an imperialist in their life and would not know one if they did (a foreign face has always been a rarity in southern Kiangsi). For Communist purposes, however, the Kuomintang are Imperialists, and of course the Japanese, and all other foreigners as well, and they are all combating the Chinese Revolution by the meanest of tricks, and thus delaying the attainment of an earthly Paradise, tinted red.

So the Communist recruit, when in the heat of battle he looks down his sights and sees at the other end of them only the sheepish face of young Liu who used to live in the next village, nerves himself with the memory of all that has been told him about the foreign capitalists who are supplying Liu's masters at Nanking with poisonous gas and aeroplanes: and duly pulls the trigger.

It is all very well to say, as most people do, that Communism in China is fundamentally an economic and agrarian problem, and that the way to solve it is to raise the standard of living outside the Red Areas, thereby convincing the peasantry within them that they have backed the wrong horse. Unfortunately, this is impossible. The mere existence of a large district controlled by rebels with a powerful army at their disposal and every motive for aggression postulates the complementary existence of a zone of military occupation surrounding that district. This is the situation to-day.

For the last three years there have been permanently garrisoned in Kiangsi between 100,000 and 200,000 Government troops, and the lot of the inhabitants (as they freely admit) could hardly have been worse if the whole province, instead of only half of it, had been in the hands of the Reds. Press gangs, conscript labour, extra taxes, and many forms of indignity and extortion have made their lives a burden to them, and in return they have received only the most inadequate protection. If anything is calculated to make the Chinese peasant turn spontaneously to Communism (or to anything else that presents itself), it is having troops permanently billeted on him.

'Permanently', unfortunately, would seem to be the word. The Nationalist generals in Kiangsi are facing a problem of great difficulty. Topographically it is much the same problem which confronts the Japanese bandit-suppression forces in most parts of Manchukuo. It is analysed in some detail in chapter 12.

The thing that struck me most on the front was that every officer to whom I spoke was thinking in terms of defence, not of attack. There is no real 'front' in Kiangsi. Fortifications have been erected round the villages and towns, and an uncoordinated system of isolated garrisons has thus been established. Outside these fortifications there are no outposts and few patrols; news of a Communist advance is the signal for the soldiers to withdraw into the villages. When I was in Kiangsi preparations were on foot for Chiang Kai-shek's autumn offensive, and it struck me as significant that – as part of these preparations for a general attack – an order had been issued to all villages of more than 200 families to build three forts if they had not got them already. Similarly, while work was going forward night and day on a huge military aerodrome at Nanchang, the capital of the province, the defences of that city, more than one hundred miles from the frontiers of the Communist territory, were being strengthened with scarcely less expedition.

In the summer of 1933 the Red Armies launched into Fukien three separate but simultaneous raids, threatened Foochow (a treaty port), and were with difficulty driven off by the 19th Route Army, the heroes of the Shanghai fighting against the Japanese; they took with them much booty and at least a million and a half dollars (Mex.) in cash. Judging by this and similar recent ventures, the present policy of Communists would seem to be to consolidate their almost impregnable position, supplementing their capital and their food supply by occasional marauding.

The Russian influence, though no longer felt directly, is still strong (the armies march under a red banner bearing the hammer and sickle), and time seems to have adapted both their doctrines and their methods to those modifications of the original models which are best suited to the nature of the people and the circumstances. At any rate, a split between the 'Trotskyists' and the 'Stalinists' which have greatly weakened the Communist Party elsewhere in China has produced no apparent repercussion in the Red Areas. There are signs that their leaders are becoming more, rather than less, sophisticated in their technique. Captured villages are no longer indiscriminately pillaged or destroyed; the wealthy and the powerful suffer, but the poor are encouraged to carry on business as usual. The role of Robin Hood is a universally popular one, and the Communists are doing their best to sustain something very like it. There can, however, be little doubt that the peasants are leading miserable lives under the Red regime; for its strength is that it is a reign of terror.

The chief weakness of the Communist policy, regarded simply in the light of a method of governing the Chinese, is that it comprises a strong element of what may be called internal iconoclasm. The oldest, the most powerful traditions in China are centred on the family, and Communism is out to break the family. By abolishing inheritance, and marriage, and ancestor-worship, and by trying to superimpose the conception of a State as the unit to live in and work for, they are defying customs so long established that they have become instincts. It is, I think, this aspect of Communism which is the limiting factor on its spontaneous generation outside the present Red Areas. Only a reproduction of the special circumstances in which the movement had its birth could result in the occurrence of a parallel outbreak elsewhere in China.

How is the situation going to develop? Is Communism a menace to the well-being of China as a whole? I doubt it. There are, it is true, two possible developments of the present state of affairs which would be, for a time, dangerous and inconvenient not only to China herself, but to foreign interests in China. One would be a northward drive by the Red Armies which would result in the cutting of the Yangtse. But this could hardly be achieved unless the bulk of the Nationalist armies were occupied elsewhere, and even if it could be achieved the Communists could not make good the position thus boldly seized, where they would find themselves for the first time facing really desperate opposition in open country.

The other alternative would be an eastward drive, culminating in the capture of either Foochow or Amoy. Here, also for the first time, their armies would confront those Imperialists in whose iniquities they have been so sedulously instructed; and it can hardly be supposed that they would confront them for very long.

These two contingencies, remote but unpleasant, represent in my opinion the limits of the aggressive harm which can be done by Communism in its present stage of development. Probably they will not arise. Hunan, to the west of the Red Areas, is an exceedingly well-run province with a decent army; she remembers with bitterness the Communist occupation of 1929 and is taking what look like effective measures to make its recurrence impossible. If the Communists try to penetrate farther into China they have a respectable barrier in their path. To the south, the well-equipped troops of Kwantung are not likely to let the Reds into their province again. To the north, a heavy concentration of Nationalist forces blocks the road to the Yangtse.

I do not think that Communism will ever be stamped out by Chinese armies, for the country is too difficult and the Reds too strong. The infection has been localized, and the probability is that for many years the same disproportionate efforts will have to be made to prevent it spreading. Gradually, perhaps, the system of investing the Red Territory will become more efficient, and the burden of the peasantry in the

2

ON THE ROAD

EVEN on the map, where journeys fairly radiate feasibility, Shanghai and Canton looked a very long way apart. The comments of Shanghai on my project did little to bring them closer together. I was confronted once more with the ghost of Mr Riley. Mr Riley was a brilliant correspondent of *The Times* who came out to China a few years ago and was almost immediately murdered in the interior. All the way from Printing House Square to Peking people had reminded me of his unhappy fate with a monotonous regularity; among strangers to whom I was introduced it was a favourite conversational opening. In the end even Mr Riley himself could hardly have wished more fervently than I that he had escaped his assassins.

But it is my experience that in foreign communities inhabiting more or less outlandish countries only one man in twenty is worth listening to on the subject of travel in the interior. The information of the other nineteen is often either second-hand or out of date; still more often it is both. So I went ahead with my preparations, which consisted mostly of collecting information about Communism from men whom I cannot, alas, thank publicly.

My first objective was Nanking. Early one morning, equipped* with a small suitcase, a rucksack, and a bottle of some chemical which was said to be capable of making even

---

*I should do wrong to omit all mention of my visiting cards. These are indispensable adjuncts to travel in the interior of China – far more necessary than a passport. They have a mollifying effect on every one, from the provincial Governor to the officious (and incidentally illiterate) sentry at his gate. They must bear, in Chinese characters, the traveller's Chinese name, which comes as near as possible to a phonetic equivalent of his own. Mine is Fu Lei Ming; it means, I believe, Learned Engraver on Stone.

the foulest water drinkable but was never given a chance of showing its worth, I left Shanghai in company with the delightful R.

R. was an Englishman attached to the Nanking Government in an advisory capacity. His task it was to formulate a scheme for the reconstruction of the Civil Service (at least I think that was it), and he brought to it, in default of previous experience of the Far East, a sense of humour, a quickness of perception, and a charm of manner which were the best possible qualifications for understanding the Chinese. The Nanking Government is an enlightened one, and its kingdom is already a Utopia – on paper. Whether that corner of Utopia which is R's province will ever be transplanted from the ideal to the real I do not know; but it will not be his fault if it is not.

We travelled to Nanking in a car – an excellent and (like most of the cars in China) an American car. The journey took us two days. They were well spent.

Shanghai is at no time a likeable city, and at no time is she less likeable than in July. The heat is bad. The humidity is worse. The brow of the village blacksmith, if I remember right, was wet with honest sweat. In England to sweat is both praiseworthy and beneficial; honest sweat, like an honest penny, is earned, and to earn anything is good. But in Shanghai during the summer you do not earn your sweat, far less deserve it. It springs into being unprovoked by exertion. Your hand, as you write, sticks to the paper; and when you lift it a powerful electric fan blows the paper across the room. When you go out to lunch your thin clothes cling to your body, and at night you either court rheumatism by sleeping under a fan or insomnia by trying to sleep without it. It is an enervating kind of heat.

To our delight, R. and I found that we had left the heat behind. The car ran swiftly along a good, unmetalled road beside the sea, which was decorated by junks and an occasional small island. The hired chauffeur was an excellent man. He came from Buriat Mongolia and answered to the name of Alec. He was fat, spoke always in thick, languid, and despondent tones, and appeared to be a man of character. His sense of humour was recondite, manifesting itself chiefly in the sudden, hoarse shouts of laughter with which he greeted the sight of a peasant working naked in the paddy fields.

At eleven o'clock we stopped, left the car, and followed a path over some low hills to the sea. Here there was a sandy cove, overlooked by some garish wooden huts, tenanted by a small colony of garish White Russians. Judging by the number of females in evidence it seemed to be a matriarchy, and R. and I, who were unprovided with bathing dresses, had some difficulty in both entering and leaving the sea without offending the laws of public decency. The bathe, however, well repaid the furtive and shameless skirmishes which led up to it.

We emerged feeling invigorated but very thirsty. Among the huts was one, rather more ramshackle than the rest, which proclaimed itself 'The Beach Café'. We sat down on a kind of veranda and ordered some beer from a Chinese boy of cretinous appearance.

I don't know why I remember that scene so well. It wasn't that there was anything wildly funny about it. But it had an element of the fantastic just sufficiently strong to underline its complete meaninglessness. It reminded me of those symbolic problem pictures which crop up from time to time in the Academy, full of howitzers in flowerbeds and skeletons in ballet-skirts and bishops neglecting their duty.

The veranda was thickly surrounded, for no reason at all, with barbed wire. There was a chicken tied to the leg of my chair with a very thick piece of black cord. The centre of the stage was occupied by a witch-like Russian lady, wearing an enormous green hat and a Cubist dressing-gown. Her companion, a small, fat man, had somehow come by a gigantic fish and the two of them, with an air of ritual, photographed each other again and again holding aloft this trophy. They used the tinest camera imaginable.

The pair, with the tethered hen and the Chinese cretin, were the principal permanent decorations of the foreground.

From time to time, however, an aged Russian, heavily whiskered but wearing only a brand-new straw hat and a tattered pair of shorts, would be dragged at high speed across the veranda by a large Alsatian dog. What this piteous figure was doing, or trying to do, it was impossible even to conjecture. Meanwhile up a bright green hill which occupied the centre of the background, there slowly crawled a procession of six priests. In their black robes, and diminished by the distance, they looked exactly like beetles. They were on their way to a mission on the summit of the hill.

When we had had enough of the warm beer and the indefinable atmosphere of this unexpected place we went back to the car. Alec was roused from the torpor into which he was able to fall at a moment's notice, and we took the road again.

In the middle of the afternoon we reached Hangchow, famous for its silks, its temples, and its lake. I had been there two years before with the delegates to an international conference. That had been a month after the invasion of Manchuria, and I remembered the special guard which had been called out to protect the Japanese delegates, and the lurid anti-Japanese posters with which the streets had been plastered. Of that great wave of popular feeling there were now no outward and few inward signs.

The lake, set among the hills of Chekiang, is indeed very beautiful. Bridges and causeways intersect it, leading from one to another of the little islands on which rich merchants have built themselves curious and splendid houses. The principal streets in the city have been modernized, and there is a foreign-style hotel, where we established ourselves for the night.

Now began the quest for Gerald. Gerald needs some explanation. I had met him only twice in my life – once, when I was at Eton, at dinner with the Provost, and once at a week-end party in the country. All I knew about him was that he had had an extremely distinguished academic career both at Eton and at Cambridge: that he had been to Mexico: that he was supposed to have lived for a time in a Welsh cave: and that he had come out to China nine months ago to do some research work, travelling 'hard' class on the Trans-Siberian Railway. I knew also that during the Jehol fighting last spring he had been up to the Great Wall with the Chinese armies as Reuter's correspondent, and that he had been arrested, though only for a short time, by the Chinese authorities behind the front line. He sounded an enterprising chap, and a potential companion for my journey to Canton; so I wanted to get in touch with him.

I knew that he had lately been living in a Buddhist monastery outside Hangchow, and R. and I set out to comb these establishments for traces of an old Etonian. In this somewhat unusual task we were greatly assisted by Mr Hsiao, a young Chinese to whom R. had a letter of introduction. He produced a car and drove it at a furious speed round the lake and out into the hills. We visited three monasteries, and drew blank at each of them. They were pleasant, silent, aimless places, standing in groves of tall trees and maintained in excellent repair by the gifts of the pious. The monks drifted about their courtyards with an air of benign detachment; visitors chattered in low voices and drank tea. At one it was admitted that there had been an Englishman staying there, who claimed that in his native country he was a member of Parliament. (This was new if rather apocryphal light on Gerald.) At another he was known, but had recently departed, leaving no clue as to his whereabouts save the address of a Buddhist organization in Shanghai.

So we returned baffled, to Hangchow, and dined with Mr Hsiao in a Chinese restaurant overlooking the lake, across which the lights of sampans moved mazily. From a room downstairs came that sound which so often accompanies meals in China – the staccato, competitive ejaculations of a party playing the 'scissors' game. In this you and your opponent shoot out your right hands at each other simultaneously, the fingers being arranged in one of three postures. A clenched fist means 'stone'; two fingers extended means 'scissors'; all five fingers extended mean 'paper'. Scissors cut paper but are broken on stone, and paper wins against stone because stone can be wrapped up in paper. It is a pleasant, childish game, and the Chinese play it endlessly on convivial occasions.

Mr Hsiao had been trained as an engineer in France, England, and America. He had been trained in the best sort of way; instead of collecting a sheaf of diplomas on the strength of academic theses, he had worked as an apprentice with big engineering firms. His life in the West seemed to me to have stabilized him; he was now a very solid citizen, talking good sense, but at the same time he was rather dull. The Chinese mind is vagrant and subtle; Mr Hsiao's had become rather literal and slow. He spoke with affection of the English, whom he appeared to respect for the right reasons. He told us amusing stories of his first days in Birmingham, and the problems presented by the time-table of lodging-house meals. He still, he said, corresponded with his landlady.

Early the next day we were on the road again. The country grew still more beautiful. It appeared that there were more shades of green than one had realized before. The rice fields were that colour which I suppose the hymn-book to mean by 'living-green'; and between them and the dark trees clustered round a shrine or a grave was a subtly graded range of variations. The hills were better wooded than is usual in that part of China, and there was always a bamboo-grove or a clump of little fir trees in sight. The houses had white walls and grey bedragoned roofs; they harmonized well with the landscape. The road, which was now cobbled, often passed over stone bridges, from whose acutely humped backs only a narrow aisle of water showed in the canal between the double rank of sampans which crowded the village moorings. We overtook many buses, all crowded, and some towing trailers on which the luggage of the passengers was attached. The fare from Hangchow to Nanking or Shanghai was only five dollars.

The bus and the road on which it runs are a new and highly significant portent in Chinese life. In the most unexpected parts of the interior you will find bus services plying regularly and on the whole efficiently. Sometimes they are operated by the provincial government, sometimes by private enterprise which pays heavily for the privilege. Save in such exceptional circumstances as prevail in Kiangsi, they are almost always run at a profit. The chassis and engine are American, the body is of local manufacture and, characteristically, designed with an eye rather to economy than to equilibrium. The bus service, as a Chinese institution, is both conceived and carried out on a far sounder basis than the railway. It requires a much smaller capital outlay, and therefore presents fewer opportunities for squeeze. A road is quicker as well as cheaper to build than a railway, and the Chinese talent for delay is accordingly a less operative factor. The running of a bus service, as compared with the running of a railway, is not only easier but offers more scope for individualism, and is therefore better suited to the Chinese character. Finally, in the event of political upheavals, a bus service is less vulnerable than a railway because its capital value is much smaller.

To the small farmer and the small trader – the two most important people in China – a bus is as good as a train, any day. Culturally, too, the buses must produce a considerable effect. The barriers of distance and of dialect are two of the most formidable obstacles to Chinese unity; and in the long, slow war of attrition which may one day wear those barriers down the buses are a potent weapon. They are a new thing; they have not been going long, but already they have gone far. Towns and villages which formerly knew each other only by name now exchange frequent visitors. The old, traditional distrust of the stranger is breaking down, new curiosities are being aroused, new contacts made. The buses were the best omen that I came across in China.

A more ancient and more deeply characteristic feature of the Chinese scene is the water-wheel. This represents the motive power in the irrigation system. In country which is at all hilly the fields are all at different levels, and the water-wheel is the link between each level. A chain of little wooden paddles, worked by a treadmill, forces the water up from one field to the next. I do not know how many centuries it is since the Chinese first evolved this primitive but ingenious

3

THE CAPITAL OF CHINA

THAT evening we reached Nanking.

Place-names lend a certain colour, a tang of actuality, to the discussion of international politics. When a man tells us that the Wilhelmstrasse is waiting for a lead from Warsaw, or that Tokyo has got her eyes on Moscow, it sounds rather grand and romantic. We are duly impressed by a hint that Rome is much nearer to Washington than she was a month ago, though the statement is on the face of it absurd. It is a harmless and even beneficent form of snobbery, this bandying of place-names by the world-minded, and it is effective for two reasons. In the first place, it fleetingly recalls the diplomatic world of Ouida and Oppenheim, that wonderful world where chancelleries are always tottering, and across which King's Messengers post madly to and fro, hotly pursued by beautiful women with a *penchant* for wearing secret treaties next the skin. In the second place, the use of place-names puts the whole rather abstract discussion on a more concrete plane and often links us personally, though remotely, with its subject; for, whereas we find it quite impossible to visualize the Japanese Government, we have a cousin in Tokyo and only last week received a postcard from him. And in any case, however little we (or our cousins) have travelled, there is in our minds some visual image – the Kremlin, the Eiffel Tower, the Acropolis – associated with the name of every capital city.

Or rather, of almost every capital city. There are exceptions and one important one. Nanking is the capital of a country with a population of 400 millions; but when anybody says, 'Well, the next move must come from Nanking', there arises in our minds none of those helpful little pictures of a building, or a monument, or a delicacy, or an exiled friend, which reinforce our interest in the policies of other capitals. Few foreigners go to Nanking, and fewer still stay there. It is indeed so little known that the producers of *Shanghai Express* were able with impunity to ignore not only the capital but the principal river of China; the latter must be crossed by ferry, and the former briefly visited, by all passengers on what the film portrayed as a through journey.

Nanking is far, though perhaps not very far, from deserving this obscurity. Of the old city, sacked in the Taiping Rebellion, little remains save the walls, breached, unkempt, no longer encircling. To-day the charm of the place lies in the contrast, sharply presented at a hundred points, between the old and the new, the real (one is tempted to say) and the unreal China.

The city is spacious. There is plenty of elbow-room, and this is rare in China. On a piece of waste land, fronting an asphalt boulevard, stands a Government office, brand new, reasonably palatial, and still not quite completed. It is not very beautiful, but it looks business-like. The sentries at its gates wear smart yellow uniforms; in spite of the broiling sun they are in full marching order, with packs, blankets, mess-tins, and water-bottles, for this gives the whole building 'face'. It is all very modern and progressive.

But behind the building there is a huddle of huts of mud and matting, and the thin blue smoke of economical cooking-fires, and a community of people whose life is as intricate and precarious as the patches on their clothes. The click of administrative typewriters is drowned by the cries of naked children escorting water-buffaloes to wallow in the numerous pools. Nine-tenths of the capital is a congeries of villages: the rest is a bold façade. When the seaplanes on the up-river service roar low overhead to land, trailing a white furrow on the yellow Yangtse, no one's attention is distracted from a shrill, bitter and inconsequently ended quarrel between two sisters-in-law over ten coppers. In the evening the tall towers of the broadcasting station stand up against the sunset; but it is a professional story-teller, prattling and posturing in a dirty alley, who has the people's ear.

For all this Nanking is a brave monument to progress, **or** to the wish for progress: a monument not without humorous decorations. There is the Stadium, where tier upon tier of empty seats rise above a sea of weeds, now so deep and dense that the cost of clearing it to hold an athletic meeting would be all but prohibitive. There is the Swimming Bath which, since it could only be filled by depriving the Orphanage of its water-supply, has long since been cracked and fissured by the sun. There is the fine large building which is not quite so fine or so large as it should have been, because the contractor shrunk it, by knocking ten per cent off all the measurements, to make sure of his profit. There is the disposition of the Government offices which, in a town where distances are enormous and all business is transacted by committees, compels every public man to spend a quarter of his working day in his car.

Although Nanking is the capital of China, Russia is the only power who has transferred thither from Peking the official headquarters of her diplomatic representatives. In this country the question of moving the British Legation to Nanking is periodically mooted.

In China it is mooted seldom, and then in a more or less academic spirit. There are two main arguments in favour of the move – one (the 'face' argument) that it would enhance the prestige of the Nanking Government, and the other that it would enable the British Minister to keep in closer touch with the currents of Chinese politics. The first argument is unanswerable, the second valid with qualifications. Though neither is likely, at any rate for the next half century, to prevail against the fundamental considerations of expense, the second argument is worth examining.

The Councillor of the British Legation is – or has been for the last few years – stationed at Nanking almost *ex officio*. Also, Nanking is within two hours of Peking by air. It cannot therefore be argued that the diplomats at Peking are wholly, or anything like wholly, out of touch with the modern seat of government. Nor is the value of closer contact either overwhelmingly or continuously apparent. In the summer of 1933, for instance, there were three men who counted in Chinese administrative circles. One of these, M. T. V. Soong, was attending the World Economic Conference in London. Another, General Chiang Kai-shek, was up-river at Kuling or Nanchang, preparing for his anti-Communist campaign. Only the third, Mr Wang Ching Wei, was in Nanking. Politics in China were as nearly at a standstill as they can be.

Peking is admittedly a backwater; but a costly and potentially insecure anchorage in midstream is not worth much if the current is liable at any moment to run, temporarily or permanently, in other channels.

I have said nothing of two other factors in the situation. One, the wishes of the diplomats themselves, who may be excused for preferring a post with many social, sporting, and climatic advantages to one without them. Two, the question of the Legation Guard which, since the Boxer siege of 1901, has been established in the British Legation, with three months' supplies for the whole community contained within its walls, and which could not be transferred to Nanking without special treaty provision.

These factors are minor ones in a situation which is governed in the last analysis by considerations of economy. Money spent on moving our Legation to Nanking would be money well spent: but only moderately well spent, and only that in a period of exceptional prosperity.

4

MINISTERS AND MISSIONARIES

Two days in Nanking yielded the inevitable crop of interviews. Of these interviews the one which it gives me most pleasure to remember was with Dr Lo Wen Kan.

I had a letter of introduction to him from Mr Quo Tai Chi, the Chinese Ambassador in London. It was addressed to 'Dr Lo Wen Kan, Minister of Foreign Affairs, Nanking'. I had carried this letter half-way round the world, and it was just my luck that on the day before I was able to deliver it Dr Lo Wen Kan was obliged to resign the Ministry of Foreign Affairs. At first I found this an embarrassing circumstance, for the superscription on my letter of introduction now seemed to be little better than a taunt. Friends of the late Minister, however, assured me that I was being hypersensitive, and I presented my letter.

I should say from my limited experience of Chinese politicians that Dr Lo Wen Kan is a rare type. He is in the first place not a rich man, and that in itself gives him a marked singularity. In the second place, he has a reputation for honesty. In the third place, he appears to take little interest in the party politics of the Kuomintang, on success in which high position at Nanking ultimately depends. He was educated at Oxford, and I seemed to detect in him a certain unserious detachment, a touch of the lackadaisical, which might have been derived from that seat of learning, once the Home of Lost Causes, and now the resort of those who deplore the fact that there are no more causes worth losing.

Dr Lo Wen Kan is a slight man, with a small moustache and hair *en brosse*. He is renowned for his taste in wine. He received me, with great courtesy and the inevitable tea, in a little summer-house built out over the pond on the shores of which his villa stood. I knew that his resignation had been tendered under compulsion, though not with reluctance, and I knew also that, for reasons too complex to be entered into here, he was being sent, into what was virtually exile, on a 'pacification mission' to Chinese Turkestan, which for the best part of a year had been torn by a three-cornered civil war. We began to discuss his journey, and he expounded his scheme for reopening the old Imperial highway to the North-West by means of convict labour. (He still retained his post as Minister of Justice, which gave him jurisdiction over the prisons. 'It is,' he said, 'a position for which I am peculiarly well qualified by experience, for I have served several terms of imprisonment myself.')

He was going to fly to Urumchi, and as we talked of it I said, politely, though with complete sincerity, that I wished I was going with him. Dr Lo Wen Kan immediately offered me a seat in his aeroplane.

It was the most tempting offer I have ever had. But to accept it would have meant scrapping my plans – now well advanced – for Canton and the Communists. Moreover, I was under contract to be back in England by November 1st, and that would be impossible if I went to Chinese Turkestan. After a fierce internal struggle I had to decline the offer.

'On how few things,' said Dr Johnson, 'can we look back with satisfaction.' To recall the things that I have done (admittedly they are few and unremarkable) gives me the minimum of pleasure. But the things that I very nearly did – ah, they are a different cup of tea. The lustre of illusion lies thick upon them. That journey to Urga with the Mongolian impresario, that cooking-pot which I so nearly stole in Brazil, the puma-hunt which only just failed to come off in Guatemala, and last of all this narrowly thwarted descent on Urumchi – these splendid possibilities are still as bright as on the day I first discerned them, outshining the stale, trite, tarnished memories of the things that really happened. In the matter of the words 'it might have been' I belong to a school of thought sharply opposed to that of Wordsworth.

On the same day that I interviewed Dr Lo Wen Kan I also interviewed his successor to the Ministry of Foreign

Affairs. This was Mr Wang Ching Wei, who, after a career unusually adventurous even for a Chinese politician, has risen to be the third most powerful man in the Nanking Government. Handsome, astute, a fluent speaker and a forceful writer, Mr Wang Ching Wei impressed me rather by his polite ability than by his personality. He told me, among other things, that he had good reason to believe that the Communists were receiving clandestine support from the Japanese. His belief, as I then suspected and now know, was baseless. I remembered that it had been reflected in an article in the *Manchester Guardian* by the late William Martin, who had recently been in Nanking; even for the ablest and most determined seekers, the truth is very hard to come by in China. Mr Wang Ching Wei very kindly promised to wire to General Chiang Kai-shek, the head of the Nanking Government and at present in Kuling, asking him to facilitate my journey to the anti-Communist front.

My next objective was therefore Kuling. On the eve of my departure Gerald unexpectedly turned up, a large young man of saturnine appearance, equipped with a knobkerry and a Chinese servant called Li. Without more ado he signed on for at any rate the first part of the journey. He was to prove in many ways an ideal travelling companion. His cheerfulness was as infinite as his curiosity, and he was more completely impervious to the effects of discomfort, boredom, and delay than anyone I have ever met.

Li was a remarkable person. He was twenty-two years old, and his home was in Shangtung, which produces probably the best type of peasant in China. Like many another young man from that province he emigrated to Manchuria, where he helped to run a store in Manchuli and worked in a bank in Harbin. Gerald had come across him during the fighting at the Great Wall. Li had attached himself to one of the many generals and/or bandits who raised a so-called Volunteer Corps to resist the Japanese invasion of Jehol, and who was no more successful than most of his kind in avoiding either defeat or insolvency. Gerald fell in with Li during the evacuation of a village and signed him on as his servant.

173

If any credit is due to anyone for the journey which we three made together, it is due to Li; he did all the dirty work, and he did it extraordinarily well. Even the best Chinese servants are seldom wholly honest; Li was. We never had the slightest hesitation in entrusting him with money, and this saved endless complications, for on our travels the currency changed with astonishing rapidity between one place and the next, and even where it remained constant, that supremely mysterious thing, the copper exchange, would alter. Li was a tireless bargainer; to pay more than you need for anything was in his view the grossest solecism.

He was also a person of resource and humour, very good at collecting information and very good at assessing its worth. Here, however, we were handicapped by the language problem. Gerald knew a few words of Chinese, I knew still fewer; Li had picked up a few words of English. We thus had a *lingua franca* adequate to the simpler contingencies of travel, but not sufficient, for instance, for the purpose of verbatim interpreting. But Li had a very quick mind, and could often tell us when, if not exactly how, an official interpreter had played us false. At any rate we managed somehow, and Li did his best to improve his English with a Chinese phrase-book which contained, among other conversational openings, the following useful sentence: 'It makes me very sad to see my concubine being sick this morning.'

He was a very likeable person, with his square face, and his broad, mischievous smile, and his instinctively faultless manner. I can see him now, padding along in his demure grey robe, all slung about with our cameras; he is scowling a little to himself, because one of us gave a five-cent tip to a carrier who had already been adequately paid.

Early the next day we boarded a river steamer and started up the Yangtse. There was a large party of French sailors on board, bound for duty on a gunboat at one of the up-river ports. On the passenger list they were anonymous, appearing only, opposite the cabins allotted to them, as 'Two French Sailors'. This element of duality was their dominant characteristic and they were seen always in pairs. This has been my only contact with the French Navy, and as a consequence I find it impossible to visualize its personnel in the singular.

The other passengers were mostly missionaries or business men of various nationalities. There were also four rich Chinese – two men and two women – who had become so very thoroughly expatriated in America that even in conversation among themselves they used the language of that country. (Many of the smarter Chinese business men in Shanghai speak nothing but English.) These four represented a type which I find extremely unattractive, and when, as quite infrequently happened, the women were insulted by the French sailors, my chivalrous instincts remained, I am afraid, dormant. They spent most of the time playing bridge. The fatter and shriller of the women was once heard to remark that she was going to wait to marry again until she found a man who was her intellectual equal. 'She's got a long time to wait,' observed my diary, at times a rather acid document.

Travel on the Yangtse is preferable in a number of ways to travel at sea. The horizon is not empty. Thatched huts cling to the dykes which precariously imprison the yellow waters, and the broad river is dotted with shipping ranging from the smallest sampan to a big steamer like our own. On the dykes women and children invigilate over contraptions which resemble a gigantic landing-net worked by a lever. From time to time the net is lowered slowly into the water and, after a due interval, withdrawn once more skywards. I must have seen some hundred of these devices at work, but I have yet to witness the capture of a fish.

Sometimes your boat calls at a little town, and from the deck you watch coolies who look frail and half-famished manhandling bulky cargo on the jetty below you with equal determination and address; the brawniest British coal-heaver could not attempt their feats. Then there are the children, who scramble savagely for the coppers you throw them and yet somehow contrive that the infants in their charge emerge unscathed from the rough-house. And there is almost certainly something else – a policeman arguing with a hawker, or a quarrel between two women, who shriek and gesture and prance to and fro in taut and curiously formal attitudes which suggest the mating antics of birds. In China there is always something worth watching.

Just before dusk on the second day we passed a little red and white temple which crowns a precipitous pinnacle of rock in midstream, and round which kites circled, a disjoined halo. Then, as night was falling, we reached Kiukiang. At Kiukiang, formerly a treaty port and a place of importance in the tea trade but now much declined, we were to disembark. Kuling, our next objective, perches on the summit of a 3,000-foot mountain called Lushan. It owes both its name and its popularity as a summer resort to missionary enterprise, which has found an anomalous outlet in the field of real estate. Some years ago a missionary, whose name I forget, acquired from the Chinese a large plot of land on the then sparsely inhabited mountain top, and in a short time the place became famous as a refuge from the sweltering heat of the Yangtse Valley. It was thought proper to change the Chinese name of Lushan to one which, while tastefully preserving an indigenous flavour, would convey to intending visitors some idea of the resort's peculiar attraction; and so it became Kuling, a *mariage de convenance* between the synthetic and the facetious as revolting as any that blazons the gateposts of suburbia. From Kiukiang a road runs to the base of Mount Lushan, which must be climbed on foot or in a chair. So we left the boat at Kiukiang.

As we were preparing to leave it there came suddenly bounding into the saloon a strange and terrifying monster. It was a female missionary. An unusually well-developed woman, she was clad only in a pair of very tight shorts and a dirty white blouse. Her aspect was *farouche*; she carried an alpenstock at the 'ready', her short gravel-coloured hair was in disarray, and her eyes flashed fire behind the lenses of her spectacles. Her formidable and uncovered legs were stained with travel. She bore down on the purser like a rogue hippopotamus.

'What's this I hear about our cabins having been given to the Van Tuylers?' she cried.

The purser stood his ground and prevaricated for dear life. There had been some misunderstanding. The male Van Tuyler, a little dim ghost of an American, drifted into the argument; but he soon retired and sat at a table, holding his head in his hands and from time to time uttering a ghostly bleat, half protest, half apology. The place began to fill up with missionaries of every shape and sex; the faces of all of them bore those traces of nervous exhaustion which are the hall-mark of the holiday-maker on his way home. A few of them were conventionally dressed, but most wore clothes which a respectable Chinese would regard as scandalous.

Gerald and I, not without reluctance, left them and made for the gangway. Several Chinese boys had come on board, and were offering paper-backed Chinese novels for sale. We stopped to examine their wares. But the books were whisked from our outstretched hands, and we found ourselves involuntarily gazing on a large selection of obscene postcards, arranged fanwise.

'Master likee nice picture?' suggested the chorus, in confidential unison.

The Church Militant had attracted incongruous camp-followers.

5

THE HOLY MOUNTAIN

WE slept that night in the least repulsive of the Chinese hotels in Kiukiang. The rooms were bare of everything save dirt and one bedstead. From downstairs there came unceasingly the rattle of mah jong. Out on the river a sampan with a band on board observed I forget which festival of the Chinese calendar by strewing the waters with sibilant fireworks, to pacify the spirits of the drowned.

At dawn next day, under grey and gusty skies, we set out for the foot of the mountain in a hired and far from rainproof Ford. A low belt of mist hid the hills. The road ended in a little village, from one mean house in which there hung a sign proclaiming in Gothic lettering, 'Ye Tabard Inne'. The sun must find increasing difficulty in setting on the influence of the Arts and Crafts.

Most of the population were chair-coolies, who earned their living by carrying holiday-makers up the hill. Disdaining their offices, we hired two carriers of frail appearance for our inconsiderable luggage, and set forth. A path wound up into the mist, changing, as the gradient grew more abrupt, into an illimitable flight of steps such as you find on every Chinese mountain. Presently we left the mist. The air grew cooler and sweeter than I had known it for months. Pagodas standing in the wooded foothills dwindled as we climbed. The sun came out, and below us the Yangtse Valley offered a fine combination of land- and water-scape. The great river on which we had been travelling twisted away into the distance, its colour a curious alluvial red. Between it and the mountains lay a lake, filled, as it seemed, with some quite different element, for here the water was an untroubled blue. Junks crawled on the river like stiff-winged insects. The elaborate criss-cross on the dykes stretched like a net across the waterish land.

It was still early, and at first we passed few people on the path. Every half mile or so there was a rest house, a little thatched shelter where a crone behind a counter offered tea and unlikely delicacies. Sometimes our bearers halted and laid down the long bamboo poles from either end of which our luggage dangled; but they never stopped for long, partly because they were much stronger than they looked, and partly because in Kuling they hoped to get a return load for the journey down.

The view was lovely and the exercise welcome. I asked no more of the climb than it already offered. But in China comedy is always at your elbow, and when we were halfway up comedy came suddenly round the corner at a brisk trot.

Comedy was represented by a lady, twin sister as it seemed to the apparition of last night. We were resting in the middle of a particularly steep ascent when she hove in sight – a great globular European woman with a face like a boot. She was clad in dark-blue shorts and a sorely tried blouse. She came tripping down the steps at a formidable rate, for she was temporarily a slave to the laws of gravity and her huge bare legs twinkled rather more rapidly, I think, than she intended. Behind her, at a staider pace, came the bearers of her discarded chair, laughing. She thundered past us with heaving flanks and nostrils distended, to disappear round the next corner, still out of control.

'Jesus-man,'* murmured Li reflectively in Chinese. He took off his hat and scratched his head.

The lady in shorts was outrunner to an exodus. The worst of the hot weather was over, and a big batch of the holidaymakers was going down to catch a boat at Kiukiang. They were a strange procession: English missionaries, German missionaries, American missionaries, and many other kinds, leavened with a few rich Chinese laymen. A patriarchal Belgian priest sat in his chair nursing a bunch of red and

*Missionary.

179

yellow flowers and smiling very sweetly. Behind him came an angry American, accompanied by two anaemic daughters in shorts. Then came a German with a large square wife, both dressed for the late Victorian tropics. Then two pretty Chinese girls, one with a ukelele on her knees, their chairs escorted by four files of little soldiers. The foreign children were all pale and mostly querulous. One could not help feeling sorry for them, condemned by a combination of heroism and piety in their parents to exchange the untasted fields and friendships of their native land for life in a country which offers few amenities to the child.

As we came near the top of the mountain the air grew keen. Coolies were wearing their padded cotton clothes – things which would not be seen down in the valley for many weeks to come. Lushan is a sacred mountain, and on the rocks beside the stairway there should have been pious inscriptions carved; but the old beliefs no longer monopolized the summit, and now the rocks bore only crudely painted advertisements for Chinese dentists and photographers.

At last, in the saddle between two minor peaks, we found Kuling. The streets by which we entered it were ancient and Chinese, but soon the place proclaimed itself as a foreigner's resort. There were hawkers selling picture postcards, and notice boards announcing whist-drives and church services, and shops offering tourist bric-a-brac and tennis balls. On the steep but well-kept gravel paths which served as streets missionaries paraded in the sunshine, and we bade our hearts rejoice at the sight of more than one college blazer. Nor were beach pyjamas altogether absent.

The principal hotel rejoices winsomely in the name of 'The Fairy Glen'. Here we installed ourselves, noting with interest that the West was taking one of its rare revenges on the East by charging higher rates to Chinese guests than to foreigners. Here also, in the middle of the morning, we made off sausages and marmalade one of the best meals I remember eating; we had started at dawn on little save tea, and it had been a long climb.

Somewhere in Kuling there were a number of people whom

we wanted to see, the greatest of them Chiang Kai-shek himself. But we felt that we had earned a 'stand easy' for the moment. Leaving Gerald incongruously absorbed by an ancient *Bystander*, I asked the way to the swimming-pool.

I fear that the interlude which followed can hardly be appreciated by those unfamiliar with China. It is said that China has an unrivalled capacity for assimilating, for merging into herself, members of other nations who come in contact with her. In Manchuria I had been told more than once that she had been exercising this capacity on the Japanese, who in certain cases, discovering that they had a thing or two to learn, were exchanging their own standards of honesty for the Chinese standards – were in fact adopting the technique of 'Squeeze'. Squeeze is, to Western eyes, a deplorably dominant feature of Chinese life; it may be described as – not exactly earning a commission – but putting yourself in a position to take a commission. Your loyalest servant, instructed to make the most trifling purchase, squeezes you without a qualm of conscience. Eminent men through whose hands pass funds humanely contributed for the urgent relief of thousands of starving flood-refugees exact squeeze as a matter of course. It is not so much a habit as an instinct; very few transactions in China are unaccompanied by squeeze.

What happened at the swimming-pool would have been unremarkable if the swimming-pool had been a Chinese institution. But it was run by foreigners, and predominantly pious foreigners at that; so the incident, which has a typically Chinese pattern, is worth recording as a sidelight on the theory stated above.

At the gate of the swimming-pool was a *guichet*, with a pleasant young American behind it. He stopped me from going in and handed me a blank form. This, which entitled the bearer to use the swimming-pool in return for a small charge, must be signed by two property holders in Kuling; there was also a medical certificate which must be signed by a doctor. He directed me to a neighbouring bungalow, whose tenant, Gosfoot by name, was both a doctor and a property holder and therefore in a position to supply two of the necessary signatures.

With that lamb-like subservience to red tape which is perhaps the most striking characteristic of civilized man, I set out in quest of Dr Gosfoot. The bell was answered by his lack-lustre daughter, who said that her father was out, but that her mother might be able to help me.

In this surmise she was right. Mrs Gosfoot, a small, fat, fierce woman, signed twice in the space reserved for property holders and offered to throw in a medical inspection as well. She was not, she explained, qualified, but that didn't really matter.

I agreed readily and prepared, though not without em-barrassment, to bare whatever portions of my anatomy were considered most suspect. To my relief Mrs Gosfoot said that it was the eyes and the feet which were most likely to contaminate the waters of the swimming-pool; what sort of condition were my eyes in?

I said I thought they were pretty good.

Mrs Gosfoot, after favouring them with a piercing stare, said that they looked all right to her too. What about my feet?

I sat down and began to unlace my shoes. Mrs Gosfoot stopped me. In the case of adults, she said, it was usual to take the would-be bather's word about the state of his feet. Could I promise that my extremities were free of skin disease?

I said I thought I could, and Mrs Gosfoot, for the third time, signed the form. I thanked her warmly and backed towards the door.

'Excuse me,' said Mrs Gosfoot in an extremely menacing voice, 'but that will be one dollar.'

It seemed a lot to pay for having one's word about one's feet taken by a woman; but it was a low price at which to buy an insight into such a demure little racket. I enjoyed my swim.

The rest of that day was spent looking for a man called Colonel Huang. He had been recommended to us by Mr Wang Ching Wei as a useful liaison man, who might be able to arrange an interview with General Chiang Kai-shek.

Colonel Huang proved elusive. Neither his name nor his rank is uncommon in China (the number of Colonels in the Chinese Army is second only to the number of Generals), and the information we collected about his whereabouts was often conflicting and always inaccurate. The settlement at Kuling clings to the side of a steep hill and is divided up into 'Lots', each of which bears a number and each of which may comprise several dwelling-places. With Li as interpreter, we went mountaineering round the Lots, picking up clues from German military advisers and Chinese minor officials and missionaries of many races. Eventually, on a breast-high scent, we ran our man to ground in a church where the wedding of two Christian Chinese was being celebrated with considerable pomp. We picketed the graveyard and sat down to wait.

At last the ceremony was over. Crackers were discharged, photographs taken – and the guests adjourned *en bloc* to a reception far away up the hill. With tongues hanging out we followed them and drew a cordon round the bungalow which was their destination.

After a long time the guests began to depart. Still there were no signs of our man, and we told Li to make enquiries. He returned with that deprecating smile which so often softens the impact of disappointment in China. Colonel Huang had left Kuling the day before; we had been on a false trail all the afternoon.

Nevertheless, we had a stroke of luck (as we thought) that evening. We went to see a German adviser who was R's colleague in his task of reconstructing the Civil Service. He was a charming though almost painfully ingenuous man, very much of the old school; after six months in China he was just beginning to suspect that Chinese officials were sometimes dilatory, inefficient, and unreliable, and the suspicion disquieted him. It was a remarkable achievement to have staved off for so long the dawn of disillusionment.

He put us on the track of one of Chiang Kai-shek's private secretaries, and this man, by good fortune, we ran down almost at once. We had sent Li home and the secretary spoke

6

GENERALISSIMO

CHIANG KAI-SHEK has hardly ever been known to give an interview to a foreign journalist, and in the end it was the sheerest luck that got me mine. All our cherished and convergent lines of approach – the telegram from Wang Ching Wei, the secretary's recommendation, the German military adviser who was to have put in a word for us – all came to nothing. The first thing that Chiang Kai-shek heard of us was our appearance on the threshold.

We made this appearance at ten o'clock the next morning, blissfully supposing that we were expected. We were not. Chiang Kai-shek was living in a small bungalow belonging to a foreign missionary. We strode confidently up to the garden gate, which was guarded without formality by half a dozen of the bodyguard armed with automatic pistols. We gave our cards to the officer in charge and Li explained who we were; but the atmosphere remained chilly and inauspicious, and we should, I think, have been denied admission had not Mme Chiang Kai-shek at that moment come out of the bungalow. Mme Chiang Kai-shek is the gifted and influential sister of Mr T. V. Soong. Another sister is the wife of Dr H. H. Kung, the President of the Bank of China, and it is in great part due to these ladies that the balance of power within the Nanking Government lies with what has been nicknamed the Soong Dynasty.

Seeing two foreigners in difficulties with her guard, Mme Chiang Kai-shek sent an aide-de-camp to deal with the situation. The aide was impressed by our references, as rehearsed by Li, and five minutes later we found ourselves sitting on the edge of cane chairs in a small, bare room furnished in the European style. On the wall hung cheap reproductions of inordinately religious pictures. The furniture was plain, unattractive, and old. The Generalissimo of the Armies of the Chinese Republic was somewhat incongruously housed.

Li was being cross-questioned elsewhere (servants are one of the principal sources of information in China). The young aide remained as our interpreter. We were told that Chiang Kai-shek was holding an important conference, but would leave it for a few minutes to see us.

He came into the room quietly, and stood quite still, looking at us. He wore a dark-blue gown and carried in one hand a scroll, evidently part of the agenda of his conference. He was of rather more than average height, and unexpectedly slim. His complexion was dark, his cheek bones high and prominent, and he had a jutting, forceful lower lip like a Habsburg's. His eyes were the most remarkable thing about him. They were large, handsome, and very keen – almost aggressive. His glances had a thrusting and compelling quality which is very rare in China, where eyes are most negative and non-committal, if not actually evasive.

We stood up and bowed. Chiang Kai-shek motioned us to sit down. I was conscious of his eyes. The interview began.

I got through the essential courtesies as quickly as possible. The Marshal replied to them with business-like and un-Oriental brevity. Then I came to our purpose. I said that China was the only country whose armies were actively and continuously engaging the forces of Bolshevism in the field, and that the world's interest in, and sympathy for, China would be stimulated by first-hand information, hitherto lacking, about what had happened on the spot. Would the Marshal allow my friend and myself to go up into Kiangsi and get that information?

The Marshal, after disconcerting me with a piercing stare, said that he would. He would wire that morning to the Governor of Kiangsi at Nanchang and instruct him to grant us every facility.

This was splendid. This was what we wanted. I thanked him warmly. And how soon did he expect to see the Red areas cleared up and the problem of Communism in China solved? Chiang Kai-shek replied, rather perfunctorily, that the Red Armies at present in the field would be wiped out by that winter; after that would come the rehabilitation of the Communist areas, for which he had already drafted plans.*

It was obvious that Chiang Kai-shek enjoyed the sound of his own voice far less than most politicians, in China and elsewhere. He was not the usual type of glib and rather impressive propaganda-monger; he did not cultivate salesmanship. He was moreover a busy man in the middle of a busy morning. I decided that we should make a better impression if we emulated his laconic methods and anticipated his wishes by cutting our interview as short as possible. I therefore asked him only one more question: When might we expect a *rapprochement* between China and Japan?

'On the Manchurian issue, never,' said Chiang Kai-shek firmly.

We rose and took our leave, with many expressions of gratitude. As we parted I received once more one of those formidable glances, of the kind which prompts an involuntary self-accusation of some grave sartorial omission. We trooped down the garden path feeling very small.

As a rule contact with the great brings out the worst in me. The more exalted a man's position, the less impressionable I become. A man's vulnerability increases in direct proportion to his eminence. The higher his place, the greater the incongruity between the real and the ideal – between the human material and the dignities it is supposed to uphold. And, by corollary, the bigger the bluff, the better worth calling. So I approach the eminent in a frame of mind in which, I regret to say, scepticism and disrespect are uppermost.

But before Chiang Kai-shek I retired abashed. Here was a man with a presence, with that something incalculable to him to which the herd instinctively defers. He was strong and

* Those plans, alas, remain in draft. In the late autumn of 1933 the elaborately prepared campaign of the Nationalist armies against the Communists in Kiangsi had already fizzled out ingloriously before the separatist revolt in the adjoining province of Fukien provided at once a distraction and an excuse for failure.

7

GRAND HOTEL

In China the wise man budgets for delays all along the line. I had expected that Chiang Kai-shek would prove inaccessible, and that it would take us at least four days to find out that this was so. Now, after only twenty-four hours in Kuling, our mission was miraculously fulfilled, and we could start on the next stage of our journey. We were jubilant.

We went down the hill that afternoon. The descent was uneventful, except that half-way down we met a young man who was driving a pig up to Kuling. The unhappy creature was no mountaineer, and at last its forelegs had refused their office, though the hind ones still had some strength left in them. The pig lay prone in the gutter, squealing, while the young man thrashed it incessantly with a switch, uttering loud and angry cries.

As usual it was a question of face, that dominant factor in Chinese life, which I can never hope to define, but only to illustrate. The young man was a cut above the coolie class, and therefore could not demean himself by adopting the obvious and only practical course of carrying the pig up the mountain slung from a pole across his shoulders. Nor could he allow himself to be defeated without a struggle by the pig's collapse. So he made a loud noise (which always helps to give you face, as the Chinese artilleryman well knows) and flogged the pig mercilessly, though he was aware that no amount of corporal punishment would get it any farther up the hill, as yet only half scaled. His face expressed a fiendish rage, but only for the sake of appearances. He was waiting for The Mediator – for some passer-by who would intervene in the strained relations between him and the pig and effect a compromise. The whole incident was cut to a traditional pattern.

In the evening we reached the village at the foot of Lushan and got a car to Kiukiang, where we were put up for the night by a Scot and initiated into the game called Pin Pool, which dominates the billiard tables of the Yangtse Valley. Gerald, who has a fine natural eye, easily defeated the local expert, and we acquired face.

Very early the next morning we boarded a train for Nanchang. It was the most irresolute of trains. After maintaining for perhaps twenty minutes its maximum speed of eighteen miles an hour, it would suddenly lose heart and draw up in a siding for a period of introspection, during which we suffered some discomfort on account of the intense heat.

We were, however, partially consoled by tangible signs of Communist depredations, which grew thicker as we approached Nanchang. Quite a large proportion of the fields were uncultivated which meant that the situation must recently have been very bad indeed. The Chinese peasant's capacity for 'Business as Usual' during disturbances is, and needs to be, extraordinary. He is as nearly impervious to political conditions as the English sportsman is to climatic; both excite awe and amazement in the foreigner for the same reasons. He allows the chaos of which you read in your newspaper to affect his daily life hardly more than it affects yours. Uncultivated fields are the symptoms either of death or exile.

Then there was a recently derailed train lying on its side, and several of the wooden bridges had been burnt down and rebuilt. Not very solidly rebuilt, I thought, and a week later we heard that a hundred soldiers had lost their lives when one of them gave way beneath a troop-train. All the stations were guarded by soldiers, and on the little hills commanding them there were trenches and small pill-box forts of recent construction.

And this, you must remember, was north of Nanchang, more than a hundred miles from the main Red area in southern Kiangsi.

Nanchang itself, which was to be the base for Chiang Kai-shek's autumn campaign, was protected as thoroughly as if it had been an advanced post. A wide circle of high barbed-wire entanglements ran all round the provincial capital, and within this a new and massive city wall was being hastily constructed. Every knoll on the outskirts was crowned by one of those little forts which from now on were to become a familiar sight.

Our train was an hour and a half late. The station was crowded with troops, among whom were the only Chinese soldiers I had ever seen wearing steel helmets. They were four in number.

The railway stops short at the river on the farther side of which the city lies. We crossed in hulks towed by a tug and, reaching the Bund, chartered rickshaws. I use the verb advisedly. Characters in old-fashioned novels were always said to 'charter a hansom'. The phrase had an even more impulsive and dashing connotation than its modern equivalent, to 'hail a taxi', and thus ran counter to the true meaning of 'to charter', which is to hire in a particular and rather complicated way. To charter a hansom, in fact, does not mean what it says; to charter a rickshaw does.

Li did the chartering, and it always took hours. Himself of a fanatically economical nature, he belonged to a race with whom bargaining is a passion and to pay any price above the minimum is to lose prestige. (In China you earn as much contempt as gratitude by an over-generous tip.) Whenever we appeared, casting among the rickshaw coolies those carefully non-committal looks which betray the potential passenger, we would be instantly surrounded by a yelping semi-circle, the slender shafts of their vehicles converging on us like the spears of some hostile tribe. Li would step forward, facing pandemonium and by his adamant parsimony increasing it. For five, perhaps for ten minutes, the process of chartering would continue with the greatest animation; and in the end it would very often be necessary for us to walk away, shaking our heads more in sorrow than in anger, until three disgruntled coolies came trotting after us, their faces expressing a sulky acceptance of Li's ultimatum.

Noise and delay are two of the chief drawbacks to travel in China, and I often used to wonder whether it was worth provoking and enduring these in their most aggravating form for the sake of a financial saving which in very few cases totalled more than a penny between the three of us. But Gerald said, and I have no doubt that he was right, that Li would lose face if we interfered with his transactions; so we gave him his head, and very soon our nervous systems became hardened to the consequences.

In the province of Kiangsi, we discovered, the rickshaw coolies do not trot, as they do elsewhere; this is probably because they have a guild powerful enough to enforce the working conditions they prefer. We proceeded, therefore, at a stately pace through the principal streets, which looked very up to date, being wide and smoothly paved with concrete subjected only to a negligible extent to the wear and tear of motor traffic.

In due course we came to a large but unprepossessing building, bearing the name of the Grand Hotel de Kiangsi, but no other trace of foreign influence.

It was the chief hotel in a provincial capital, and I suspect that it was typical. It had about six storeys, built round a dark courtyard which served as an entrance-hall, airshaft, and urinal. This place was infested, as indeed were all other parts of the hotel, by people who would in the West have been thought to have no business there: soldiers; relatives of the servants, coolies who had brought a message, coolies who had not brought a message, and a substantial number of persons who seemed to have decided, like the suburban housewife, to slip into something loose and have a good lie-down. We took a large and comparatively clean room without – once more, paradoxically, for reasons of face – haggling about the price.

For two nights then, and two later, the Grand Hotel de Kiangsi was our headquarters, and we came to know its sounds and smells fairly well. I am peculiarly well qualified for travel in the Far East by having practically no olfactory sense, and it is therefore the sounds that I remember best, though Gerald assured me that the smells were not less remarkable. The sounds were continuous, reaching a crescendo in the hot hours after midnight. The crash of mah jong: the urgent clamour of the 'scissors' game; the unendurable voices of singing girls entertaining officers on their way to the front: a gramophone with a limited repertoire of Chinese records: a bugle in the courtyard below our window, where men drilled with an air of tolerant amusement: the snoring of servants sprawled in the passage outside: and, eternally punctuating all these noises, the vigorous sound of spitting. It was not a bad hotel, but I would not choose it for a quiet week-end.

Many foreigners, when they travel in the interior of China, burden themselves with a large roll of bedding and a lot of food in tins. Gerald and I had none of these things, and never felt the lack of them. The beds in the hotels, and the k'angs in the inns, were of course no softer than the floor; but the quilt provided for you to lie on, if it could not in any circumstances have been called clean, was never as thickly populated with vermin as it looked to be on first sight. Neither of us was badly bitten. As for the food, it varied; but while there is rice there is hope, and there was always rice. Some of the meals we had were excellent.

The only real discomfort was the heat – a heat not to be kept at bay, as it is in the Treaty Ports, with a battery of electric fans and many long, cool drinks. In Nanchang, where there was no electricity, the place of the fans was taken by a primitive form of cloth punkah, divided into two sections, and having the words 'FAIR WIND' embroidered across it in large, erratic capitals. Very few of the people who used these punkahs can have had any idea of what the words, or even the letters, were; I often wondered how they came to be established there, and by what infallible instinct the poorer householders, whose punkahs boasted only one section, always chose the noun and not the adjective to adorn it.

In Nanchang we worked quickly and had luck. The first person we interviewed was Mr Hsiao, who was not a member of the Provincial Government but an outsider appointed by Chiang Kai-shek as a sort of Food Controller; his mission was to effect an economic blockade of the Red Areas. He was an extremely intelligent man, and spoke good English. He told us that Communism in China was not an economic problem, as most people supposed, but a political one; far the most important feature of the anti-Communist operations was the food blockade.

Next we interviewed the Governor of Kiangsi, Mr Hsiung. He told us that Communism in China was not a political problem, as most people supposed, but an economic one; in the course of an extensive survey of the measures which were being taken to suppress the Reds he made no mention of the food blockade. He was a small, alert man, wearing a smart blue uniform. He received us at the yamen, in the last of many courtyards. Though the buildings were ancient, and their courts pervaded by the proper atmosphere of sleepy tranquillity, the administrative offices had an air of modernity. Telephones not only rang, but were promptly answered. There were files of Chinese newspapers, and good maps. The Governor's car, standing in the shade of a banyan tree outside, had bullet-proof shutters over the windows which looked as if they came straight from Chicago.

Both the Governor and his Food Controller gave us a great deal of information about the Communists; such of it as we were able to confirm is summarized in my conclusions in an earlier chapter. The general impressions that I got in Nanchang were that the Red Armies were a formidable and incalculable striking force; that everyone was afraid of them; and that the measures which were being taken against them were ambitious but unreliable. We were told, too, of many schemes for the future – Utopian projects for railways, and co-operative markets, and agricultural credits. They were paper schemes, and likely to remain so; but for a province as sorely afflicted and as impoverished as Kiangsi to have worked them out even on paper was an achievement. The traveller in China finds everywhere grandiose and enlightened plans which seem doomed to remain indefinitely plans and nothing more; and after a time, perhaps, he grows impatient and sceptical of these castles in the air. This, I think, is a wrong attitude. Castles, especially in the modern style, are difficult, expensive things to build; this straining after rarely attainable civic ideals is in itself a healthy phenomenon, and must in time (for the Chinese are at heart an intensely practical people) produce some positive and tangible result. The result may be only a tithe of what was aimed at, but it is at least something.

The provincial government, though apprehensive for our safety, very kindly arranged for our journey by car to advanced posts on the anti-Communist front; we were told that we could leave Nanchang on the morning of our second day there. The interim was filled in with rather aimless activities. We walked out to the gigantic aerodrome which was being hastily constructed by forced (but paid) labour on the outskirts of the city, dodged the sentries, and inspected the ten assorted machines which were already there; they included a special bomber of Chiang Kai-shek's, a huge tri-motor Ford. Coolies, working night and day in shifts, were levelling the field and constructing a concrete runway which would be proof against the rains. It was all very impressive, but I suspected (and later confirmed this suspicion) that aeroplanes were no more use against the Reds than they were against the bandits in those parts of Manchuria which are, like southern Kiangsi, mountainous and densely wooded.

The Governor invited us to dinner, and Li replied formally on an imposing sheet of *The Times* notepaper. In China your calligraphy is an important clue to your social status; it serves something of the purpose of your Old School Tie in England, but is of course much better fitted to serve it. Li wrote a good hand, and as we watched him painting the delicate lovely characters on that sheet of paper with the London address we hoped that we had acquired face by conforming to a good tradition.

Perhaps we had. But the dinner was not what we hoped. The considerate Chinese had thought, mistakenly, that we

8

THE RENEGADE

EARLY the next day (this was in the last week of August) we started for the front. From Nanchang two roads run – one slightly east, the other slightly west, of south – towards the borders of the Communist territory. We went first down the eastern road, which was held, more or less continuously, by Nationalist troops as far as a small town called Nanfeng, about a hundred miles from Nanchang. We hoped to reach Nanfeng.

I have spoken already, and I shall probably speak again, of the anti-Communist 'front'. Actually there was no front in the accepted sense of the word – no continuous line, that is, held by the government troops. The south of the province is mountainous, and the mountains are the Communists' strength. A low but thickly wooded spur of these hills runs northwards towards Nanchang into the V formed by the two roads which I have mentioned, and from this spur attacks may be launched at any moment upon the military posts along either road. The villages on each of them have changed hands repeatedly, and a situation has often been created in which Communist forces were threatening Nanchang while the advanced Nationalist posts farther south had not even been molested.

While we were in Kiangsi things were fairly quiet. The main, organized Red Armies were marauding to the eastward, in Fukien, from which province, laden with booty, they were with difficulty driven out by the Nineteenth Route Army, the quondam heroes of the Shanghai fighting against the Japanese, and afterwards the mainstay of the short-lived separatist movement in Fukien. Such trouble as arose while we were with the troops was created by gangs of men whose attachment to the Communists' cause had exalted their

status from that of bandits to irregular detachments of the
Red Armies.

We set off early in the morning in a car, which was followed
by a bus containing Li, our luggage, and two guards of a
cheerfully horrific aspect, armed with Mauser automatics.
We had with us in the car two representatives of the provincial government: the intelligent, willowy, and (as we were
to discover) rather vague Mr Hsiao, and a Mr Chen, a
twenty-six-year-old graduate from Harvard, who held a
potentially important post on one of the numerous Bureaux
of Reconstruction which were waiting for a military victory
to give them something to reconstruct.

Mr Chen's was an unhappy case. He was a lugubrious
young man, with a large, sour face and a loud, harsh voice.
He had been educated at Harvard, a process which he had
taken very seriously. 'I never went to a picture, I never
looked at a girl, I never played cards, I never had any fun at
all. I just worked and worked and worked,' he told me once
in a pathetic burst of self-revelation. But the West, though he
had lived there ascetically, had made him fastidious; it was
typical of him that he inhabited the Chinese Y.M.C.A. at
Nanchang, for the sake of the bathroom and the foreign
cooking. Much worse, he was at heart out of sympathy with
his country. For a Chinese he had singularly little tolerance
and less humour. His constructive zeal clashed with his
critical faculties. America (this happens very rarely) had
destroyed his faith in the ancient, indigenous set of values on
which the progressive Chinese can fall back in moments of
despair; there were no compensations for him. His country
seemed to him to be in a hopeless state; but his affection for
it had withered in the West, and the impulse to regenerate
was more or less academic. The desire to do something was
cancelled out by the desire to point out the futility of doing
anything. Mr Chen was in truth disgusted with China; it
made him very unhappy.

I realized quite soon that we were suffering from the same
handicap that I had suffered from with Mr H. in Jehol – that
we were, in other words, visiting a military area under

civilian auspices. As we left Nanchang we overhauled column after column of reinforcements on their way up to the front; but neither Mr Hsiao nor Mr Chen was able to tell us where they were going, or why, or to what division they belonged, or why they had no rifles. There lingered in them something of the Chinese gentleman's disdain for the soldier, and they were not pleased when we asked them those questions on military subjects which were all-important to our investigations. They sought to divert our attention to admirable but irrelevant amenities of a civilian nature, and we dutifully inspected the headquarters of the bus service, and a war memorial put up to a general who had fallen fighting for Chiang Kai-shek in the Northern Expedition of 1926, and a charming Taoist monastery whose walls had been decorated by troops lately billeted there with vivid anti-Communist posters.

We were also taken over an agricultural school, which stood a little way back from the road about twenty miles from Nanchang. Here, at any rate, was a project which was no longer on paper. Founded by the provincial government, the school was now said to be self-supporting. It was run by a cheerful, modest young man – the very best type of young Chinese. I have said before that the curse of China is ineffectiveness. As you travel through the country you find a continuous pleasure in the charm, the humour, the courtesy, the industry, and the fundamentally reasonable outlook of the inhabitants: but all the time you are missing something, and you are hardly conscious of what it is until you meet somebody – like this boy – who is effective: who really means to do what he says he is going to do: who can resist the fatal lure of compromise: who can rise superior to his enervating and obstructionist surroundings: who gets things done. Such a man puts your respect for the Chinese on a less academic plane.

The school was on holiday. As we were conducted round the dormitories it was strange to see, pinned to the wall above a bed, one of those preternaturally shiny and romantic postcards which are sold by small newsagents in English seaside resorts. It was a typical specimen; a glossy young man in a high stiff collar was engaged in the dual task of gnawing a girl's left ear while forcing her to eat an unusually large rose. By another bed there was a photograph of a Japanese geisha girl; when I called Mr Hsiao's attention to it he seemed embarrassed and said it was a joke.

We drove on along a fairly good road. The country was down-like and not very thickly cultivated. There were many deserted fields, but the bus service ('Business as Usual') was running regularly, though the company's receipts showed that seventy-five per cent of their passengers were military, and soldiers travel free or know the reason why. In most of the little villages we stopped and drank tea with the bus company's local representative, for Mr Hsiao, in addition to his post as Food Controller, had something to do with transport and was making a tour of inspection. In this way we picked up a lot of miscellaneous local information.

Late in the afternoon we reached Fuchow, where we were to stay the night. It was a small town, dominated by a rather unfortunate Roman Catholic cathedral. After a good meal at an inn, we trooped off to the yamen to pay our respects. Here we were received with great courtesy and some delicious sweet cakes by the local magistrate, a fat man with a benign and babyish face, and the Special Commissioner, a charming dotard with the *distrait* inconsequence of a P. G. Wodehouse peer. He fairly poured forth information on every conceivable subject, all of it having a markedly Utopian flavour. He was, by virtue of his office, in charge of the local militia or defence corps, a somewhat imponderable force armed with spears. He had some photographs of this well-intentioned rabble. They were huge photographs, neatly rolled up in pretty little cardboard boxes decorated with a coloured design, and he took a touching pride in them; they were his *pièce de résistance*. I can see him now, playing Santa Claus to us, deliberately tantalizing us (as he thought) by the slowness with which he undid the boxes, unrolling each photograph inch by inch with hands that trembled with excitement.

But his charm could not blind us to the fact that we were barking up the wrong, the civilian tree. We began to make tentative, circuitous inquiries about military headquarters. Was it true that they had some Communist prisoners in Fuchow? At last without, I think, offending our civilian hosts, we engineered a call on the military.

From headquarters an officer took us to what he called the Reform House. This was a place where captured or repentant Communists were turned into better men. In a small, hot, over-crowded room (our retinue was by this time greatly swollen) we interviewed the chief prisoner, who appeared, as far as I could judge, to be in supreme command of the establishment.

The head prisoner was a remarkable young man. He had spent six years in the ranks of the Third Red Army Corps; then, sickening not so much of the theory of Communism as of its bloody practice, he had with difficulty escaped and surrendered to the government forces. He was a small, demoniac-looking man, with a face like a weasel; his hair stood up like a palisade above it. He spoke with great rapidity and vehemence, and my interpreter – Mr Chen from Harvard – professed himself amazed at his fluency and command of rhetoric. I questioned him for an hour, at the end of which the atmosphere in that tiny room was like a Turkish bath.

When I had finished we all trooped out into the now twilit courtyard, where the inmates of the Reform House were drawn up on parade, two hundred strong. Some of them could not have been more than ten years old, but they all wore military uniform (though they carried no arms), and the little ex-Communist put them through drill which was as good as any that I saw in China. We were impressed, and, through Chen, asked the weasel-faced leader to say so. He made a short, barking speech, and dismissed the parade. He was an unusually effective man, and as we walked back to the yamen I wondered whether there were many more like him within the Red Areas. At a guess I should say that there are, for it has always seemed to me that the degree of success attained by the Communist movement in China must be largely due to its power of attracting, and exploiting to the full, young men of exceptional ability. Some of the ablest work being done in China to-day is being done by young men (a minority of them Russian-trained) holding subordinate administrative positions in the Red Areas. If this was not so the movement would have been broken before now.

Before dinner we called, in a state of considerable exhaustion, on the Catholic Mission, where three delightful American fathers gave us beer to drink and with it a new lease of life. They confirmed much of our information about the iniquities of the Reds, but pointed out (what we had already begun to suspect) that from the point of view of the peasants the government troops were just as bad. A long day ended with dinner at the yamen, outside which there was a venerable cannon cast by a British firm in the eighteenth century.

9

THREE MILLION MEN AT ARMS

NEXT day, very early, we left Fuchow for Nancheng, the next place of importance along the road south. (I must apologize for these Chinese names. Nanchang is the capital of Kiangsi: Nancheng is the second, and penultimate, stop on the road thence to the borders of the Red Area: and Nanfeng, beyond it, is the most advanced post held by government troops in that sector.) We made the usual stops for tea and cakes at the bus stations in the villages, passed the usual aimless columns of troops, each with a long tail of limping stragglers, and once were held up at the point of a temperamental-looking musket by the Food Controller's economic cordon. The countryside was getting hillier. In that part of the province it has a curiously English look. Villages cluster in the shade of great trees, among which you do not at first discern the curling and outlandish eaves which brand as Oriental the quiet grey walls and roofs. But the strongest suggestion of your own country comes from the magpie houses – black beams on white plaster – which abound in Kiangsi but which I never saw elsewhere.

We reached Nancheng in time for lunch. It is a small, compact, walled city, dominated by an inordinately romantic white fort perched on a hill outside the north gate. As a rule (to which Fuchow was an exception) roads in the interior skirt the towns, whose streets are too narrow to admit traffic, and we found that we must leave our luggage at the bus station outside the walls, for lack of a military permit to bring it in. Another reminder that we were under the wrong auspices.

Nancheng was full of soldiers – poor-quality troops, like all the permanent garrisons on the outskirts of the Red Areas, and far below the standard of Nanking's best divisions. Here you must forgive a brief digression on the subject of the Chinese soldier.

The Chinese soldier is commonly regarded as a joke by foreigners, and as a pest by compatriots. He is mercenary. He often is, and always looks, absurdly young. His military record shows, on paper, far more of cowardice than of courage, and too frequently it is cowardice in a particularly disgraceful context. In billets he very seldom pays for what he eats; and the division to which he belongs was almost certainly created by diverting some part of the national or provincial revenue from more legitimate and needful expenditure. Should his general meet with a reverse, whether military or financial, he will be turned loose on a district which is probably far from his home, with a rifle, a few rounds of ammunition, and a grievance against society. It is ten to one that his next appearance will be as a bandit.

As things stand, he is a nuisance, unmitigated by his usefulness in a time of national emergency; his only redeeming feature is his cheerfulness, and even that is too often soured by shortage of pay and rations. Small wonder that the people hate him. Take, for instance, the case of a town like Nancheng. Apart from the periodic incursion, during major but invariably unsuccessful campaigns, of better-class troops from Nanking, the town had been garrisoned for the past three years by the *n*th division. The *n*th division came from the North. They were strangers, with a different language and a different diet from the people on whom they were quartered. Their discipline had never been good, and it must have been hard to maintain even at its normal low level in that labyrinthine town, where billets were inevitably scattered and where there was no place inside the walls which could be used as a parade ground. Once you marched your men in you virtually lost control of them.

Most of the time there was nothing for the troops to do. Their vile marksmanship could not be improved, for lack of ammunition to practise with. Their equipment was ridiculous. In a file of four men you would often see three different makes of rifle (the commonest was Japanese). The home-made stick-bombs which dangled by lengths of old string from their belts looked (fortunately for the passer-by's peace of mind) about as likely to explode as the dumb-bells which they resembled. Only a crack division can afford leather equipment; these men carried their cartridge clips in cotton bandoliers, and one day I saw half a dozen of these spread out in the sun to dry after being washed with the ammunition inside them. The nth division were, at best, caterpillars of the commonwealth. Those romantically situated forts were prosaically evacuated at the first serious threat of danger, and expeditions which marched out against the Reds returned minus their rifles and their officers.

There you have a picture of the Chinese soldier at his worst. It is an accurate picture, but it is also unjust. For the curious thing is that the Chinese soldier has it in him to be a very good soldier. He inherits all the advantages of the Japanese soldier except his military traditions. Though you might not think it to look at him he has great strength and endurance. He can live on next to nothing. He is often a man of courage and resource, and he will be loyal to a good master. On regular pay and a full stomach his high spirits combine with his fatalism to keep his *morale* high, even when things are going badly. Add to this that every Chinese is some sort of a craftsman by nature so that this is no reason why, if he could be shown some good cause to take this particular craft seriously, he should not become as adept at drill and musketry as he is at other more difficult and even less indigenous trades.

Why, then, is he in practice such a contemptible failure? Why is he a liability all round – a liability to the foreign bond-holder, whose railway dividends are diverted into a pay-chest with which the soldier's general eventually absconds, a bitter liability to the peasant who is taxed to maintain him, forced to house him free, press-ganged into building his roads, and whose life he does no more to protect than a scarecrow would?

Why? Because of his leaders. His leaders have almost never given him a chance. For every Chinese battle that is won by strategy and tactics, nine are won by a particularly unscrupulous form of commercial diplomacy. Though there have been exceptions, the average Chinese general fights only as a last resort; he makes war by secret negotiation, under cover of a cloud of bombastic and defiant telegrams. Most battles are lost and won before a shot is fired. While the leading troops are coming to grips an armoured train containing the less powerful general slips out of the station at his base away from the fighting, while the telegraph office discharges a last shameless *feu de joie* of heroics. For a time the general will live, on the bribe which bought his departure, in one of the foreign settlements, till crisis again coincides with opportunity. Then once more he will take the field, if that is the right expression.

And even if the general is loyal to his own cause, it will be strange indeed if all his divisional commanders are. If the big man cannot be bought, or is too expensive, some of the little men may well be content with a safe return – in both senses of the phrase – before the bottom drops out of the market.

So the Chinese soldier goes into battle in the expectation of what would be, for anyone else, the bitterest disillusionment. Is it to be wondered that his name as a fighter is mud? The anti-climax of the Jehol campaign in the spring of 1933 is typical of the conditions under which he is expected to show his mettle. The Japanese columns, mechanized but numerically weak, were advancing on the Great Wall, whose passes offered the Chinese a series of positions which must have been temporarily impregnable if held with any degree of resolution. But scarcely any preparations were made to receive the enemy. No adequate entrenchments were dug in the frozen ground. Anti-tank defences were not erected till the Japanese were almost in sight. For all this, and for the hopeless confusion prevailing on the short Chinese lines of communication, there was no excuse at all, for the Chinese had been amply forewarned.

In most of the passes only the most pitiable show of resistance was put up. They were held by the Young Marshal's troops, and rumours were current at the front that Chiang Kai-shek had quarrelled with the Young Marshal and meant to sacrifice his men by sandwiching them between the Japanese and his crack Nationalist troops from the south. These rumours were typical of many, and it is not in the least important whether they were true; the point is that, even in this national emergency, they sounded so highly probable that the soldiers threw away on the strength of them a splendid chance of winning the world's sympathy, if nothing else. The Japanese forced the Wall without difficulty, and then, when it was too late, some of the Nanking regiments fought gallantly for a cause already lost. Also, incidentally, young men and girls of the Chinese Red Cross worked in the front line with conspicuous bravery and resource; but then they had no leaders to let them down.

The Chinese is an individual with a shrewd commercial instinct. To profit and advantage himself and his family he will show immense industry, skill, and courage; for decent pay and a good master he will do all that is required of him and more. That this is true of the Chinese in war as well as in peace was shown by Gordon's levies against the T'aipings, and, more conclusively, by the British-officered Wei Hai Wei Regiment, which was disbanded after an honourable career just before the Great War.

But under bad conditions – the sort of conditions under which ninety per cent of Chi na's threemillion armed men are serving to-day – the soldier would be a fool by his own standards if he fought well. And there are not many fools in the nth or any other division.

10

NOBBLED

THE walls of Nancheng were incredibly thick, and to go through the gate was to traverse a tunnel. At the end of this we were stopped by soldiers armed only with what seemed to be metal ram-rods. The Food Controller beamed with a paternal pride. This was part of his blockade; every sack of rice or anything else was probed with these stabbing ram-rods before it was allowed in or out of the city. Smugglers of ammunition to the Reds were thus apprehended.

As a matter of fact, the Food Controller was very nearly apprehended himself, for he was carrying a little portfolio, and his zealous minions (to whom, since they were illiterate, his name, and rank, or even his visiting card, meant nothing at all) tried to impound it. When one is much in the company of the Chinese one becomes almost as sensitive to somebody else's loss of face as to somebody else's bereavement; but the scene, though painful, was short, for an officer arrived and all was well.

Among familiar smells, familiar stares, familiar noises, and familiar heat, we trudged through narrow stone-flagged streets. They were very ancient streets; down the centre of each the wheelbarrows of generations had worn a deep, smooth groove in the stone, as direct and unwavering as a tram-line. Presently we reached the yamen.

Here we were welcomed by the Special Commissioner, a fluttering ineffectual little man of considerable charm, who retailed to us opinions on the local situation which were too obviously fathered by his wishes. We listened politely, and then, since it was still early in the day, began to inquire about the possibility of getting farther down the road before nightfall. We hoped, we said, to pay a more protracted visit to Nancheng on our way back.

Ah, but we must wait for some refreshment, said the Commissioner; just a little refreshment, something to restore our energies after our tiring drive.

We beamed, groaning inwardly. We knew that we were in for a twenty-course meal in the middle of the afternoon.

I had sensed already, in Mr Hsiao and especially in Mr Chen, a reluctance to continue our journey farther than Nancheng. I for my part was determined to reach Nanfeng, which, you remember, was the most advanced post held by government troops and which had recently been beseiged by the Red Armies. While we waited for lunch I began trying to secure our line of advance.

In this it looked at first as if I had an ally. He was a young officer who had been trained in Japan, a brusque, sardonic man with no nonsense about him. I questioned him in such a way that his answers must throw some light on our prospects of proceeding to Nanfeng, and at first that light was a reassuring one. Then I made the Westerner's usual mistake of pressing my point too hard, of being too obvious and too specific, of trying to get them to commit themselves; and the tide turned against me.

Maps were produced – maps on which the southward road ran between two perilously converging seas of red, and around which was built up a very pessimistic estimate of our chances of reaching Nanfeng alive. The Japanese-trained officer, hitherto so seemingly impatient of civilian qualms, was rallied to his countrymen's aid by the common horror of my forth-right methods – methods which at a committee meeting in London would have seemed despicably circuitous – and he coined for the occasion rumours of an impending Red attack on Nanfeng. Even if we got there, he now said, we should never get out again.

Someone else weighed in with the all too plausible theory that we might get in and we might get out, but we should never get back; spies would report our arrival, and our car would be ambushed in the hills on our return journey. Foreign hostages would mean a great deal to the Communists.

We adjourned to the next room for lunch. The debate

still raged, behind a screen of compliment and circumlocution. We were handicapped (for none of them knew English) by having to plead our cause through a hostile intermediary, Mr Chen; but here Li came in useful, for Mr Chen knew that, limited though our *lingua franca* was, we used Li as a check on his interpreting whenever we suspected distortion or suppression.

Responsibility: that was what they feared. No one would accept responsibility for holding us up; no one would accept responsibility for letting us go on. With bland, ingenuous faces they shuffled responsibility hastily from one to the other, like children playing Hunt the Slipper. It was impossible to corner them; we might as well have tried to pick up mercury with our chopsticks.

At the end of the meal, when the rice bowls had been emptied, the Special Commissioner suddenly got up and made a long, formal speech of welcome, in which of course there occurred no reference to the issue uppermost in everybody's mind. Gerald replied with a speech of thanks (Gerald was far better than I was at the essential courtesies). I was then called upon, and made what in China passes for a fighting speech. I lavished praise on almost every aspect of life in China and, more specifically, in Kiangsi, and then passed on to an account of Japanese iniquities in Manchuria. The bandits there, I said, were a problem very similar in many respects to that presented by the Communists here; and, strongly though I (of course) disapproved of the Japanese, I had nothing but gratitude for the courtesy and efficiency with which they had facilitated my investigation of the bandit problem. They had acted as though they had nothing to hide, nothing which they were ashamed of my seeing; they had even allowed me to accompany an expedition into the heart of the bandit territory. But in this, I pointed out, they were wise; it was in their own interests. For it enabled me to send back to the great newspaper which I had the honour to represent not only a fuller and fairer, but a more readable account of the true situation. In the meantime, what a fine town Nancheng was. . . . And so on.

This speech dragged in the element of face and had some effect. But not enough. The best we could get was a compromise. There was a small fortified post forty *li* down the road to Nanfeng (three *li* go to a mile) and our hosts would find out by telephone from the commander of it whether we could go there without danger. We could then return before nightfall and sleep in Nancheng. We accepted this proposal as a *pis aller* and the meeting broke up.

Poor Mr Chen! I doubt if he ever travelled forty *li* in greater discomfort in his life. In the first place, he was suffering from acute physical fear, and incessantly searched the excellent cover along the roadside with apprehensive eyes. In the second place, I behaved diabolically towards him. I adopted an air of whimsical resignation, as if I had made up my mind that we should never see Nanfeng. 'Well, well, what can one expect in China?' was the line I took. But as I prattled innocently away I levelled against the unhappy Mr Chen indirect and roundabout charges of cowardice, inconsistency, breach of faith, and mendacity – failings, which, I implied, bade fair to bring disgrace, not only on himself, but on his province and indeed on all China. The whole English-speaking world was waiting on tenterhooks for *The Times* to reveal the truth about Communism in China. How could the truth be told if I was prevented from going to Nanfeng? And what would the English-speaking world think of Mr Chen, who was instructed to take me there and didn't?

Poor Mr Chen, threatened with the world-wide exposure of his native and quite pardonable ineffectiveness as the motive power behind large-scale anti-foreign machinations, became perturbed as well as embarrassed. My absurd accusations were all implied and could not be specifically refuted; Mr Chen's attempts to clear himself got him into even deeper waters. At last he lost his nerve altogether and spontaneously volunteered to go behind the civil authorities and appeal to military headquarters for a pass to Nanfeng. I knew that he would of course arrange for an unfavourable answer to be returned; but I felt that we had scored a moral victory on a difficult and unfamiliar wicket.

By now we had reached the post which was our destination – a small village lying on both banks of a river, which was crossed by the usual bridge of boats. Beyond the village on the eastern bank a ridge was crowned with a bright new fort, and when we had routed out the commander in the village we walked up to inspect it. At least we walked and the commander, rather surreptitiously, ran. Ours had been a surprise visit, and it was necessary to wake up the garrison.

It was a nice, sturdily built little fort, of a medieval pattern: the sort of fort which has been erected in China for many centuries. By the time we arrived its battlements were duly decorated with a sentry, bare-legged, juvenile, and self-conscious, who stood gazing eastward with rapt eyes towards the marches of Fukien. We were told that a Communist attact was expected at any moment from that quarter. The fort was garrisoned by about a dozen men, and stocked with provisions for five days in case of siege; the water-supply did not look to me as if it would last that long. Though it was less than a year old the fort had already changed hands twice. The Reds had captured it in the preceding spring, the defenders, for lack of promised reinforcements, being driven back into the river, where most of them were drowned.

At this place we got a sidelight on the intelligence methods practised by the government forces. In the anti-Communist, as in the anti-bandit campaigns, intelligence is an all-important factor. The trouble is that peasants within the Red Areas are too effectively terrorized to give away useful information, while dislike of the Nationalist troops makes peasants on the fringes equally uncommunicative. Spies have to be bought, and for a stiff price. That price had just gone up. Two members of a small civilian patrol, sent out from this post three days ago, had been captured by the Reds and beheaded; the survivors were now demanding six dollars a day instead of four. Four dollars a day is fantastically high pay in that part of the world.

We drove back to Nancheng in an atmosphere of some constraint. Mr Chen brooded over his wrongs, we over what we conceived to be our rights. We arrived only just in time –

to get inside the walls before they shut the gates for the night; our luggage was still in quarantine outside.

In the city we parted. Mr Chen departed to the yamen with a last half-hearted promise to interview military head-quarters about a pass before he went to bed. We made for the Catholic Mission, where we hoped to sleep.

11

HAVEN

It had been a tiring day. Few things take it out of you so
much as trying to pin down a set of utterly unreliable people
to a course of action to which they are rootedly opposed;
and when you have to do most of it through a recalcitrant
interpreter the strain is substantially increased. The Catholic
Mission gave us just the reception we needed to restore our
morale.

This time the Fathers were Irish. They had taken over the
Mission from the French. It was a gaunt, rather cheerless
building, standing in a large compound which also contained
a church and a vegetable garden, and which was at present
packed with refugees whose homes had been devastated by
the Communists. To these the Fathers gave food and shelter
free.

It is certainly difficult, and I am afraid it is impossible, to
translate into words the impression which that small community produced on me. The traveller passes through many
countries, but the world is too much with him; or, if not too
much, at any rate all the time. All the time he is haggling
or hustling or scheming: coping with contingencies or antici-
pating them. Everyone he meets, from the mandarin to the
muleteer, he meets (to some extent) on a business footing.
Either he wants something of them or they want something
of him; or both. Usually both. The muleteer wants higher
pay; the traveller wants a quicker pace. The mandarin wants
a public pat on the back; the traveller wants a passport in a
hurry. All the time he is fighting a guerrilla war, a war of
attrition. Truces are frequent; but they are clouded by the
certainty that hostilities will soon be renewed. All the time –
immediate or impending, acknowledged or unacknowledged
– there is conflict, conflict, conflict.

214

It is the same, of course, in other walks of life. The traveller is not the only one who seems to himself to have embarked on a petty, inglorious Hundred Years War, a dateless and unprofitable struggle. But, both for the traveller and in more sedentary though not less strenuous lives, there are moments when the dust evaporates and the heat is cooled – when for a brief interval one feels oneself translated to another world: truces unclouded by the coming war. On the top of a hill, or swimming in an unsuspected bay, or as often as not in far more unlikely, less spectacular, surroundings the conviction suddenly descends that the world is a better place than one had supposed.

The Mission at Nancheng provided me with such a moment. It was as if we had suddenly happened on a very good club of an unusual kind. The Fathers' talk was lit by humour and comprehension. One of them was ill, another lately lamed; their lives were in danger from the Reds, their property in danger from the whites. They were in daily contact with misery and suffering in their acutest forms, and their efforts to alleviate them were handicapped by a heart-breaking multiplicity of obstacles. They were worn out by the heat of the summer. They had few comforts, and we were the first strangers they had seen for months.

Yet you would have supposed from their bearing that they were the most fortunate of men, so cheerful were they, so humorously apologetic for the limitations of their hospitality, so full of an unwistful curiosity about the outside world. Theirs were incongruous circumstances in which to find content, yet with them you had the feeling that you were as near to true felicity as you would ever be. I remember them with admiration, and occasionally with envy.

They gave us an excellent dinner and a great deal of beer and told us stories against themselves and against the Chinese. Like most Catholic missions in China, they were full of inside information, and they had much valuable news of the Communists, culled from refugees. When we told them how our plans for reaching Nanfeng were likely to be thwarted, they flung themselves into the intrigue with great zest, and immediately sent a chit round to the local general (who was a convert of theirs) asking him to receive us early the next day. We went to bed with the pleasant feeling that we still had a shot in our locker.

When it was light the next morning I went with one of the Fathers into their church, which was a large rather than a beautiful building. Matins were being sung. The nave was full of Chinese, chanting their prayers in a devout sing-song. A few of them were respectable citizens, but most of them were refugees in rags. Children stood wondering among the kneeling forms, picking their noses with an air of abstraction. Sunlight filtering through the crude stained-glass windows made lurid and luminous the immaculate black heads of the women.

As we strolled back to breakfast the Father remarked that nothing in foreigners so powerfully attracted the curiosity of the Chinese as their habit of walking in step; the most eccentric behaviour earned you fewer stares than the carrying out of a normal activity in a way which could never occur to the Chinese, whose tripping paces are at no time synchronized.

We had breakfast, and then said good-bye with a very real regret. I tried to make the Fathers accept a donation for their mission, but they would have none of it. I have never known kinder hosts, or more unforgettable hospitality.

From then on our intrigue was triumphantly successful. The General (who of course had heard no word from the perfidious Mr Chen) produced a military pass without demur, and by nine o'clock we were ready to take the road for Nanfeng. In our hearts we knew that we should see nothing there which we had not seen already; but the struggles of the last twenty-four hours had invested the place with a desirability, an irresistible lure, beside which Eldorado itself had no more than the casual appeal of a railway poster. It had been a point of honour that we should reach Nanfeng; and now, with luck, we were going to.

As we waited for the crestfallen and now genuinely terrified Mr Chen, I watched reliefs for the nth division marching

into Nancheng. They were poor troops – little slouching
men in grey with gigantic cart-wheel straw hats lined with
oiled paper, which acted as a protection against both sun and
rain. These hats looked silly, but they were both practical
and cheap. Most of the men carried umbrellas slung across
their backs, and here and there in the column a soldier had
a singing bird in a little cage. Umbrellas and larks on active
service! How the superior West enjoys its laugh at the expense of the Chinese soldier! Yet nobody finds it funny when
an English platoon takes a gramophone into the front line;
and a song-bird, which is the only kind of potted music the
nth division can afford, is a lesser burden than a gramophone.
As for the umbrellas, they are not only lighter but far cheaper
than waterproof capes, which are in any case nowhere pro-
curable in Central South China. The Chinese soldier is not
as funny as he sounds.

The column included a detachment of stretcher-bearers,
which gave the no doubt illusory impression that it meant
business. A few of the officers were mounted on Szechwan
ponies, which are smaller and prettier animals than the
Mongols in the North. There are very few ponies in Kiangsi;
this always seemed to me curious for the grazing looked good,
and the country was sufficiently open to have made a pony
a more valuable asset than in most parts of South China. As
I watched the troops march past I suddenly realized that I
was standing outside a regimental armourer's shop. The regimental armourer had taken a rifle to pieces and was furbish-
ing up its component parts on an old razor strop.

At last Mr Chen arrived, and we were off. We passed the
post which we had visited the night before and got into
country which grew steadily wilder. The road twisted along
roughly parallel to the river, and I could not restrain myself
from pointing out to Mr Chen how admirably adapted to
an ambush was almost every one of its sharp and numerous
corners. Mr Chen's large face was disconsolate, and pale
green in colour. Our bus had been commandeered by the
military, so the guards were no longer with us. All along the
road were recently dug trenches, relics of a successful Com-

munist advance towards Nancheng a month ago. None of the fields were under cultivation.

Whenever we passed a military post Mr Chen would stop the car and question the commander about conditions farther down the road; he hoped to elicit an excuse for turning back. But the commanders, being, I think, familiar with conditions only as far as their eyes could see, failed to furnish an excuse, and we went on. Every time we passed a peasant on the road Mr Chen would turn sharply in his seat and watch the man until he was out of sight; he expected to see him go bounding up the hillside to inform the Communist outposts of our passing.

But nothing ever seems to happen to me and we reached Nanfeng safely, acknowledging with what dignity we could muster the salutes of an unforeseen guard of honour. Nanfeng is a small and very picturesque town, split by the river and dominated by an exceptionally tall pagoda. An ancient wall of great thickness runs round it, and its defences have been strengthened by a rash of little forts. Five months before we came there Nanfeng was hotly besieged by the full force of the main Red Armies under the redoubtable Chu Teh. The garrison held out stoutly, but after a fortnight their ammunition was exhausted and the town was on the point of falling. It was only saved by aeroplanes which flew down from Nanchang and dropped fresh supplies of ammunition. The year before, however, it had been occupied for some time by the Reds.

The town, as we walked through it to the yamen, bore no outward traces of these stormy vicissitudes. Business as Usual; though there was of course less business. We were received with China's unfailing courtesy by the magistrate, and, wise from experience, succeeded in forestalling lunch and arranging instead a visit to military headquarters. Before we parted, the magistrate produced one of the Communist coins, minted in Shuikin, the capital of the Red Area; these coins, with notes bearing the head of Lenin, make up a currency which is remarkable, even in these inflationary days, for the paucity of backing behind it. The coin was a twenty-cent piece, dated 1933, and bearing the hammer and sickle in addition to the star which is the emblem of the Kuomintang. The magistrate (as we afterwards discovered from Li) made us a present of it. But Mr Chen – alas for Harvard! – pretended that it was meant for the Governor of the Province, to whom, he said, he would hand it over when we got back to Nancheng; so we never saw it again.

Afterwards, forgetting this incident, Mr Chen confessed in an unguarded moment that he had a passion for coins, and owned a collection which included an American cent for every year since 1882.

12

THE RATTLE OF MUSKETRY

AT military headquarters we drank tea, in the cool, pillared hall of what had once been a temple, with the officer in charge. As we were talking the telephone rang. My instinct, which is sometimes oddly infallible, told me that the message concerned us.

It did. As Mr Chen listened to the conversation there spread slowly over his face that greenish tinge which it had worn in the car; I could guess the nature of the message.

At last the officer put down the receiver and spoke in grave tones to Mr Chen. Mr Chen, still more sepulchrally, passed the information on to us.

It did not, as a matter of fact, amount to much. A military post half-way between us and Nancheng reported that firing had broken out along the road. It was thought that a Communist attack was developing. The road might be cut at any moment.

It sounded to me like a vague, panicky rumour, probably released only to ensure that we did not loiter in Nanfeng, where real danger was expected to threaten soon. I said that we would stick to our plan of going back to Nancheng that evening unless any more specific warning were received. Mr Chen licked his lips and fanned himself with that emblem of the West – a boater. We set out to inspect the defences.

From the turreted walls we looked south-west towards the high and densely wooded mountains which will, I think, for many years prove an impregnable bulwark to the main Communist area. In those hills campaigning is about as difficult as it could be. The only communications are narrow stone-flagged paths along which troops must march in single file. Little of the land is cultivated, and such food supplies as do exist can be stripped by the Communists in retreat. An invading army must carry its own victuals with it and – since animal transport is out of the question – on its own backs. All movement is perforce slow and, in the inevitable absence of good information about a highly mobile enemy, usually ineffective. I do not think that there is in China to-day even the nucleus of an army capable of clearing the Red Areas in southern Kiangsi.

We examined the defences which had withstood so well the siege of last spring, and heard from the officer of the Communists' tactics in the field. What had impressed him most was the dash with which they charged – sometimes, admittedly, behind a screen of boys armed with spears on whom the defenders emptied their magazines unprofitably. They had had he thought, about one hundred rounds a man; their machine-guns had been well used, though they were obviously short of ammunition. They had treated prisoners well.

The Nanfeng garrison I took to be better than most. It was found by the 8th Division, and quartered mostly in forts outside the town; this obviated that relaxation of discipline in billets to which I have referred elsewhere. Moreover, the 8th Division had been there, on and off, for four years; the inhabitants were used to them, liked them, and in some cases had even married them.

The Catholic Fathers had told us the night before that one of their number was still on outpost duty in Nanfeng, and our tour of the walls brought us near a Christian church. So we said good-bye to the officer, arranged to meet Mr Chen at the car in an hour's time, and called on Father Duffy.

Father Duffy was a giant of a young man with red hair and a disarming brogue. On seeing us, his first action was to send a boy to haul up several bottles of beer from the bottom of the well, which is the only refrigerator in the interior of China. We talked and drank. Father Duffy, apparently unconscious of the fact that he already qualified as a hero and was in a fair way to qualify as a martyr, treated his precarious situation in Nanfeng as a source of comedy only. The Reds, during their occupation of the town, had desecrated his church and damaged the mission; and those of their troops who were quartered in it could clearly never have passed even the most elementary examination in sanitation and hygiene. Broken windows, splintered doors, and a thick layer of red paint over the outside of the buildings testified to anti-Christian sentiments which may have had their origin in Moscow but were more likely to be merely a symptom of anti-foreignism.

One thing that Father Duffy told us threw light on a puzzling question. Were there any foreigners working in the Red Areas? The best information – and it was very good information – available in Shanghai indicated that there were. But hitherto the most diligent inquiries in Kiangsi had failed to produce confirmation for this theory. Almost everyone we spoke to – civil and military authorities, renegades and refugees – had heard of the foreigners; had met those who had seen them; could specify their number (which was generally two) and their nationality (which was either German or Russian, more usually the latter); but had not, unfortunately, actually come across them themselves. From the evidence we had collected I felt convinced that there had been foreigners – probably two Russians – acting as advisers to the Communists, but that they had either left the Red Areas or else no longer occupied positions of importance in them.

What Father Duffy said confirmed the first of these conclusions – that there had once been foreigners with the Reds, and that they had held sufficient power to be widely known and feared. When things were quiet in the Nanfeng district Father Duffy had gone out on a round of visits ('itinerating', the Panters called it in Jehol) to converts in outlying villages on the fringe of the Communist area. No one would accompany him so he travelled alone. More than once his appearance was the signal for the evacuation of the village; the people recognized him afar off as a foreigner and at once associated him with the Communists; which seemed to show that Shanghai's information had once been accurate and was now wildly out of date.

Father Duffy's company was so congenial, and his beer so

cool, that we were late for our appointment with Mr Chen. He was awaiting us in a state of profound and growing agitation, and we were bustled into the car without delay. More firing had been heard on the Nancheng road, and Mr Chen disliked the prospect of the drive only less than he feared the possibility of being marooned in Nanfeng by a Communist advance. As we drove off there was a strong suggestion of the tumbril about our car. Mr Chen was a Sydney Carton without the comfort of a Sydney Carton's convictions.

It was a beautiful evening, and the chance of an ambush lent the peaceful landscape a dramatic quality which it had lacked that morning. The military posts along the road had been instructed to redouble their precautions on our behalf; from points of vantage round the isolated little forts sentries waved a conjectural All Clear with flags. On the long stretches between the forts our driver approached the corners with unwonted caution. Even Li seemed subdued.

But of course nothing happened. We got through without so much as a false alarm. If there had been fighting near the road nobody seemed any the worse for it. Mr Chen's complexion reverted slowly to its normal hue, and we reached Nancheng in such good time that we were able to push straight on to Fuchow, where Gerald and I spent the night with the American Catholics.

Next day, in spite of a slight *contretemps* when our bus was driven too impetuously on board a ferry, we were back at the Grand Hotel de Kiangsi.

13

NIGHTMARE

THERE were, you remember, two roads running south from Nanchang. Of these we had now explored the more easterly. There remained the other, whose terminus – a village called Kian – was, like Nanfeng on the first road, the farthest stronghold of the government troops. We had been promised a visit to Kian.

But when we presented ourselves – this time at military headquarters – the authorities hedged. The road, they said, was not good; there were various difficulties. . . . Eventually it transpired that within the last few days the Communists had gained possession of a large section of the road and had burnt the bridges on it. Kian could be reached only, if it could be reached at all, by boat down the river; a journey of several days. By road we could go no farther south than a place called Hsinkan.

Very well, we said, we would go to Hsinkan. Headquarters kindly promised a car and a guide.

And what a car! Or rather, what a driver! We left Nanchang for the second time at dawn on the morning after we had returned to it. Myself, I can remember little of the journey to Hsinkan. Something in last night's Chinese food had got under the guard of a normally ostrich-like digestion, and I would have welcomed death. The driver gave me every chance of doing so. The Hsinkan road ran through low-lying country on top of a narrow embankment. The Chinese peasant has about half as much traffic sense as a Buff Orpington, and peasants were for some reason plentiful that morning. Some of them had brought their water-buffalo with them, some a flock of geese.

This substantial proportion of the agrarian population the driver dismissed as figments of his imagination. There can be little doubt that, in some form or other, they *appeared* to him, for he acknowledged their existence by a savage increase of speed, whenever an increase of any kind was possible. He pressed his foot on the accelerator almost subconsciously, as he might have passed his hand across his brow, to banish what he took to be an hallucination. I think he was drunk.

We reached Hsinkan, by a miracle, with no blood on our hands, and still in possession of our lives. In this village, which had lately been recaptured from the Reds and was surrounded by a high stockade, we presented ourselves at the headquarters of the fire brigade. Why we took this course I never discovered; we were in the charge of a rather incalculable man, and it was he who decided on it.

His name was Colonel Fan. He was young for his rank, being only twenty-three, but his rise had been rapid; he had joined the army two years ago, and was now on the point of retiring. He spoke excellent English, wore a smart blue uniform, and was full of a negative charm. But there was about him a certain vagueness and inconsequence, a willingness to fall in with any idea coupled with a complete inability to carry it out, which prevented him from being an ideal guide. After a long and desultory conversation with the chief of the fire brigade (who, to my infinite regret, was in undress uniform) Colonel Fan was persuaded to conduct us to military headquarters.

The commander of the garrison was from Shantung. The men of that province might be called the Scots of China; not because they exemplify any of those characteristics which music-hall tradition associates with the North British, but because they are to be found in the remotest parts of China, as Scots are to be found all over the world, displaying great enterprise and great industry. Li was from Shantung, and the number of his co-provincials whom he came across at every stage of our travels was astonishing.

I was by this time feeling very low indeed, and the kindly commandant lent me his wooden bed while he gave the rest of us lunch and the local news. After lunch we drove on (the driver had mercifully sobered down) to his outposts a few miles farther down the road. The country looked devastated. Houses were deserted, and some of them burnt to the ground: hardly any of the fields were tilled.

The headquarters of the outpost line were in a farm which stood in a grove of ancient trees and bristled with sentries who handled their Thompson sub-machine guns with a terrifying casualness. The officer in charge gave us what information he could and confirmed the current theory that the road beyond this point had been cut by the burning of all the bridges a few days ago. He also gave us some pineapple out of a tin. We said good-bye and started back.

It was the hottest day of the journey. As we sat in the car, waiting for Colonel Fan to come on board, a thing happened for which I still reproach myself. A little boy appeared at the window of the car. He was wearing military uniform, but he could not have been more than twelve. One arm was in a sling, and filthy bandages partially covered some very bad sores on his legs; he hopped along with the help of a crutch.

He held out his hand to us, and began to speak in a plaintive, urgent voice. His face was puckered in that disconcerting way which sometimes makes it hard to decide whether a child is going to laugh or cry. We asked Li what he was saying.

It seemed that he came from farther south. His family had been massacred by the Communists, and he had taken arms against them with a Nationalist division. But now his commander had been defeated and he himself was wounded. He wanted to get to Hankow, where his mother's family lived. Would we give him a lift?

While this was being translated the driver had given the boy a dollar and was shooing him away. The child began to cry in an automatic, almost perfunctory way; it looked as if he had wept a good deal lately.

I was at the time, what with one thing and another, not much more than semi-conscious. Before I was really alive to the situation Colonel Fan had returned, jumped into the car, and given the driver an order which crystallized his determination to have nothing to do with the boy. The small desperate hand was dislodged from the coachwork, and the car shot forward. We left him, crying, in the middle of the hot and empty road.

In spite of our tardy protests Colonel Fan refused to turn back. Our relations with him were thereafter somewhat strained, and in Hsinkan he refused to let us photograph a prehistoric armoured car on the enigmatic but sufficient grounds that 'it would not be nice'.

On the way back we stopped at a place called Changshu. Our objective was the Catholic Mission. But the Chinese, poor pagan souls, had not yet learnt to differentiate between the various brands of Christianity, and the 'Jesus-men' to whom we were directed turned out to be two elderly Protestant ladies from Bavaria. They were charming; they gave us cold water to drink, which sounds a small favour but which in the interior of China you appreciate very much. Yes, they had heard of the Catholics; they could even direct us to their Missions (it was within a bow-shot of their own). But they had never met the Fathers.

They had never met the Fathers. It was less of an admission than a boast; it was made with a self-righteous sniff. When they made it I could not help thinking that there was a lot to be said for Lord Melbourne's verdict on religion; it was all right as long as you didn't let it interfere with your private life. For here were two gallant ladies in exile relentlessly ignoring the only other white people they had a chance of seeing from one year's end to the next. For a long time they had been neighbours; often they had shared a common peril, always they had shared the same discomforts and the same difficulties. Yet they had never allowed themselves to meet. What, I wonder, may have been the effect on the observant Chinese, to whom the West is for ever counselling the virtues of unity and co-operation?

When we did at last find the Catholics, we were received with great kindness by Father Breuker, a nervous bearded Dutchman. His hospitable impulses, for ever unexpectedly recurring, threw him into a state of extreme agitation. His conversation, rapid rather than fluent, was conducted impartially in four languages – English, French, German and Chinese; just as we had unravelled the thread of his discourse, he would bound to his feet with a reproachful exclamation and from a cupboard produce a bottle of home-brewed beer, or a corkscrew, or another box of matches, or a twist of tobacco, at the same time apologizing with tears in his eyes because he had not produced them earlier. His embarrassment and mortification were painful to see.

Difficult though he was to understand, he gave us some useful information. He had once spent three weeks hiding in the hills from the Reds, and was able to confirm at first hand what we had heard of their anti-matrimonial campaign, which had had some success with the younger generation.

It was late when we left him, and Nanchang was still far away. It was not very much nearer when we had a puncture. For some reason we found it impossible to get the spare wheel on, so the puncture was mended; but as soon as the wheel was in position the tyre went flat again. It looked as if we should have to spend the night where we were, in the middle of a desolate expanse of pea-nut fields.

Leaving Li and the driver to make a last assault on the spare wheel, Gerald and I walked on with Colonel Fan. I had been restored, by somewhat drastic means, to health, and was ready for some food, my first for twenty-four hours. We walked for a long way in the twilight, under a cool grey sky, and eventually got some tea at the hut of a man who appeared to be a gooseherd on a considerable scale.

The prospect of sleeping by the car meant cleaner lying and better ventilation than the Grand Hotel de Kiangsi could offer, and was not unwelcome. The prospect of sleeping on an empty stomach was another matter. Colonel Fan was not much help. Reluctant to admit a state of emergency which would demand the use of his own initiative, he smiled politely and pretended that nothing had happened. Occasionally he said, in a very cheerful voice, 'The gates of Nanchang will be shut by now', or 'It is going to rain, I think'.

So we were relieved when a sudden blaze of light down the road showed that the headlights had been turned on. This meant that the car was in running order again; our proximity to the Communists had made it unsafe to use the lights while she was out of action. In due time the car appeared, and we headed once more for Nanchang; superhuman exertions had managed to affix the spare wheel, and the driver hoped that good luck would keep it in position.

It did. The driver was infected with something of his pristine verve, and we reached Nanchang in record time, annihilating in our progress only one very large dog. After some delay the huge gates were opened to admit us, and by midnight Gerald and I were asleep. Not all the noise in the world – and most of it seemed to be temporarily concentrated in the Grand Hotel de Kiangsi – could have kept us awake.

14

RAIN ON THE WINDSCREEN

THE next morning was occupied by a round of farewell visits. By the middle of the next afternoon we were on the road again, going west.

Our objective was Changsha, the capital of Hunan. From Shanghai it had looked as if, in order to reach this place, one would have to retrace one's steps from Nanchang to the Yangtse, take a boat to Hankow, and thence travel south to Changsha by the first and only completed link of the Canton–Hankow Railway. But in Nanchang we learnt that a cross-country journey by road (uncompleted) and rail (alleged) was possible. It was on the first stage of this that we were now embarking.

We crossed the river by sampan. A lot of troops were being ferried over to Nanchang in hulks from the railhead on the opposite bank. They had a few mules and ponies with them, and one of the former, slipping off the narrow gang-plank into the river, delayed the embarkation of the whole contingent for some time.

Of our two days' journey from Nanchang to Pinsiang on the borders of Kiangsi and Hunan there is not much to tell. The road was very bad; large parts of it were still under construction, and rivers were negotiated by ferries with a lackadaisical technique. On the first day the country was rolling and empty, its soil a Devonshire red. On the second it was wilder and had a more obviously romantic beauty; there were big hills, thickly wooded and reputed to harbour tigers. We were drawing away from the territory of the Communists, and traces of their depredations were rarer now, though even here each village had its quota of little new forts.

I remember only one moment distinctly. On the evening

of the first day we ran into a storm so violent that we had to halt the two cars in a darkened world for fear that they would be blown off the road. We took shelter in a little temple. It was inhabited by a minor official of the busy company and his numerous family. They were charming people who pressed upon us tea and cakes while a neglected telephone rang, petulant and incongruous, among old images with gilded, non-committal faces.

When the worst of the storm was over we went on. It was still raining, though in the west the evening sky was clean and yellow. Through the blurred windscreen the world lost what was outlandish in its shapes and colours; all that I could see was a drab road running on into the dusk between hills that were no longer specifically Chinese. I fell victim to a faint nostalgia. It was September, and I thought of the familiar September things that China was denying me. Rain on the windscreen. . . . For me that typified September: rain on the windscreen, dusk, a bad road between hills, a yellow light in the west, the smell of wet clothes. I thought of the road winding up from Alt a Chaorin over Black Rock and down at last to the Lodge; I imagined the harsh smell of a dead stag in the back of the car, and the feel of the rifle in its sodden case between my knees. I remembered other roads of the same sort and for the same reasons; the road from Sollas, which runs round the north of the island back to Sponish and which one travelled always wet to the waist from the snipe-bogs; and an earlier road on Ardnamurchan, along which the first and therefore memorable rabbits were brought in triumph home. . . .

On these roads the windscreen had shown something not very different from what it showed me now: dark, leaping hills distorted by the swimming glass. But inside the car there was a contrast, and for a moment, softening, I wished myself on those other roads, down which one jolted towards the certain expectation of scones, and a hot bath, and shared laughter. But nostalgia is a superfluous luxury in the traveller's equipment, and it was not so very difficult to resign oneself to the anticipation of rice, and interminable courtesies, and a wooden bed in an inn, with perhaps some compensating dash of comedy thrown in as a relish.

Most of the comedy on this stage of our journey was provided by Mr Tu. Mr Tu was a dreamy, gentle old man, so fragile, and so altogether negative that I never looked at him without thinking of the phrase, 'You could have knocked me down with a feather'. Feathers might have proved a very real source of danger to Mr Tu.

Though Mr Chen from Harvard, reluctantly faithful, was still with us, Mr Tu was in charge of the party. He was an official in the Department of Foreign Relations in the Kiangsi Provincial Government. When I asked him what function his department fulfilled, and with which foreign powers his province might be said to have relations, he gave a little reedy laugh and said that it was difficult to explain. I dare say it was.

As far as we were concerned Mr Tu was an obstructionist, and his tactics as such were highly instructive. Pinsiang was the terminus of a little railway which ran thence to Changsha and it was our aim to reach it in time to catch a train on the evening of the second day. With this aim Mr Tu had expressed at the outset the liveliest sympathy. It could be done, he said, and he was going to see that it was done; for his part, he was only too anxious to make his own absence from Nanchang as short as possible, so the faster we travelled the better he would be pleased.

But even as he said it he hardened his heart against us. Not because he disliked us; not because he wanted to involve either us or himself in any unnecessary delay. But he had a profound, probably unconscious, and certainly instinctive disapproval of our haste. It was all wrong, this preoccupation with time, this undignified cross-country scramble, his living with one eye on the clock. It was un-Chinese. It was in bad taste. Mr Tu proceeded to teach us a lesson.

It was a lesson for which I have an immense theoretical respect, though I find it difficult, and even impossible, to learn. I know it is foolish to be, even for the best of reasons, in a hurry, and my reasons are seldom in the last analysis the best. But a sense of proportion which is either hopelessly under- or hopelessly over-developed makes it impossible for me to take any of my own activities seriously; and I therefore make a point of carrying them out, whenever possible, in circumstances which give me no time to think. If you undertake to do a thing against time you have at least one opponent worth beating; and a victory in that field bulks, for the moment, just sufficiently large to obscure your otherwise inconvenient doubts as to whether the thing was worth doing at all. It is a *modus vivendi* for which I share the just and profound contempt of Mr Tu and all China.

The tactics of Mr Tu's delaying action were delightfully unobtrusive. When the car was ready to start Mr Tu would be found to have disappeared. If a long meal looked like ending, Mr Tu would make another speech. If a halt was objected to, Mr Tu would agree that it was inadvisable; but the halt would take place. The process of being delayed was almost painless. It was effected by the traditional methods. No reasons were advanced, no excuses given; it simply came to pass. In this respect the gentle and old-fashioned Mr Tu was a great contrast to the alert and modern Mr Chen, whose Western training made him fall, dismally and without dignity, between two stools. On our former journey to Nanfeng Mr Chen had been actuated by the same obstructionist motives, conscious and unconscious, as Mr Tu; but he tried to play a Chinese game by Western rules. He allowed himself to be involved in arguments, pinned down to statements, confuted out of his own mouth. Mr Tu merely smiled, agreed, changed the subject, and had his way.

So it was not until dusk on the second day that we reached Pinsiang. The younger members of the population had not, I think, seen a foreigner before and we were followed everywhere by a large crowd of excited children. We were both very tired, and I had a mild fever; we wanted nothing more than a long sleep. But the local Commissioner invited us to a banquet, and the laws of etiquette forbade refusal. Groaning, we burrowed in the rucksack for clean shirts.

The banquet did not begin till ten o'clock, and at first only the extreme discomfort of our stools prevented us from going to sleep where we sat. It was a very good, very formal meal. There were seventeen courses. We were toasted repeatedly in *samshui* of a more than ordinary potency. Gradually we began to wake up. By the birds'-nest soup we had the table laughing. Toasts became still more frequent; no heel-taps were allowed. Speeches started when the Peking duck was served. I made five, all rather delirious. By the time the meal was over it was beyond question that we had been a big social success. Two minor officials were under the table and the Commissioner had to be helped downstairs.

15

RAIL AND ROAD

FIVE hours later we boarded the train, which made off at a
brisk walking pace in the direction of Nanchang. I seem to
remember (the fever made my impressions of that morning
rather imprecise) that we had bidden affectionate farewells to
Mr Tu and Mr Chen, and that our two guards had been
suitably rewarded. We had also received, with the apathy of
exhaustion, the news that a station ten miles down the line
had been raided by Communists the night before, and its
garrison of six soldiers killed.

The railway from Pinsiang to Changsha is not of the best.
On the sleepers the rails are held in position – or something
like it – by spikes instead of by the more customary bolts.
There are two classes of passenger-accommodation – Goods
and Cattle; between these the chief difference in comfort is
that Goods is open, whereas Cattle has a roof. In the latter
class we were fortunate enough to secure a corner seat.

The truck was very full, and its passengers made, as always
in China, a pattern of humanity so intricate and so seemingly
well-established, with their babies and their bundles and their
bowls of rice, that one thought of them rather as a community
than as a carriage-full of strangers. Next to me there was a
woman with a baby. The babies who were my neighbours in
public conveyances in China all fell into one of two categories:
babies who appeared to be dead, and babies who appeared to
be dying. This one belonged to the former, and preferable,
category. Beyond the woman were two soldiers, one of
whom had a fiddle. On the opposite bench their officer was
sleeping, stretched out full length; when presently we crossed
the border into Hunan a tough and well-accoutred Hunanese
captain told him that he was occupying more than his share
of space and made him sit up. This most unusual occurrence

was a tribute to the discipline of the Hunanese armies, which we afterwards discovered to be of a very high level.

Next to the officer there were three fat schoolgirls on their way back to college in Changsha. They wore European dress and clearly belonged to rich families. At one station a special meal had been ordered for them in advance, and our average rate of progress can be gauged from the fact that, when we started again with unexpected punctuality, the man who had brought the meal on board was able, without mishap, to leave the train half a mile farther on, holding a tray piled high with bowls.

There were the usual quarrels, the usual gambling games, the usual children being sick. The soldier with the fiddle played it with excruciating assiduity. At every station hawkers came on board with fruit and tea and cakes and less obviously edible delicacies; they generally travelled on with us as far as the next station, and, when unable to force their way through the crowded carriages or alternatively when approached by the ticket collector, would climb up on to the roof of the carriageway and thus pass unchallenged up and down the train. The journey lasted eight hours.

We found that we were very tired when we reached Changsha. It was not merely a bodily fatigue, for we had had but little physical exertion. We seemed to have petered out all round. Our voices sounded unnatural, our speech was slow and blurred, and it required a tremendous effort to finish our sentences. At the time I was annoyed at this, and found it unaccountable. But afterwards I realized that we had had no rest at all since we left our steamer at Kuikiang over a fortnight ago, and that the tempo of our progress had been fairly rapid. We had covered a lot of ground, in very hot weather, and we had been using our brains all the time. I am not one of those who regard all travel as intrinsically tiring; but we had been travelling at fairly high pressure, and when you are doing that you need an occasional 'stand easy' – a quiet evening, or a good dinner (not a banquet), or a long sleep. We had somehow missed these things; so I suppose there was some excuse for the dazed and fumbling condition in which we reached Changsha and presented ourselves at the office of the Commissioner of Customs, to whom I had a letter of introduction.

The Commissioner of Customs was just what we wanted. A delightful Pickwickian American in a bottle-green coat, he took us completely under his wing. In his house on the island where a small foreign community lives (Changsha was until recently a Treaty Port) we stayed for that night and the next. We departed with full stomachs and very nearly clean.

During our one day in Changsha we succeeded in interviewing the Governor of Hunan, General Ho Chien. We found him at the University on the far side of the river. He was about to set out on a picnic, at which he was entertaining, in an idyllic and somehow Shakespearean manner, the visiting Governor of Hupeh. Ho Chien's indescribably shifty appearance is belied by his excellent record during the last few years. Hunan is one of the best governed and most progressive provinces in China. Its people are sturdy and independent, and there prevails among them a tradition of squirearchy which is all too rare in modern China, where most landlords are rich absentees living in luxurious security in one or other of the foreign concessions. Hunan is the only province in which I have travelled where you occasionally see something roughly corresponding to the English country house; in most other parts the big families, if they still live in the provinces, live behind high walls in the heart of the larger towns.

Both from Ho Chien and from an extremely able young A.D.C., with whom we afterwards played Corinthian bagatelle in his westernized villa in Changsha, we heard more of the Communists. Though they captured Changsha in 1928, they have since been driven out of the province; there are, however, small isolated gangs still operating in the east and the north-west, by whom an Italian missionary had been decapitated two days before. The Hunan troops (which, as I have said, are of unusually high quality) wage a vigorous campaign of counter propaganda against Red influence, and from each company three men are selected, by means of an oratorical competition, to preach orthodoxy in the villages where they are garrisoned.

On September 4th we got up at five o'clock, said good-bye to our charming host, took rickshaws to the outskirts of the city, and there caught a bus. On a Chinese bus service it is, unfortunately, impossible to reserve seats in advance; if the tickets were sold overnight they would, I suppose, be cornered by speculators and resold to the public (like the seats for a successful play in New York) at a greatly increased price. The would-be passenger is therefore obliged to turn up in plenty of time and use his elbows relentlessly when the bus arrives.

After a fierce struggle we and a score of other people got seats. The bus service in Hunan is almost beyond reproach. We were thirteen hours on the road that day, and covered the best part of two hundred miles. The bus was ferried with the utmost expedition across two sizeable rivers. The road, though unmetalled, was well engineered, kept in excellent repair, and lined with an embryo of young trees; in England it would have passed for a good second-class highway. At every halt tickets were religiously punched. so that we, who came in time to be the oldest inhabitants of the bus, were left eventually with the merest shred of paper heavily eroded with perforations. Soldiers were not allowed to travel free, and one of them, who stepped out into the middle of the road and attempted to hold us up at the point of his umbrella, narrowly escaped annihilation. The bus service is run by the provincial government; I should imagine that it makes a handsome profit after paying for the maintenance of the roads.

The hilly and well-wooded country had a prosperous air, and was at times exceedingly beautiful. In the middle of the morning we passed Hengshan, one of the five sacred mountains of China and a popular terminus for pilgrim traffic; all save its lower slopes were hidden by mist. Still, we had a good day's run. The passengers were packed like sardines, but as long as the bus was in motion the heat was not uncomfortable. The seating accommodation of a Chinese bus does not, however, cater for the long-legged foreigner, who finds that his hard seat, so inconveniently close to the one in front of it, is something of a Little Ease. His height is also a disadvantage, greatly increasing the risk of concussion when the vehicle passes at full speed over the not infrequent irregularities of the road.

In the early afternoon we reached a little town called Hengchow, where we had to change buses. While we were eating a bowl of sweet gruel bought from an old surprised man who I think regarded us as some kind of vision or hallucination, we were intrigued to discover that this time we were not the only foreign passengers. An American lady in pince-nez had mysteriously appeared. She was amorphous and silver-haired, and wore an expression of the utmost benignity. She was returning to her mission, down the road at Chenchow, and when she heard that that was where we meant to spend the night she kindly but rashly offered to put us up.

Partly owing to a puncture, we did not reach Chenchow until long after it was dark. The missionary was surprised to find that no one had come to meet her. We got a carrier for the party's luggage and set off to walk to the mission, which was a mile away on the outskirts of the town. When we reached it the lady's surprise increased. The gates of the compound were locked and no lights were showing. Our unworthy hopes of a sensational explanation were dashed by her theory that her companion in the mission, a much younger English lady, was probably staying at the girls' school.

We set to work to storm the mission, and eventually managed to effect an entry. A messenger was sent to the school, and presently returned with the second missionary, a young woman with a fine face, dark, rather haunted eyes, and terribly nervous hands. The two of them showed us the greatest kindness. At dinner it was amusing to watch Li, shy but alert, keeping an anxious eye on our technique with the cutlery and surreptitiously copying it. He had been for so long our mentor in matters of etiquette that it gave us a strange feeling of superiority to have the position for once reversed. We slept in a deserted and unfurnished house in the mission compound, which had been despoiled and gutted by the Reds in 1928.

At dawn we were off again. On our way to the station we visited a temple which contains a famous portrait of Confucius. The temple was a splendid though desolate place, on whose cracked steps fantastic dragons sprawled among the weeds. On the walls there were exquisite carvings in relief. The place was deserted save for a family of peasants who acted – nominally – as caretakers.

We found at last the portrait of Confucius. It was delicately cut upon a seven-foot slab of dark grey stone. The sage stared at us with inexpressive eyes. At his feet, on a pile of straw, lay a little soldier in a ragged uniform. His face was grotesquely swollen. Dark-brown matter issued from his ear. It was clear that he had not long to live. The scene was perhaps allegorical.

We fetched the soldier some water and commended him to Confucius and the caretakers. There was nothing else to do.

At the bus station we found that our impulsive vehicle had left early with a full complement of passengers. That was our first and last stroke of bad luck, and it mattered very little, for at noon we caught another.

It was such a bus as I hope never to meet again. We were hardly inside it when it dashed away and passed murderously through the little village, roaring. Its body was of an even more cumbrous and top-heavy design than usual, and so full of passengers that we could hardly breathe. Yet it gadded down the twisting mountain road like a thing possessed. It seemed as if our stripling driver had constituted himself president of a suicide club, with its thirty passengers as members: life members. For him chasms were a challenge, corners a spur, and he appeared to cherish a belief, analogous to, but stronger than, that held by our chauffeur on the Hsinkan road, that all water-buffaloes are a form of mirage, dissolving when approached.

Worst of all, he was not a good driver. He was rank bad. His cornering was contemptuous but inept, and as he flashed between the low stone parapets of narrow bridges it was hard to tell whether he was desirous or oblivious of the dried-up river bed far below them. Usually I am imperturbable in a car; conceit, not courage, supplies a reassuring though baseless conviction that I am not meat for a coroner's inquest, that it will not be me this time. But in that bus I was terrified.

We covered forty miles in just over sixty minutes, and then, thank God, the road ended. Its next link was still under construction. We took, with alacrity, to our feet.

16

THE LOVELY RIVER

From Nichang, the place where the road ended, we faced the welcome prospect, after all these sedentary days, of a fourteen-mile-walk over the hills; this would bring us to a little village across the Kwangtung frontier, whence we should get a sampan down the Pei River for the last stage but one of our journey to Canton. It was still only the middle of the day, so we set about hiring carriers for our luggage, from which, for fear that it would be searched at the provincial frontier, we extracted and concealed about our persons a remarkable collection of Communist propaganda, given us, together with some Red seals and banners, by the authorities in Kiangsi. We did not want our political sympathies to be misinterpreted.

Carriers were harder to hire than usual. On the day before a party of three merchants had been stripped, robbed, and beaten by bandits on the path which we were to follow, and the coolies put a higher commercial value on their qualms than Li considered reasonable. I don't know what it is about me, but there seems to exist – I have remarked on this before – between me and the criminal classes in the Far East some queer and constant time-lag. Jam to-morrow, jam yesterday, but never jam to-day. Just up the road, a little way down the line, the day after or the day before I pass that way, the worst happens. The day I am there is a *dies non*.

And so it was on this occasion. We came at last to terms with carriers, and paid them half their wages in advance to leave with their wives, to soften the blow of a potential bereavement. Two young Chinese students, bound for Canton, joined our party on the theory that there is safety in numbers, and we set out from the village at a good round pace. The path we travelled was an ancient one, being flagged and for part of its length lined with an avenue of firs. All through the afternoon we walked, following the path over the curious and savage hills and down into gullies from whose solid walls of rock the heat of the sun leapt out at us. The country was extraordinarily beautiful. All the hills in China – at least all the hills that I have seen – have an oddly artificial look. They rise suddenly and take quaint shapes; they never sprawl. They are exactly as they are portrayed in Chinese art; they seem to have been enlarged from a delicate and fanciful miniature, with complete success. It is a mannered landscape, and it has great charm.

Occasionally we halted to drink tea and rest the carriers. With their tottering yet indefatigable gait they set a rapid pace. Our two Chinese fellow-travellers, so slight, so reedy in appearance, padded happily along, fanning themselves with their straw hats and seeming not to feel at all the effects of a march of which, from one glance at their physique, you would have judged them wholly incapable. When the path went up or down a hill, the flags became steps; of this form of highway the only criticism possible is that you must watch your feet too much, thereby missing things which are beautiful or strange in the countryside around you.

There were no bandits; there was not even a frontier post. Only one incident enlivened our journey. We reached a point where the path crossed the last, half-constructed lap of the motor road down which we had been whirled that morning. Here it ran in a cutting made in the flank of a steep hill. Coolies were working in the cutting, and there were more coolies far up the hillside above it. The bed of the cutting was full of huge boulders which were to form the foundations of the road.

Over these boulders we picked our way with some difficulty, jumping from one to the other like the most maladroit of goats. In the middle of them I stopped, poised on a pinnacle, to take a photograph. The others went on ahead.

Suddenly I heard shouts, followed by the dull sound of an explosion from the hillside above me. Looking up, I found that I was now alone in the cutting. The smoke of a blasting charge floated out against the blue sky, and a large, a really enormous rock was bounding savagely down the hill.

I had no doubts as to where it was going to land. It was going to land on me. This opinion was shared by the men who had released it, a wildly gesticulating fresco of manikins two hundred yards above me. I made a prodigious leap from my rock to the next. The galloping boulder, which now looked to me about the size of the Isle of Wight, scored one of its increasingly rare contacts with the hillside, kicked up a cloud of dust, and slightly changed its direction. It was still coming straight for me.

The prospect of a game, however short, of catch-as-catch-can between me and a large segment of South China clearly appealed to the spectators but left me cold. I decided that, if one had to be squashed, it was better to make, figuratively speaking, no bones about it. I descended, with all possible dignity, into a cranny between two boulders and shut my eyes.

With a sound to which the Fall of the House of Usher was as the dropping of a pin, the mass of rock landed among the boulders ten feet away and lay, miraculously, dead. It hardly splintered at all, and none of the splinters came my way. We continued our journey.

The only other thing worth relating about that walk was a coincidence, trivial but striking. I had been telling Gerald, as we went along, about a journey which I had undertaken the year before, as one of an expedition which had pursued a ludicrous course across the Central Plateau of Brazil in search of the legendary Colonel Fawcett. We were discussing the strange immortality of the lost explorer – how after eight years one was still continually coming across references to him. Suddenly Gerald stooped and picked up a scrap of news-paper. It was printed in English. The only complete para-graph on it announced the return, empty-handed, of yet another American expedition from the jungles of Matto Grosso; although defeated, they were still convinced, the newspaper said, that Fawcett was alive.

Gerald and I pointed out to each other what a small place the world was. It is always better to observe the rites.

Presently we climbed the last pass. Below us lay the village of Pingshek, squeezed in between the foothills and the river, and pricked by three little white forts which stood on knolls among the huddled houses. The river wound away southward through a valley embossed with shaggy and fantastic rocks, hundreds of feet high; beyond it was a great climbing wall of mountains, remote and insubstantial in the evening light. The sun was setting behind us; as we went down towards the village the shadows on the eastern slopes were cool.

The village inn was not a very good one. Li, for whom the linguistic problem now loomed larger with every step we took, was at sea with the local dialect; the feeling that he was losing face with us, and perhaps being swindled by the inhabitants, made him very unhappy. 'South man not good,' he muttered, and shook his head in a disconsolate way. His disgust was increased when the local soldiery came to examine our passports. Having seen few if any foreigners before, they took us for Japanese and made an outcry. They were soothed only after an impassioned speech by the student from Canton, whose ethnology was providentially more advanced than theirs.

We got a room opening on to the stone roof of the inn, on which I slept under an enormous moon; the small white forts stood up out of a nacreous haze which hung low above the river and shone as if they had been made of silver. Although the local wine was good, the dinner was the worst of the journey – so bad, indeed, that it took me half a minute's mastication to discover that a morsel, selected with chopsticks in an uncertain light, was in fact the left claw of a chicken. At this we lodged a complaint and the proprietress, a woman of spirit, beat her cook over the head with a stool. The dish was sent down again to the kitchen. On its return it was found to contain, among other things, the chicken's beak. After that we gave it up.

At dawn the next morning we went down to the river, where the sampan which we had chartered the night before was beached with many others on the mud. High above us (the river was low) men and women were cleaning their teeth and performing other tasks associated with reveille from the jutting windows of wooden houses on the water-front. Our crew brought eggs and vegetables and little shreds of pork to the sampan, where, in the tunnel-shaped cabin of matting, rice was already cooking in a big black pot.

Only the distant peaks were warmed by sunlight as we pushed off from the foreshore, on which scavenging curs with hostile eyes moved slowly, stiff from sleep. A man lying on the bows of the boat next to ours woke and lay staring at us, too amazed to blink. His face was full of apprehension and perplexity, for he had come from oblivion straight to a world in which two giants of an unorthodox colour monopolized his field of vision. He was still staring as we dropped downstream.

The water came from the mountains and was swift and green, not the drab yellow of the rivers of the plains. In the bows our three rowers, standing, plied their long thin-bladed oars. The master of the boat managed the ponderous twenty-foot steering-oar which trailed behind us limply. He had a crafty but uninteresting face. We made a little deck of loose planks in the stern, and the student from Canton, treading first on one, then on the other of the projecting ends, fell twice, with fearful force, into the bilge.

A little mist still drifted on the surface of the water: the bluer smoke of the village we had left behind us hung above it in a series of half-formulated tiers. The beauty of the river increased as we descended. Great pinnacles of rock, as high as a hill and oddly tufted with vegetation rose about the river bed; the summit of one of them, by a freak, had the exact outline of a monstrous camel, kneeling.

We were the first boat away from Pingshek, but others were following us, a leisurely, equidistant procession which the straight stretches of the current's course revealed. Soon we began to pass boats coming upstream. The men poling them put the crutch of the pole in the hollow between neck and shoulder, then, bending almost double, ran down the broad gunwales of the boat with a great shouting song. In passages where the current was swift the boat was hauled by trackers who, straining at a long rope, cried in shrill chorus as they stumbled along the shore. Every boat, however full of cargo, was also the home of a family; only the poultry, the animals, and the smallest babies played no part in the day's work of poling, steering, cooking, and washing clothes. Each sampan reflected, in cross-section, the peasant's unremitting struggle for existence.

In the middle of the morning we came to a place where the river had to pass through a high range of mountains. Here was the head of the Gorges, and from now on there would be an element of danger in the journey, though only a small one. Within sound of the rapids a little temple was perched on a cliff, looking downstream over the white and leaping waters. We landed and climbed to it up a flight of steps. In obscurity, before a rank of gods full of that pantomimic fury which seems so often to be the hall-mark of divinity in China, our crew offered prayers for a safe run, lit joss-sticks, and let off crackers. The dark temple was pungent with smoke and incense. Outside in the sunlight, a long diagonal of bent, half-naked trackers stamped a formal design across the wide steps which led downwards to the river. Slowly, with cries, their straw sandals slipping on the stone, they hauled a sampan up the rapids by a rope tied to her mast-head. As she reached clear water at the top they broke into a trot and disappeared round a bend in the rocky tow-path, chanting a triumphant sing-song. We went back to our boat.

In the Gorges there were nearly fifty separate rapids. They did not look very bad, and they were not as bad as they looked. With memories of another river in another country, where twelve months ago these things had been encountered on a grander scale and under less expert guidance, I watched the local technique with interest. The steering was as much from the bows as from the stern, and with the long beam which was the forward tiller a certain amount of rather inartistic prodding and fending off was done. The river though low, ran fast, and we felt as if we were travelling like the wind as we plunged down the steep, broken chutes between the rocks. We struck several times, but always with impunity; the flat and rather flexible bottom of the sampan slid easily over obstacles which seemed to have been worn smooth by the passage of her unnumbered sister ships. The worst that had happened to us was to lose our lunch, which was upset by a collision that felt as if it must have split the boat; as the meal consisted only of a thin soup made of rice and some imponderable kind of cucumber, this was no great misfortune.

All through the afternoon we were carried swiftly down the Gorges. The hills, tall and Tyrolean, now rose more closely on either side of our winding course. We were in a narrow corridor, roofed by the blue sky. In between the rapids we hoisted a patched rectangular sail; the crew whistled fervently, and with an air of concentration, for a breeze, so that I wondered on which side of the world that superstition was born. The eastern bank, far above us, was scarred with cuttings, and hordes of men, clinging to the steep face like flies, were at work on the railway which will one day (perhaps in five years, if all goes very well) link Canton with Hankow and thus with Peking. We did our best to rejoice at these symptoms of progress towards the great and desirable goal of mechanization; but it was not without a certain reactionary glee that we learnt of the existence of a spirit to whom they were anathema. This spirit – a kind of unicorn, according to the boatmen, who pointed out to us the crag in which he lived – was doing his best to hold the pass against the forces of civilization, and had on one occasion gone so far as to overwhelm a hundred labourers with an avalanche. The final issue of the struggle, they seemed to think, was still in doubt; but it was clear that they did not regard the unicorn as being engaged in a forlorn hope.

At last we left the rapids and came out into a plain. We passed a fisherman; in his little boat sat twenty fishing cormorants, and at every lurch of it they hunched their wings in protest with comical unanimity. (Is there perhaps always something comical about unanimity?) The hills behind us were black against a yellow sky, and, where the river wound, tall grey sails stalked through the silent fields like ghosts. Through a land from which the colour was being drained we moved slowly and in silence towards the lights of a village.

That was almost the last stage of the journey, and the best.

The sampan was beached on a foreshore above which electric light shone fiercely in many of the windows; we were getting back to what the parvenu West understands by civilization. Men with flashlights and a peremptory manner came on board and searched for opium. We dined on shore, but slept in the open air on the unaccommodating boards of the sampan.

The village, which was called Lokchong, was railhead. There were, however, no trains, and the next morning, after a long, hot wait, we bumped over an inferior road in a bus to Shuichow. This, our last bus-ride, was enlivened by the Chinese lady next to me who was inordinately sick.

At Shuichow there were trains, but only in the early morning. We had to wait a day. In Kwantung the rights of women seem to be regarded as inconsiderable. The carriers at the bus terminus were all female, and our luggage was carried a mile under a blazing sun by two ladies, one not a day under seventy, the other much younger but pregnant. Neither of them turned a hair.

Shuichow was brisk and up to date; the local garrison were the best-disciplined troops we had seen since Nanking. In the afternoon we were surprised, while bathing naked in the river, by a mixed party of foreign missionaries. Apart from this shameful incident, our stay was uneventful.

Next day, after a five-hour train journey which seemed luxury to us but might not have appealed to anyone lacking our fund of odious comparisons, we reached Canton. We were thinner, swarthier, much dirtier, but only about twenty pounds poorer than when we had started out, nearly a month ago. The route which we followed has not, I believe, been previously covered in its entirety by a foreigner, nor is there any earthly reason why it should have been.

Still, it is a good journey.

FINIS

LIGHTS pricked the dusk between wind and water. I stood on deck and watched England swim towards us, a long indeterminate ribbon of opacity which widened slowly. Around me my fellow-passengers were preparing for the supreme moment, the moment of homecoming. . .

'Oh, *there* you are. I thought you were never coming. . . . '

'What did you do with my landing card?'

'But you said *you* were going to tip the wine-steward. . . . '

'Well you'll just have to unpack the book and give it back to her.'

'How should *I* know?'

'You can't have looked properly, that's all I can say. . . . '

'Yes, dear, I know, but . . . '

'There's not time, I tell you.'

'No, sir, I haven't seen her.'

'You *don't* mean to say you've lost the keys?'

'She says she won't come up till the ship docks.'

'You might have known we'd want some change. . . . '

'Oh, well, have it your own way.'

'If you don't declare them, I shall.'

'George is quite old enough to look after his own things.'

'It's not *my* fault. . . . '

'Hi! Maude! *Maude*. . . . '

Travelling by one's self, I reflected has many advantages. Katherine Mansfield once wrote in her *Journal*, 'Even if I should, by some awful chance, find a hair upon my bread and honey – at any rate it is my own hair'. There are moments in every journey when the equanimity of even the most fatalistic traveller breaks down and he stands revealed in an unbecoming posture of dejection, panic, or annoyance. If he is alone, the moment passes, damaging only his self-respect; if he is not alone, its effects are less ephemeral. Somebody else's bread and honey has been spoilt.

It is easy enough for one man to adapt himself to living under strange and constantly changing conditions. It is much harder for two. Leave A or B alone in a distant country, and each will evolve a congenial *modus vivendi*. Throw them together, and the comforts of companionship are as likely as not offset by the strain of reconciling their divergent methods. A likes to start early and halt for a siesta; B does not feel the heat and insists on sleeping late. A instinctively complies with regulations. B instinctively defies them. A finds it impossible to pass a temple, B finds it impossible to pass a bar. A is cautious, B is rash. A is indefatigable, B tires easily. A needs a lot of food, B very little. A snores, B smokes a pipe in bed. . . .

Each would get on splendidly by himself. Alone together, they build up gradually between them a kind of unacknowledged rivalry. Allowances are always being made, precedents established; each, in his darker moments, looks back on the journey they are making and sees it lined, as if by milestones, with little monuments to his own self-sacrificing tolerance. Each, while submitting readily to the exotic customs of the country, endures with a very bad grace the trifling idiosyncrasies of the other. The complex structure of their relationship, with its queer blend of nobility and baseness, its accretion of unforeseen drawbacks and unforeseen compensations, bulks larger and larger, obtruding itself between them and the country they are visiting, blotting it out. . . .

Occasionally you find the ideal companion; exactly a year ago I had returned to England with such a one. But the ideal companion is rare, and in default of him it is better to make a long journey alone. One's company in a strange world.

MORE ABOUT PENGUINS
AND PELICANS

For further information about books available from Penguins please write to Dept EP, Penguin Books Ltd, Harmondsworth, Middlesex UB7 ODA.

In the U.S.A.: For a complete list of books available from Penguins in the United States write to Dept CS, Penguin Books, 625 Madison Avenue, New York, New York 10022.

In Canada: For a complete list of books available from Penguins in Canada write to Penguin Books Canada Ltd, 2801 John Street, Markham, Ontario L3R 1B4.

In Australia: For a complete list of books available from Penguins in Australia write to the Marketing Department, Penguin Books Australia Ltd, P.O. Box 257, Ringwood, Victoria 3134.

In New Zealand: For a complete list of books available from Penguins in New Zealand write to the Marketing Department, Penguin Books (N.Z.) Ltd, P.O. Box 4019, Auckland 10.

Hindoo Holiday

J. R. ACKERLEY

J. R. Ackerley's classic journal of his experiences as companion to the Maharajah of Chhokrapur is, said Evelyn Waugh, 'a book difficult to praise . . . temperately'. Marvellously observed and extremely funny, it extracts the irony, absurdity and farce of life in India in the twenties, as well as the dignity and richness of an ancient culture.

'His humour is the humour of pity and love. He is an artist in understanding' – V. S. Pritchett

Mani

PATRICK LEIGH FERMOR

The Mani is a remote and untouched region of the Greek Peloponnese, and its inhabitants one of the wildest and toughest peoples. Patrick Leigh Fermor's remarkable account of his journey through the peninsula unlocks the secrets of a people and culture whose roots stretch back to Byzantium.

'The masterpiece of a traveller and scholar' – *Illustrated London News*

A Reed Shaken by the Wind

GAVIN MAXWELL

Between Baghdad and Basra lie 2,000 square miles of unexplored marshland waste, inhabited by the Ma'dan, a tribe whose primitive way of life has remained unchanged for thousands of years. Gavin Maxwell went to live among these people and describes their strange existence in this classic travel book.

'He writes so well and effortlessly that his experiences become our own' – *Sunday Times*

'A work of art' – *Spectator*

A Choice of Penguins

Slow Boats to China

GAVIN YOUNG

It needed twenty-three agreeably ill-assorted vessels and seven months to transport Gavin Young by slow boat from Piraeus to Canton – seven months crowded with adventure, excitement and colour. His account of a fantasy come true memorably distils the people, places, smells, conversations, ships and history of the places he encountered in a quite exceptional book.

'Storms, fleas, pirates, bad food and bureaucrats . . . Mr Young suffered what he did to entertain us' – Anthony Burgess in the *Observer*

The Chinese

DAVID BONAVIA

'I can think of no other work which so urbanely and entertainingly succeeds in introducing the general Western reader to China' – *Sunday Telegraph*

'A timely book, informative, enlightening, intimate, based on personal experience, in which the reader quickly and easily gets to know the Chinese in their everyday life, at home, the city factory and country commune. Following, are insights into the fluctuating functions and fortunes of the inevitably strangling bureaucracy and the fields of education, medicine, commerce, the law, industry, consumerism, the arts – and politics' – Walter Tyson in the *Oxford Times*